Nine Fantastic Tales!

- Lucifer comes to earth seeking help from a physics professor and his well-bosomed wife. Hell is about to be invaded by alien demons....

- A majestic tree quenches its thirst for life by capturing the soul of a dying space man. . . .

- A quiet rural village quakes when its beloved mascot—an ancient war machine—awakens to fulfill its real purpose. . . .

- An interplanetary detective blunders again and again as she tries to stop illegal planet smashing for a multi-D thriller. The planet is earth. . . .

Books by Keith Laumer

The Best of Keith Laumer
Fat Chance
The Glory Game
A Plague of Demons
Retief and the Warlords
Retief: Emissary to the Stars
Retief of the CDT
Retief's War

Published by POCKET BOOKS

THE BEST OF KEITH LAUMER

A KANGAROO BOOK
PUBLISHED BY POCKET BOOKS NEW YORK

Distributed in Canada by PaperJacks Ltd., a Licensee of the trademarks of Simon & Schuster, a division of Gulf+Western Corporation.

POCKET BOOKS, a Simon & Schuster division of GULF & WESTERN CORPORATION
1230 Avenue of the Americas, New York, N.Y. 10020
In Canada distributed by PaperJacks Ltd.,
330 Steelcase Road, Markham, Ontario.

ISBN: 0-671-83268-9

First Pocket Books printing March, 1976

10 9 8 7 6 5 4 3 2

POCKET and colophon are trademarks of Simon & Schuster.

Printed in Canada

ACKNOWLEDGMENTS

"The Planet Wreckers" copyright © 1967 by UPD Publishing Corporation.
First published in *Worlds of Tomorrow*.

"The Body Builders" copyright © 1966 by UPD Publishing Corporation.
First published in *Galaxy*.

"Cocoon" copyright © 1962 by Ultimate Publishing Company, Inc. First
published in *Fantastic*.

"The Lawgiver" copyright © 1970 by Harry Harrison. First published in
The Year 2000, edited by Harry Harrison. Reprinted by permission of
Doubleday & Company, Inc.

"Thunderhead" copyright © 1967 by UPD Publishing Corporation. First
published in *Galaxy*.

"Hybrid" copyright © 1961 by Mercury Press, Inc. First published in *The
Magazine of Fantasy and Science Fiction*.

"The Devil You Don't" copyright © 1970 by Anne McCaffrey. First published in *Alchemy and Academe*, edited by Anne McCaffrey. Reprinted
by permission of Doubleday & Company, Inc.

"Doorstep" copyright © 1961 by UPD Publishing Corporation. First published in *Galaxy*.

"A Relic of War" copyright © 1969 by The Condé Nast Publications, Inc.
First published in *Analog: Science Fiction-Science Fact*.

CONTENTS

5

This book is for
Marte,
who understands

INTRODUCTION

The facts of Keith Laumer's career are these: he is a serious and gifted writer; his work shows great range, versatility, and technical sophistication; and he has written some of the most excellent stories of our time within the science-fiction genre. Most of his popular reputation is based upon the single series of adventure stories built around a hero called Retief, a galactic diplomat who averts wars and outwits conspirators and villains in a world 600 years in the future.

The artist can seldom predict his own posterity. Sir Arthur Sullivan, for instance, considered himself a major composer, yet his serious operas, symphonies, and oratorios are largely unknown today. When Sullivan teamed up with William Schwenck Gilbert and set Gilbert's humorous librettos to popular melodies, he did not imagine he was creating the music that would make him famous for generations to come. Sullivan's serious works are seldom heard, but the world will always love Gilbert and Sullivan.

The Retief series is Keith Laumer's Gilbert and Sullivan. He has kept the series going almost from the outset of his career. The magazine pieces and novels have sold in the millions throughout the world. And a decade and a half later the series is still going strong. The demand for it seems inexhaustible.

Now, I do not mean to minimize the accomplishment of this fascinating series. The Retief stories are exciting pieces featuring humor and poltical satire (unusual for the genre), and it is easy to understand their immense popularity. Laumer writes adventure as well as any science-fiction writer, and there are some marvelous technicians around.

The Best of Keith Laumer contains some of his finest work, and it will be a rich experience for those readers who have never wandered outside of Retief's amazing world. Keith Laumer knows his audience well, and he respects them far more than most.

From the outset of his remarkable career—he was an Air Force officer who left the military in the late 1950s to become (almost immediately) a successful full-time writer—Laumer has shown the quality and range demonstrated here. It is a quality and range that has taken him not only through the parameters of modern science fiction but outside the genre, to mysteries and novels. His published work is reprinted and anthologized constantly; his new work constantly expands his audience. Laumer has remained prolific in success, which in itself is a remarkable accomplishment.

I think that this collection contains some of his finest stories. I particularly recommend "The Lawgiver" and "The Body Builders"—they amply demonstrate his gifts and may be an education for newer members of his audience. *Pace* Sullivan: Retief will live on, but so will the rest of Laumer.

—BARRY N. MALZBERG

Teaneck, N.J.
August, 1975

THE PLANET WRECKERS

1

In his shabby room in the formerly elegant hostelry known as the Grand Atumpquah Palace, Jack Waverly pulled the coarse weave sheet up about his ears and composed himself for sleep.

Somewhere, a voice whispered. Somewhere, boards creaked. Wind muttered around the loosely fitted window, rattling it in its frame. The pulled-down blind clacked restlessly. In the room above, footsteps went three paces; clank; back three paces; clank . . . .

Drat the fellow, Waverly thought. *Why doesn't he stop rattling his chains and go to bed?* He turned on his other side, rearranged the pillow of the consistency of bagged sawdust. Beyond the partition, someone was whistling a strange, unmelodic tune. It was hot in the room. The sheet chafed his neck. Next door, voices muttered with a note of urgency. Waverly made out the words *magma* and *San Andreas fault.*

"Geology, at ten minutes past midnight?" he inquired of the mottled wallpaper. Above, bedsprings squeaked faintly. Waverly sat up, frowning at the ceiling. "I thought the clerk said he was putting me on the top floor," he said accusingly. He reached for the telephone on the bedside table. A wavering dial tone went on for five seconds, then cut off with a sharp click.

"Hello?" Waverly said. "Hello?"

The receiver was dead against his ear.

"If this weren't the only hotel in town," Waverly muttered.

He climbed out of bed, went to the high window, raised the roller shade, looked out on a view of a brick wall ten feet away. From the window next door, a pattern of light and shadow gleamed against the masonry.

Two silhouettes moved. One was tall, lean, long-armed, like a giant bird with a crested head and curious wattles below a stunted beak. The other resembled an inverted polyp, waving a dozen arms tipped with multifingered hands, several of which clutched smoking cigars.

"Trick of the light," Waverly said firmly. He closed his eyes and shook his head to dispel the illusion. When he looked again, the window was dark.

"There, you see?" He raised the sash and thrust his head out. Moonlight gleamed on a bricked alley far below. A rusted fire escape led upward toward the roof. Leaning far out, Waverly saw the sill of the window above.

"No lights up there," he advised himself. "Hmmmm."

Faintly, he heard a dull rattle of metal, followed by a lugubrious groan.

"True, it's none of your business," he said. "But inasmuch as you can't sleep anyway . . ." Waverly swung his legs over the sill onto the landing and started up.

As he reached the landing above, something white fluttered out at him. Waverly shied, then saw that it was a curtain, billowing out from an open window.

Abruptly, a feminine sob sounded from within. He poked his head up far enough to peer over the window sill into darkness.

"Is, ah, something the matter?" he called softly. There was a long moment of silence.

"Who's there?" a dulcet female voice whispered.

"Waverly, madam, Jack Waverly. If I can be of any help?"

"Are you with the Service?"

"I'm with ISLC," Waverly said. He pronounced it as a word "islick." "That's International Sa——"

"Listen to me, Wivery," the voice was urgent. "Whatever he's paying you, I'll double it! And you'll find the Service not ungrateful."

"No payment is necessary for aid to damsels in distress," Waverly returned. "Er, may I come in?"

"Of course! Hurry up, before one of those slimy Gimps steps out for a stroll up the wall and sees you!"

Waverly climbed quickly in through the window. The room, he saw, was a mere garret, cramped under a low ceiling. It appeared to contain no furniture other than a dimly seen cot against one wall. A vague form moved a willowy arm there. Waverly moved toward it.

"You don't have a molecular disassociator with you?" the melodious voice queried urgently. "There's not much time left."

"Ah . . . no, I'm afraid not. I——"

"They mean to strap me to my own twifler, set the warperators at two and a half busters and aim me toward Neptune," the feminine voice went on breathlessly. "Can you imagine anything more brutal?"

Waverly groped forward. "Now, now, my dear. Don't be upset."

As he reached the cot, his hand fell on stout links looped around the foot rail.

He fumbled, encountered the blocky shape of a hefty padlock.

"Good lord! I thought—that is, I didn't actually think——"

"That's right. Chained to the bed," there was a slight quaver in the voice.

"B-but—this is preposterous! It's criminal!"

"It's an indication of their desperation, Wivery! They've gone so far now that nothing short of the most drastic measures can stop them!"

"I think this is a matter for the authorities," Waverly blurted. "I'll put a call through immediately!"

"How? You can't get through."

"That's right; I'd forgotten about the phone."

"And anyway—I *am* the authorities," the soft voice said in a tone of utter discouragement.

"You? A mere slip of a girl?" Waverly's hand touched something cool, with the texture like nubbly nylon carpeting.

"I weigh three hundred and seventy pounds, Earth equatorial," the voice came back sharply. "And we Vorplischers happen to be a matriarchal society!"

A pale shape stirred, rose up from the rumpled bedding. A head the size of a washtub smiled a foot-wide smile that was disconcertingly located above a pair of limpid brown eyes. A hand which appeared to be equipped with at least nine fingers reached up to pat a spongy mass of orange fibers matted across the top

of the wide face. Waverly broke his paralysis suffi-
ciently to utter a sharp yelp.

"Shhh!" the sweet voice issued from a point high in
the chest. "I appreciate your admiration, but we don't
want those monsters to hear you!"

2

"Fom Berj, Detective Third Class, at your service,"
the creature soothed Waverly. "I'm not supposed to
reveal my identity, but under the circumstances I think
it's only appropriate."

"D——delighted," Waverly choked. "Pardon my falling down. It's just that I was a trifle startled at your,
ah, unusual appearance."

"It's perfectly understandable. A neat disguise, don't
you think? I made it myself."

Waverly gulped. "Disguise?"

"Of course. You don't think this is my natural look,
do you?"

Waverly laughed shakily. "I must confess that what
with all this creeping around in the dark, I *was* ready
to leap to conclusions." He peered at the massive form,
more clearly visible now that his eyes accommodated
to the dim light. "But what are you disguised as, if you
don't mind my asking?"

"Why, as a native, of course. The same as you are,
silly."

"As I am what?"

"Disguised as a native."

"Native of where?"

"Of this planet."

"Oh, of course." Waverly was backing toward the

window. "Of this planet. A native . . . I take it you're from some *other* planet?"

The detective laughed a rippling laugh. "You have a jolly sense of humor, Wivery. As if a Vorplischer were native to this patch of wilderness."

"And the people who chained you up—are they from, ah, Vorplisch, too?" Waverly made conversation to cover his retreat.

"Don't be absurd. They're a mixed bag of Broogs, Limpicos, Erwalts, Glimps and Pud knows what-all." Fom Berj rattled her manacles. "We'd better do something about these chains in a hurry," she added briskly.

As Waverly reached the window, an eerie, purplish glow sprang up outside, accompanied by a shrill warbling. Waverly retreated hastily.

"I think that's them arriving with my twifler now," Fom Berj said tensely. "It's a brand-new model, equipped with the latest in antiac gear and the new infinite-capacity particle ingesters. You can imagine what *that* means! My frozen corpse will be three parsecs beyond Pluto before my Mayday beep clears the first boost station."

"Frozen corpse? Pluto?" Waverly gobbled.

"I know it sounds fantastic, but disposing of an agent of the Service is a mere bagatelle to these operators, compared with what they're planning!"

"What *are* they planning?" Waverly choked.

"Don't you know? I thought you were working for Izlik."

"Well, he, ah, doesn't tell us much. . . ."

"Mmmm. I don't know about that Izlik. Sometimes I wonder just how deep a game he's playing. By the way, where *is* he?"

"He was delayed by a heavy cloud cover over Ypsilanti," Waverly improvised. "He'll be along later." His eyes roved the room, searching for an escape route. "You were saying?" he prompted in an obscure instinct to keep the detective talking.

"They're making a Galacular," Fom Berj said solemnly.

"A . . . Galacular?"

"Now you see the extent of their madness. An open violation of Regulation 69723468b!"

There was a sharp series of bumping sounds above. "Better hurry with that molecular disassociator," Fom Berj said.

"What's a Galacular?" Waverly was close to the door now. He froze as something made a slithery sound beyond it.

"A multi-D thriller," Fom Berj was explaining. "You know, one of those planetary debacle epics."

"What sort of debacle?" Waverly recoiled at a sound as of heavy breathing outside the door.

"Floods, quakes, typhoons—you know the sort of thing. Audiences love them, in spite of their illegality. The first scene they're shooting tonight will be a full-scale meteor strike in a place called Montana."

"You mean—a *real* meteor?"

"Of course. According to my informant, they've grappled onto a cubic mile or so of nickel-iron that was parked in a convenient orbit a few million miles out, and nudged it in this direction. I would have stopped it there, of course, but I blundered and they caught me," the detective sighed. "It should make quite an effective splash when it hits."

"They're going to wreck an entire state just for a—a spectacle?" Waverly choked.

"I see you're not familiar with the Galacular craze. To be accepted by discriminating multi-D fans, nothing less than a genuine disaster will serve."

Up above on the roof, heavy feet clumped; something massive bump-bumped.

Fom Berj's voice was icy calm. "Now, Wivery, it's true we Vorplischers pride ourselves on our coolness in the face of peril, but WILL YOU GET THESE DAMNED CHAINS OFF ME BEFORE IT'S TOO LATE!"

Waverly darted to the window. "Don't go away," he called over his shoulder. "I'll be right back!"

It took Waverly forty-five seconds to descend to his room, snatch up his sample case, hastily examine his tongue in the mirror and retrace his steps to the attic. He opened the case, lettered International Safe and Lock Corporation, took out a tool shaped like a miniature crochet hook, turned to the lock.

"Hmmm. A variation on the Katzenburger-McIlhenney patents," he muttered. "Child's play . . ." He probed delicately in the wide key slot, frowning as he worked.

"Hurry, Wivery!" Fom Berj cried.

Waverly wiped perspiration from his forehead. "It's trickier than it looked," he said defensively. "Apparently they've employed a double-reserve cam action."

Feet clumped on stairs, descending from the roof. A mutter of hoarse voices sounded in the hall, just beyond the door. The latch rattled. Waverly reached for his sample case, rummaged among the odds and ends there, came up with a cylindrical object. He sprang to the door, hastily engaged the chain latch just as the doorknob turned cautiously. The door creaked, swung open two inches, came to rest against the chain. A beaklike nose appeared at the opening, followed by a hand holding a gun.

Aiming coolly, Waverly directed a jet of menthol shaving cream at a pair of close-set eyes just visible above the nose. They withdrew with a muffled shriek. The gun clattered on the floor. Waverly snatched up the weapon, jammed it in his waistband, dashed back to the lock. Five seconds later, it opened with a decisive *spongg!* Fom Berj emitted a delighted squeak, rolled off the bed as the chains clattered to the floor. Waverly gaped at the cluster of supple members on which the bulky detective rippled swiftly across to the window. Outside the door, excited twitters, burbles and growls sounded interrogatory notes. The doorknob rattled. Something heavy struck the door.

"To the roof!" Fom Berj flowed through the window and was gone. The door shook to a thunderous impact. Waverly sprang to the window. On the landing, he looked down. A round, pale face with eyes like bubbles in hot tar stared up at him. He yelped and dashed for the roof.

Pulling himself up over the parapet, Waverly looked across an expanse of starlit roof, at the center of which an object shaped like a twelve-foot gravy boat rested lightly on three spidery jacks. The upper half was a clear plastic, hinged open like a mussel shell. Fom Berj was halfway to it when a small, sharp-featured head appeared over its gunwale. The monkeylike face split vertically, emitted a sharp cry and dived over the side. The boat rocked perilously as Fom Berj swarmed up and in; she turned, extended a long, three-elbowed arm to Waverly, hauled him up as something popped nearby. Pale chartreuse gas swirled about the canopy as it slammed down. The detective lurched to a small, green-plush-covered contour seat, groped for the controls. Waverly scrambled after her, found himself crowded into a restricted space which was apparently intended as a parcel shelf.

"Which way is Montana?" the detective inquired over a rising hum that sprang up as she poked buttons on the padded dash.

"Straight ahead, about a thousand miles," Waverly called.

"Hold on tight," Fom Berj cried as the little vehicle leaped straight up. "On optimum trajectory, the trip will take close to half an hour. I don't know if we'll be in time or not."

3

Level at 100,000 feet, the twifler hummed along smoothly, making the whispering sound which gave it its name. Its velocity was just under 1850 MPH.

"Hurry," Waverly urged.

"Any faster at this altitude and we'd ablate," Fom Berj pointed out. "Relax, Wivery. We're doing our best."

"How can I relax?" Waverly complained. "The headroom is grossly inadequate."

"Well, you know the Q-stress engine produces a lens-shaped field with a minor radius proportional to the reciprocal of the fourth power of the input. To give you room to stand up, we'd need a diameter of about half a light-year. That's unwieldy."

"Hmmm. I wondered why flying saucers were shaped like that. It never occurred——"

"It seems to me you're pretty ignorant of a lot of things," Fom Berj studied Waverly with one eye, keeping the other firmly fixed on the instrument panel.

"I seem to note certain deficiencies in your costume, when it comes to that," he pointed out somewhat acidly. He eyed the three padded foundation garments strapped around the bulbous torso. "Most local beauties consider two of *those* sufficient," he added.

"You don't know much about these locals. They're mammary-happy. And if two of a given organ are attractive, six are triply attractive."

"What are you trying to attract?"

"Nothing. But a girl likes to make a good impression."

"Speaking of impressions—what are you planning on doing about this meterorite? You *did* say a cubic mile?"

"I was hoping to disintegrate it outside the outer R-belt, if possible, but I'm afraid we're running a little late."

"A thing that size——" Waverly felt the sweat pop on his forehead—"will vaporize the crust of the earth for miles around the point of impact!"

"I hate to think of what it will do to the native wild life," Fom Berj said. "Their feeding and mating habits will be upset, their nests destroyed——" Fom Berj broke off. "Oh, dear, I'm afraid we're too late!"

Ahead, a glowing point had appeared high in the

sky. It descended steadily, becoming rapidly brighter. Waverly braced his feet as the twifler decelerated sharply, veering off. The glaring point of fire was surrounded by a greenish aura.

"It's about three hundred miles out, I'd say," Fom Berj commented. "That means it will strike in about thirty seconds."

A faint, fiery trail was visible now behind the new star. Through the clear plastic hatch, Waverly watched as a beam of blue light speared out from the swelling central fire, probed downward, boiling away a low cloud layer.

"What's that?" Waverly squeaked.

"A column of compressed gases. It will be splashing up a nice pit for the actual body to bury itself in."

A pink glow had sprung up from the surface far below. The approaching meteor was an intolerable point of brilliance now, illuminating the clouds like a full moon. The light grew brighter; now Waverly could see a visible diameter, heading the streaming tail of fire. Abruptly it separated into three separate fragments, which continued on parallel courses.

"Tsk," Fom Berj clucked. "It exploded. That means an even wider distribution . . ."

With appalling swiftness the three radiant bodies expanded to form a huge, irregular glob of brilliance, dropping swiftly now, darting downward as quick as thought——

The sky opened into a great fan of yellow light more vivid than the sun.

Waverly squinted at the actinic display, watched it

spread outward, shot through with rising jets of glowing stuff, intersperse with rocketlike streaks that
punched upward, higher, higher, and were gone from
view—all in utter silence. The far horizons were
touched with light now. Then, slowly, the glare faded
back. The silver-etched edges of the clouds dimmed
away, until only a great rosy glow in the west marked
the point of the meteorite's impact.

"Fooey," Fom Berj said. "Round one to the opposition."

Waverly and the Vorplischer stared down at the
mile-wide, white-hot pit bubbling fifty thousand feet
below and ten miles ahead.

"You have to confess the rascals got some remarkable footage that time," Fom Berj commented.

"This is incredible!" Waverly groaned. "You people—whoever you are—were aware that this band of
desperadoes planned this atrocity—and all you sent
was one female to combat them?"

"I'll disregard the chauvinistic overtones of that remark," Fom Berj said severely, "and merely remind
you that the Service is a small one, operating on a
perennially meager appropriation."

"If your precious Service were any sort of interplanetary police force, it wouldn't tolerate this sort of
sloppy work," Waverly said sharply.

"Police force? Where did you get an idea like
that? I'm a private eye in the employ of the Game
and Wildlife Service."

"Wildlife——" Waverly started.

"Brace yourself," Fom Berj said. "Here comes the
shock wave."

The twifler gave a preliminary shudder, then wrenched itself violently end-for-end, at the same time slamming violently upward, to the accompaniment of a great metallic *zonnggg!* of thunder.

"I shudder to imagine how that would have felt without the special antiac equipment," the detective gasped. "Now, if we expect to intercept these scoundrels in the act of shooting their next scene, there's no time to waste."

"You mean they're going to do it *again?*"

"Not the same routine, of course. This time they're staging a major earthquake in a province called California. They'll trigger it by beaming the deep substrata with tight-focus tractor probes. The whole area is in a delicate state of balance, so all it will take is the merest touch to start a crustal readjustment that will satisfy the most exacting fans."

"The San Andreas Fault," Waverly groaned. "Good-by, San Francisco!"

"It's the Sequoias I'm thinking of," Fom Berj sighed. "Remarkable organisms, and not nearly so easy to replace as San Franciscans."

4

The twifler hurtled across the Rockies at eighty thousand feet, began to let down over northwestern Nevada, an unbroken desert gleaming ghostly white in the light of a crescent moon. Far ahead, San Francisco glowed on the horizon.

"This gets a trifle tricky now," Fom Berj said. "The recording units will be orbiting the scene of the action at a substratospheric level, of course, catching it all with wide-spectrum senceivers, but the production crew will be on the ground, controlling the action. They're the ones we're after. And in order to capture these malefactors red-handed, we'll have to land and go in on foot for the pinch. That means leaving the protection of the twifler's antiac field."

"What will we do when we find them?"

"I'd prefer to merely lay them by the heels with a liberal application of stun gas. If they're alive to stand trial, the publicity will be a real bonus, careerwise. However, it may be necessary to vaporize them."

Decelerating sharply, Fom Berj dropped low over the desert, scanning the instruments closely.

"They've shielded their force bubble pretty well," she said. "But I think I've picked it up." She pointed. Waverly detected a vague bluish point glowing on a high rooftop near the north edge of the city. "A good position, with an excellent view of the target area."

Waverly held on as the flier swooped low, whistled in a tight arc and settled in on a dark rooftop. The hatch popped up, admitted a gust of cool night air. Waverly and the detective advanced to the parapet. A hundred yards distant across a bottomless, black chasm, the blue glow of the fifty-foot force bubble shone eerily. Waverly was beginning to sweat inside his purple pajamas.

"What if they see us?" he hissed—and dropped flat as a beam of green light sizzled past his head from the bubble and burst into flame.

"Does that answer your question?" Fom Berj was crouched behind the parapet. "Well, there's no help for it. I'll have to use sterner measures." She broke off as the deck underfoot trembled, then rose in a series of jarring jerks, dropped a foot, thrust upward again. A low rumble had started up. Brick came pelting down from adjacent buildings to smash thunderously below.

"Oh, oh, it's started!" Fom Berj shrilled. Clinging to the roof with her multiple ambulatory members, the detective unlimbered a device resembling a small fire extinguisher, took aim and fired. Waverly, bouncing like a passenger in a Model T Ford, saw a yellow spear of light dart out, glance off the force bubble and send up a shower of sparks as it scored the blue-glowing sphere.

"Bull's-eye!" Fom Berj trilled. "A couple more like that, and——"

The whole mountainside under the building seemed to tilt. The parapet toppled and was gone. Waverly grabbed for a stout TV antenna, held on as his feet swung over the edge. Fom Berj emitted a sharp scream and grabbed for a handhold. The vaporizer slid past Waverly, went over the edge.

"That does it," the detective cried over the roar of crumbling mortar. "We tried, Wivery!"

"Look!" Waverly yelled. Over his shoulder, he saw the force bubble suddenly flicker violet, then green, then yellow—and abruptly dwindle to half its former diameter. Through a pall of dust, Waverly discerned the outlines of an elaborate apparatus resembling an oversized X-ray camera, now just outside the shrunken blue bubble. A pair of figures, one tall and thin, the other rotund and possessing four arms, dithered, scrabbling at the dome for entrance. One slipped and disappeared over the roof's edge with a mournful yowl. The other scampered off across the buckling roof, leaped to an adjacent one, disappeared in a cloud of smoke and dust.

"Did you see that?" Fom Berj cried. "They've had to abandon their grappler! We've beaten them!"

"Yes—but what about the earthquake?" Waverly called as the roof under him bounded and leaped.

"We'll just have to ride it out and hope for the best!"

Through the dust cloud, they watched as the blue bubble quivered, swam upward from its perch, leaving the abandoned tractor beamer perched forlornly on the roof.

"Let them go," Fom Berj called. "As soon as the ground stops shaking, we'll be after them."

Waverly looked out toward the vast sprawl of lights, which were now executing a slow, graceful shimmy. As he watched, a section of the city half a mile square went dark. A moment later, the twinkling orange lights of fires sprang up here and there across the darkened portion. Beyond the city, the surface of the Pacific heaved and boiled. A dome swelled up, burst; green water streamed back as a gout of black smoke belched upward in a roiling fire-shot cloud. The moonlight gleamed on a twenty-foot wavefront that traveled outward from the submarine eruption. Waverly saw it meet and merge with the waterfront, sweep grandly inland, foaming majestically about the bases of the hills on which the city was built. The long, undulating span of the Golden Gate bridge wavered in a slow snake dance, then descended silently into the bay, disappeared in a rising smother of white. More light went out; more fires appeared across the rapidly darkening city. A deafening rumble rolled continuously across the scene of devastation.

Now the backwash of the tidal wave was sweeping back out to sea, bearing with it a flotsam of bars, billboards, seafood restaurants and automobiles, many of the latter with their headlights still on, gleaming murkily through the shallow waters. Smoke was forming a pall across the mile of darkened ruins, lit from beneath by leaping flames. Here and there the quick yellow flashes of explosions punctuated the general overcast.

"G-good Lord," Waverly gasped as the shaking under him subsided into a quiver and then was still. "What an incredible catastrophe!"

"That was nothing to what it would have been if they'd had time to give it a good push," Fom Berj commented.

"The fiends!" Waverly scrambled to his feet. "Some of the best bars in the country were down there!"

"It could have been worse."

"I suppose so. At least the San Franciscans are used to it. Imagine what that tidal wave would have done to Manhattan!"

"Thanks for reminding me," Fom Berj said. "That's where the next scene is due to be shot."

5

"The scare we gave them should throw them far enough behind schedule to give us a decent crack at them this time," Fom Berj said, staring forward into the night as the twifler rocketed eastward. "They only have the one production unit here, you know. It's a shoestring operation, barely a hundred billion dollar budget."

Waverly, crouched again in his cramped perch behind the pilot, peered out as the lights of Chicago appeared ahead, spread below them and dwindled behind.

"What do they have in mind for New York? Another earthquake? A fire? Or maybe just a super typhoon?"

"Those minor disturbances won't do for this one," Fom Berj corrected him. "This is the climactic scene of the show. They plan to collapse a massive off-shore igneous dike and let the whole stretch of continental shelf from Boston to Cape Charles slide into the ocean."

"Saints preserve us!" Waverly cried.

"You should see what they'd do on a Class-A budget," Fom Berj retorted. "The local moon would look quite impressive, colliding with Earth."

"Ye gods! You sound almost as if you approve of these atrocities!"

"Well, I used to be a regular Saturday-afternoon theatergoer; but now that I've attained responsible age, I see the folly of wasting planets that way."

The blaze of lights that was the Atlantic seaboard swam over the horizon ahead, rushed toward the speeding twifler.

"They're set up on a barge about five miles offshore," the detective said as they swept over the city. "It's just a little field rig; it will only be used once, of course." She leaned forward. "Ah, there it is now!"

Waverly gaped at a raft of lights visible on the sea ahead.

"Gad!" he cried. "The thing's the size of an Australian sheep ranch!"

"They need a certain area on which to set up the antenna arrays," Fom Berj said. "After all, they'll be handling a hundred billion megavolt-seconds of power. Now, we'll just stand off at about twenty miles and lob a few rounds into them. I concede it will be a little messy, what with the initial flash, the shock wave, the fallout and the storms and tidal waves, but it's better than letting them get away."

"Wait a minute—your cure sounds as bad as the disease! We're a couple of miles from the most densely populated section of the country! You'll annihilate thousands!"

"You really *are* hipped on conservation," Fom Berj said. "However, you can't cure tentacle mildew without trimming off a few tentacles. Here goes . . ."

"No!" Waverly grabbed for the detective's long arm as the latter placed a spatulate finger on a large pink button. Taken by surprise, Fom Berj yanked the limb back, struck a lever with her elbow. At once, the canopy snapped up and was instantly ripped away by the hundred-mile-per-hour slipstream. Icy wind tore at Waverly's pajamas, shrieked past his face, sucked the air from his lungs. Fom Berj grabbed for the controls, fought the bucking twifler as it went into a spin, hurtling down toward the black surface of the sea.

"Wivery! I can't hold it! Vertigo! Take over. . . ." Waverly barely caught the words before the massive body of the feminine detective slumped and slid down under the dash. He reached, caught the wildly vibrating control tiller, put all his strength into hauling it back into line. The flier tilted, performed an outside loop followed by a snap-roll. Only Waverly's safety harness prevented him from being thrown from the cockpit. He shoved hard on the tiller, and the twifler went into a graceful inverted chandelle. Waverly looked "up," saw a vast spread of dark-glittering, white-capped ocean slowly tilting over him. With a convulsive wrench of the tiller he brought the Atlantic down and under his keel and was racing along fifty feet above the water. He dashed the wind-tears from his eyes, saw the lights of the barge rushing at him, gave a convulsive stab at four buttons at random and squeezed his eyes shut.

The twifler veered sharply, made a sound like ripped canvas and halted as suddenly as if it had dropped an anchor. Waverly pitched forward; the harness snapped. He hurtled across the short prow, clipping off a flagstaff bearing a triangular pink ensign, fell six feet and was skidding head over heels across the deck of the barge.

For a moment, Waverly lay half-stunned; then he staggered to his feet, holding a tattered strip of safety harness in one hand. The twifler was drifting rapidly away, some ten feet above the deck of the barge. He scrambled after it, made a despairing grab at a trailing harness strap, missed, skidded into the rail and clung there, watching the air car dwindle away downwind.

Behind him, a brilliant crimson spotlight blared into existence. Hoarse voices shouted. Other lights came up. The deck, Waverly saw, was swarming with excited figures. He ducked for the cover of a three-foot scupper, squinted as the floodlight caught him square in the face. Something hard was pressing into his hip. He groped, came out with the compact automatic he had jammed into the waistband of his pajamas. He raised the gun and fired a round into the big light. It emitted a deep-toned *whoof!,* flashed green and blue and went out.

"Hey!" a rubbery voice yelled. "I thought you boobs stuck a fresh filament in number twelve!"

"Get them extra persons in position before I put 'em over the side," another voice bassooned.

"Zero minus six mini-units and counting," a hoot came from on high.

The gobbling mob surged closer. Waverly clutched the pistol, made three yards sideways, then rose in shadow and darted toward a low deckhouse ahead. He rounded its corner, almost collided with an apparition with coarse-grained blue wattles, two-inch eyes of a deep bottle green, a vertically hinged mouth opening on triple rows of coppery-brown fangs, all set on a snaky neck rising from a body like a baled buffalo robe shrouded in leathery wings; then he was skittering backward, making pushing motions with both hands.

"Hasrach opp irikik!" the creature boomed. "Who're youse? You scared the pants off me in that getup! Whaddya want?"

"Izlik s-sent me," Waverly improvised.

"Oh, then you want to see the boss."

"Ah, yes, precisely. I want to see the boss."

"You want the feeding boss, the mating boss, the leisure-time boss, the honorary boss, the hereditary boss or the compulsory boss?" The monster snapped a blue cigar butt over the rail.

"The, er, boss boss!"

"Balvovats is inside, rescripting scene two. Din't you hear what happened out on the coast?"

"As a matter of fact, I just got in from Butte——"

"How did the fireball routine go?"

"Very impressive. Ah, by the way, how long before things get underway here?"

"Another five minutes."

"Thanks."

Waverly sidled past the horror, made for a lighted doorway fifty feet away. Above, invisible behind banked floodlights, someone was gabbling shrilly. Two beings appeared at the entrance as Waverly reached it. One was an armored creature mincing on six legs like a three-foot blue crab. The other appeared to be a seven-foot column of translucent yellow jelly.

"Here, you can't go in there," the crablike one barked. *"Ik urikik opsrock,* you know that!"

"Wait a minute, Sol," the gelatinous one burbled in a shaky voice like a failing tape recorder. "Can't you see he's just in from location? Look at the costume."

"A lousy job. Wouldn't fool anybody."

"What you got, Mac? Make it fast. Balvovats is ready to roll 'em."

"Ip orikip slunk," Waverly said desperately.

"Sorry, I don't savvy Glimp. Better talk local like the style boss said."

"It's the rotiple underplump!" Waverly barked. "Out of the way, before all is lost!"

"I got to have a word with Mel about his runners, which they're a little too uppity to suit me." Waverly caught the words as the two exchanged glances and moved from the doorway. He stepped through into a room dazzling with light and activity. Opposite him, a fifty-foot wall glittered with moving points of light. Before it, on high stools, half a dozen small orange-furred creatures bristling with multi-elbowed arms manipulated levers. On a raised dais to the left, a circular being with what appeared to be four heads shouted commands in all directions at once, through four megaphones.

"Okay!" Waverly heard the call. "We're all ready on one, three and four! What's the matter with two and five?"

"Here, you!" A scaled figure in a flowing pageboy bob thrust a sheaf of papers into his hand. "Take this to Balvovats; he's got holes in his head!" Waverly gaped after the donor as it turned away. The noise around him made his ears ring. Everything was rushing toward a climax at an accelerating pace, and if he didn't do something fast . . .

"Stop!" he yelled at the room at large. "You can't do this thing!"

"It's a heart-breaker, ain't it, kid?" a bulging being on his left chirruped in his ear. "If I would have been directing this fiasco, I'd of went for a real effect by blasting the ice caps. Now, *there's* a spectacle for you! Floods, storms——"

"Here, take these to Balvovats!" Waverly shoved the papers toward a passing creature resembling a fallen pudding. The bulgy being nictated a membrane at him, snorted, said, "Okay, okay, I'm going, ain't I?" and pushed off through the press. At a discreet distance, Waverly followed.

6

The room the impressed messenger led him to was a circular arena crowded with screens, dials, levers, flashing lights, amid a cacophony of electronic hums and buzzes, all oriented toward a central podium on which was mounted a red and white, zebra-striped swivel chair, wide enough to accommodate triplets.

"Where's Balvovats?" The unwitting guide collared a jittery organism consisting of a cluster of bristly blue legs below a striped polo shirt.

"He stepped over to Esthetic Editing for a last-minute check," a piping voice snapped. "Now leggo my shirt before I call the shop steward!"

"Give him these!" The bulbous intruder handed over the papers and departed. Waverly faded back behind the column-mounted chair, looked around hastily, put a foot on a rung——

"Two minutes," a PA voice rang. "All recorder units on station and grinding."

"Hey, you, back outside on Set Nine! You heard the two-minute call!" Waverly looked down at a foot-high composition of varicolored warts mounted on two legs like coat-hanger wire.

"Mind your tone, my man," Waverly said. "Balvovats sent me. I'm sitting in for him. Is the, er, power on?"

"Cripey, what a time for an OJT! Okay, sir, better get on up there. About a minute and a half to M millisecond."

Waverly clambered to the seat, slid into it, looked over an array of levers, pedals, orifices, toggle switches and paired buttons with varicolored idiot lights. "Don't monkey with the board, it's all set up," the warty one whined at his elbow. "I balanced her out personal. All you got to do is throw the load to her when you get the flash and push-field is up to full Q."

"Naturally," Waverly said. "It wouldn't do at all to push, say, this little green button here . . . ?"

"If you got to go, you should've went before you come in here. Better tighten up and wait. You only got fifty-one seconds and you're on the air."

"How about the big blue one there?"

"What for you want more light on deck? The boys are crying their eyes out now."

"This middle-sized yellow one?"

"The screens is already hot, can't you see 'em? Boy, the greenies they send out to me!"

"I know; this immense black lever is the one——"

"You don't need no filters, for Pud's sake! It's night-time!"

Waverly ran both hands through his hair and then pointed to various levers in turn: "Eenie, meenie, minie, moe . . . ."

"Lay off that one you called 'minie,' " the instructor cautioned. "You touch that, you'll dump the whole load onto the left stabilizer complex——"

A door banged. Waverly looked up. A vast, white-robed being with arms like coiled boa constrictors had burst into the room, was goggling stem-mounted eyes like peeled tomatoes at Waverly.

"Hey—come down from there, you!" the new arrival bellowed. The snaky arms whipped up toward Waverly; he ducked, seized the forbidden lever, and slammed it home.

A shudder went through the seat under him; then the floor rose up like a stricken freighter up-ending for her last dive. A loud screech sounded in Waverly's ear as the warty being bounded into his lap and wrestled with the big lever. He rolled sideways, dived, saw the vast form of Balvovats cannon past and carom off the control pedestal, ophidoid members flailing murderously. Lights were flashing all around the room. A siren broke into a frantic, rising wail. Gongs gonged. Waverly, on the floor now and clinging to a cabinet support, saw an access panel pop open, exposing a foot square terminal block. "In for a penny, in for a pound," he muttered and grabbed a handful of intricately color-coded leads and ripped them loose.

The resultant cascade of fire sent him reeling backward just as a baseball-bat-thick tentacle whipped down across the spot he had been occupying. A dull *boom!* rocked the deck plates under him. Smoke poured from the ruined circuitry. He tottered to his feet, saw Balvovats secure a grip on a stanchion and haul his bulk upright.

"You!" the giant bellowed and launched itself at Waverly. He sprang for the door, tripped, rolled aside as the door banged wide. A gaggle of frantic spectacle-makers hurtled through, collided with the irate director. On all fours, Waverly pulled himself up the slanted deck and through the door.

In the corridor, the blare of gongs and sirens was redoubled. Buffeted by milling technicians, Waverly was spun, jostled, shoved, lifted along the passage and out onto the windswept deck. All around, loose gear was sliding and bounding down the thirty-degree slant. Waverly threw himself flat, barely avoiding a ricocheting cable drum, clawed his way toward the high edge of the barge.

"There he goes!" a bull-roar sounded behind him. He twisted, saw Balvovats winching himself upward in close pursuit. One extensible member lashed out, slapped the deck bare inches short of Waverly's foot. He groped for the automatic. It was gone. Ahead, a superstructure loomed up at the barge's edge, like a miniature Eiffel Tower. He scrambled for it, got a grip on a cross-member and pulled himself around to the far side. Balvovat's questing arm grabbed after him. He held on with both hands and one foot and delivered a swift kick to the persistent member; it recoiled, as a yell sounded from the darkness below. The deck lights had failed, leaving only the feeble gleam of colored rigging lights. Something struck the cross-bar by Waverly's head with a vicious *pwangg!* He clambered hastily higher.

On deck, someone had restored a spotlight to usefulness. The smoky beam probed upward, found Waverly's feet, jumped up to pin him against a girder fifty feet above the deck.

"A fat bonus to the one that nails him!" Balvovats' furious tones roared. At once, spitting sounds broke out below, accompanied by vivid flashes of pink light. Waverly scrambled higher. The spotlight followed him. Across the deck, a door burst open and smoke and flames rushed out. Waverly felt a shock through the steel tower, saw a gout of fire erupt through curled deck plating below.

"We're sinking!" a shrill voice keened.

"Get him!" Balvovats boomed.

Waverly looked down, saw white water breaking over the base of his perch. In the glow of the navigation lights, half a dozen small creatures were swarming up the openwork in hot pursuit. Something bumped him from behind. He shied, felt another bump, reached down and felt the hard contours of the automatic, trapped in the seat of his pajamas.

"Lucky I had them cut generously," he murmured as he retrieved the weapon. Something *spangled* beside him, and a near-miss whined off into the darkness. Waverly took aim, shot out the deck light. Something plucked at his sleeve. He looked, saw torn cloth. Below, a red-eyed ball of sticky-looking fur was taking a bead on him from a distance of ten feet. He brought the automatic up and fired, fired again at a second pursuer a yard below the leader. Both assailants dropped, hit with twin splashes in the darkness below.

"Decks awash," Waverly said to himself. *"Dulce et decorum est, pro patria, et cetera."*

Another explosion shook the stricken barge. The tower swayed. A shot whined past his face. Another struck nearby.

"Get him, troops? Get hiburbleburble . . . ." Balvovats' boom subsided. Waverly winced as a hot poker furrowed his shin. He saw a flicker of movement revealed by a blue rigging light, put a round into it, saw a dark body fall with a thin bleat. The spout of fire rising from the hatch on the high edge of the deck showed a white smother of foam washed almost to the survivors clinging to the rail. A gun burped below, chipped paint by Waverly's hip. He shifted grips, leaned far out and placed a shot between a pair of overlapping, egg-white eyes. They fell away with a despairing wail.

Abruptly, the fire died with a hiss as a wave rolled entirely across the deck. Waverly felt the tower shake as a breaker thundered against it, bare yards below where he clung. The lower navigation lights gleamed up through green water now.

There was a whiffling sound above. Waverly clutched his perch convulsively, looked upward.

"Fom Berj!" he yelled.

A dark ovoid shape settled down through the night toward him. He saw the cheery glow of running lights, the gleam reflected from a canopy.

"But . . . but our canopy blew away . . ." he faltered.

The twifler hove to, six feet above his head. A face like a plate of lasagna appeared over the edge. Squirmy hands, gripping an ominous-looking apparatus with a long barrel, came over the side, aimed at Waverly. A whirring sound started up. He brought up the pistol, squeezed the trigger——

There was an empty click.

"Superb!" the creature above exclaimed, extending a large grasping member over the side to Waverly. "What an expression of primitive savagery! Great footage, my boy! Now you'd better come aboard where we can talk contract in peace!"

7

"I'm afraid I don't quite understand, Mr. Izlik," Waverly said dazedly, trying not to stare at the leathery-hided bulk draped in a Clan Stewart tartan, complete with sporran and Tam o'Shanter. "One moment I was teetering on top of a sinking tower, with a horde of furry atrocities snapping at my heels—and ten minutes later . . ." He looked wonderingly at the luxuriously appointed lounge in which he sat.

"I left my yacht anchored here at two hundred thousand feet and dropped down to spy out what Balvovats was up to," the entrepreneur explained. "I confess I wasn't above purloining a little free footage of whatever it was he was staging. Then I saw you, sir, in action, and presto! I perceived the New Wave in the moment of its creation! Of course, I secured only about three minutes' actual product. We'll have to pad it out with another hundred hours or so of the same sort of action. I can already visualize a sequence in which you find yourself pursued by flesh-eating Dinosaurs, scale a man-eating plant for safety and are attacked by flying fang-masters, make a leap across an abyss of flaming hydrocarbons and, in a single bound, attain the safety of your twifler, just as it collides with a mountaintop!"

"Ah . . . I appreciate your offer of employment," Waverly interposed, "but I'm afraid I lack the dramatic gift."

"Oh, it won't be acting," Izlik handed over a slim glass of pale fluid and seated himself across from his guest. "No, indeed! I can assure you that all my productions are recorded on location, at the actual scenes of the frightful dangers they record. I'll see to it that the perils are real enough to inspire you to the highest efforts."

"No." Waverly drained his glass and hiccupped. "I

appreciate the rescue and all that, but now I really must be getting back to work——"

"What salary are you drawing now?" Izlik demanded bluntly.

"Five hundred," Waverly said.

"Ha! I'll double that! One thousand Universal Credits!"

"How much is that in dollars?"

"You mean the local exchange?" Izlik removed a note book from his sporran, writhed his features at it. "Coconuts . . . wampum . . . seashells . . . green stamps . . . ah! Here we are! Dollars. One Unicred is equal to twelve hundred and sixty-five dollars and twenty-three cents." He closed the book. "A cent is a type of cow, I believe. A few are always included in local transactions to placate Vishnu, or something."

"That's . . . that's over a million dollars a month!"

"A minute," Izlik corrected. "You'll get more for your next picture, of course."

"I'd like to take you up on it, Mr. Izlik," Waverly said wistfully. "But I'm afraid I wouldn't survive long enough to spend it."

"As to that, if you're to play superheroes, you'll naturally require superpowers. I'll fit you out with full S-P gear. Can't have my star suffering any damage, of course."

"S-P gear?"

"Self-Preservation. Developed in my own labs at Cosmic Productions. Better than anything issued to the armed forces. Genuine poly-steel muscles, invulnerable armor, IR and UV vision, cloak of invisibility

—though of course you'll use the latter only in *real* emergencies."

"It sounds——" Waverly swallowed. "Quite overwhelming," he finished.

"Wait!" a faint voice sounded from the floor. Waverly and Izlik turned to the cot where Fom Berj was struggling feebly to sit up.

"You wouldn't . . . sink so low . . . as to ally yourself . . . with these vandals . . . ." she gasped out.

"Vandals!" Izlik snorted. "I remind you, madam, it was I who took in tow your derelict twifler, which was bearing you swiftly toward a trans-Plutonian orbit!"

"Better annihilation—than help . . . from the likes of you . . ."

"I, ah, think you have an erroneous impression," Waverly put in. "Mr. Izlik here doesn't produce Galaculars. In fact, he's planning a nice, family-type entertainment that will render the planet wreckers obsolete."

"The day of the Galacular is over!" Izlik stated in positive tones. "What is a mere fractured continent, when compared with a lone hero, fighting for his life? When I release my epic of the struggle of one beleaguered being, beset by a bewildering bestiary of bellicose berserkers, our fortunes will be made!"

"Oh, really?" Fom Berj listened to a brief outline of the probable impact on the theatrically minded Galactic public of the new Miniculars.

"Why, Wivery—I really think you've solved the problem!" she acknowledged at the end. "In fact—I don't suppose——" She rolled her oversized eyes at Izlik. "How about signing me on as leading lady?"

"Well—I don't know," Izlik hedged. "With a family-type audience, there might be cries of miscegenation . . . ."

"Nonsense. Take off your disguise, Wivery."

"To be perfectly candid, I'm not wearing one," Waverly replied with dignity.

"You mean——" Fom Berj stared at him. Then a titter broke from her capacious mouth. She reached up, fumbled at her throat, and with a single downward stroke, split her torso open like a banana peel. A slim arm came out and thrust the bulky costume back from round shoulders; a superb bosom emerged, followed by a piquant face with a turned-up nose topped by a cascade of carrot-red hair.

"And I thought I had to conceal my identity from *you!*" she said as she stepped from the collapsed Vorplischer suit. "And all this time you were really a Borundian!"

"A Borundian?" Waverly smiled dazedly at the graceful figure before him, modestly clad in a wisp of skintight gauze.

"Like me," Fom Berj said. "They'd never had hired me in my natural guise. We look too much like those Earth natives."

"Here," Izlik interrupted. "If you two are the same species, why is it that she's shaped like *that,* and you're not?"

"That's part of the beauty of being a, um, Borundian," Waverly said, taking the former detective's hand and looking into her smiling green eyes. "Go ahead and draw up the contracts, Mr. Izlik. You've got yourself a deal."

THE BODY BUILDERS

1

He was a big bruiser in a Gendye Mark Seven Sullivan, the luxury model with the nine-point sensory system, the highest-priced Grin-U-Matic facial expression attachment on the market and genuine human hair, mustache and all.

He came through the dining room entry like Genghis Kahn invading a Swiss convent. If there'd been a door in his way he'd have kicked it down. The two lads walking behind him—an old but tough-looking utility model Liston and a fairly new Wayne—kept their hands in their pockets and flicked their eyes over the room like buggy whips. The head waiter popped out with a stock of big purple menus, but the Sullivan went right past him, headed across toward my table like a field marshal leading a victory parade.

Lorena was with me that night, looking classy in a flossed-up Dietrich that must have set her back a month's salary. She was in her usual mood for the usual reason: she wanted to give up her job at the Cent-Prog and sign a five-year marriage contract with me. The idea left me cold as an Eskimo's tombstone. In the first place, at the rate she burned creds, I'd have to creak around in a secondhand Lionel with about thirty percent sensory coverage and an under-

43

sized power core; and in the second, I was still carrying the torch for Julie. Sure, Julie had nutty ideas about
Servos. According to her, having a nice wardrobe of
specialized outfits for all occasions was one step below
cannibalism.

"You and that closet full of zombies!" she used to
shake her finger under my nose. "How could a girl
possibly marry you and never know what face she'd
see when she woke up in the morning!"

She was exaggerating, but that was the way those
Organo-Republicans are. No logic in 'em. After all,
doesn't it make sense to keep your organic body on
file in the Municipal Vaults, safe out of the weather,
and let a comfortable, late-model Servo do your walking and talking? Our grandparents found out it was a
lot safer and easier to sit in front of the TV screen
with feely and smelly attachments than to be out
bumping heads with a crowd. It wasn't long after that
that they developed the contact screens to fit your eyeballs, and the plug-in audio, so you began to get the
real feel of audience participation. Then, with the big
improvements in miniaturization and the new tight-
channel transmitters, you could have your own private
man-on-the-street pickup. It could roam, seeing the
sights, while you racked out on the sofa.

Of course, with folks spending so much time flat on
their backs, the Public Health boys had to come up
with gear to keep the organic body in shape. For a
while, people made it with part-time exercise and
home model massage and feeding racks, but it wasn't
long before they set up the Central File system.

Heck, the government already had everything about
you on file, from your birth certificate to your finger-

prints. Why not go the whole hog and file the body too?

Of course, nobody had expected what would happen when the quality of the sensory pickups and playbacks got as good as they did. I mean the bit the eggheads call "personality gestalt transfer." But it figured. A guy always had the feeling that his consciousness was sitting somewhere back of his eyes; so when the lids were linked by direct hookup to the Servo, and all the other senses tied in—all of a sudden, you were *there*. The brain was back in Files, doped to the hairline, but you—the thing you call a mind—was there, inside the Servo, living it up.

And with that kind of identification, the old type utilitarian models went out of style, fast. People wanted Servos that expressed the real inner man—the guy you should have been. With everybody as big and tough as they wanted to be, depending on the down payment they could handle, nobody wanted to take any guff off anybody. In the old days, a fellow had to settle for a little fender-bending; now you could hang one on the other guy, direct. Law Cent had to set up a code to cover the problem, and now when some bird insulted you or crowded you off the Fastwalk, you slugged it out with a Monitor watching.

Julie claimed it was all a bunch of nonsense; that the two Servos pounding each other didn't prove anything. She could never see that with perfect linkage, you *were* the Servo. Like now: The waiter had just put a plate of *consomme au beurre blanc* in front of me, and with my high-priced Yum-gum palate accessory, I'd get the same high-class taste thrills as if the soup was being shoved down my Org's mouth in person. It was a special mixture, naturally, that lubricated my main swivel and supplied some chemicals to my glandular analogs. But the flavor was there.

And meanwhile, the old body was doing swell on a nutrient-drip into the femoral artery. So it's a little artificial maybe—but what about the Orggies, riding around in custom-built cars that are nothing but substitute personalities, wearing padded shoulders, contact lenses, hearing aids, false teeth, cosmetics, elevator shoes, rugs to cover their bald domes. If you're going to wear false eyelashes, why not false eyes? Instead of a nose bob, why not bob the whole face? At least a fellow wearing a Servo is honest about it, which is more than you can say for an Orggie doll in a foam-rubber bra—not that Julie needed any help in that department.

I dipped my big silver spoon in and had the first sip just under my nose when the Sullivan slammed my arm with his hip going past. I got the soup square in the right eye. While I was still clicking the eyelid, trying to clear the lens, the Liston jarred my shoulder hard enough to rattle my master solenoid.

Normally, I'm a pretty even-tempered guy. It's my theory that the way to keep a neurotronic system in shape is to hold the glandular inputs to a minimum. But, what with the big event coming up that night, and Lorena riding me hard on the joys of contract life, I'd had a hard day. I hopped up, overrode the eye-blink reflex, made a long reach and hooked a finger in the Liston's collar going away.

"Hold it right there, stumblebum!" I gave the collar a flick to spin him around.

He didn't spin. Instead, my elbow joint made a noise like a roller skate hitting loose gravel; the jerk almost flipped me right on my face.

The Liston did a slow turn, like a ten-ton crane rig, looked me over with a pair of yellow eyes that were as friendly as gun barrels. A low rumbling sound came out of him. I was a little shook but mad enough not to let it bother me.

"Let's have that license number," I barked at him. "There'll be a bill for the eye and another one for a chassis checkup!"

The Wayne had turned, too, and was beetling his brows at me. The big shot Sullivan pushed between the two of them, looked me over like I was something he'd found curled up in a doorway.

"Maybe you better kind of do a fade, Jasper," he boomed loud enough for everybody in the restaurant to hear. "My boy's got no sense of humor."

I had my mouth open for my next mistake when Lorena beat me to it:

"Tell the big boob to get lost, Barney; he's interrupting what I was saying to you."

The Sullivan rolled an eye at her, showing off his independent suspension. "Shut your yap, sister," he said.

That did it. I slid my left foot forward, led with a straight left to the power pack, then uppercut him with everything I was able to muster.

My right arm went dead to the shoulder. The Sullivan was still standing there, looking at me. I was staring down at my own fist, dangling at my side. Then it dawned on me what was wrong.

For the moment, I'd forgotten I was wearing a light sport-model body.

2

Gully Fishbein, my business manager, Servo-therapist, drinking buddy, arena trainer and substitute old-maid aunt had warned me I might pull a stunt like this some day. He was a Single-Servo Socialist himself, and in addition to his political convictions, he'd put a lot of time and effort into building me up as the fastest man with a net and mace in show business. He had an investment to protect.

"I'm warning you, Barney," he used to shove an untrimmed hangnail under my nose and yell. "One day you're gonna get your reflexes crossed and miss your step on the Fastwalk—or gauge a close one like you was wearing your Astaire and bust the neck of that Carnera you wasted all that jack on. And then where'll you be, hah?"

"So I lose a hulk," I'd come back. "So what? I've got a closet full of spares."

"Yeah? And what if it's a total? You ever heard what can happen to your mind when the connection's busted—and I do mean busted—like that?"

"I wake up back in my Org body; so what?"

"Maybe," Gully would shake his head and look like a guy with dangerous secrets. "And maybe not . . ."

While I was thinking all this, the Sullivan was getting his money's worth out of the Grin-U-Matic. He nodded and rocked back on his heels, taking his time with me. The talk had died out at the tables around us. Everybody was catching an ear full.

"A wisey," the Sullivan says, loud. "What's the matter, Cheapie, tired of life outside a repair depot?"

"What do you mean, 'Cheapie'?" I said, just to give my Adam's apple a workout. "This Arcaro cost me plenty . . . and this goon of yours has jarred my contacts out of line. Just spring for a checkup and I'll agree to forget the whole thing."

"Yeah." He was still showing me the expensive grin. "I'll bet you will, pint-size." He cocked an eye at the Wayne. "Now, let's see, Nixie, under the traffic code, I got a couple courses of action, right?"

"Cream duh pansy and let's shake a ankle, Boss. I'm hungry." Nixie folded a fist like a forty-pound stake mallet and moved in to demonstrate his idea.

"Nah." The Sullivan stopped him with the back of his hand against his starched shirt front. "The guy pops me first, right? He wants action. So I give him action. Booney." He snapped his fingers and the Liston thumbed a shirt stud.

"For the record," the Sullivan said in a businesslike voice. "Notice of Demand for Satisfaction, with provocation, under Section 991-b, Granyauck 6-78." I heard the whir and click as the recorder built into the Liston's thorax took it down and transmitted it to Law Central.

All of a sudden my mouth was dry.

Sometimes those Servo designers got a little *too* realistic. I tapped a switch in my lower right premolar to cut out the panic-reaction circuit. I'd been all set for a clip on the jaw, an event that wouldn't be too good for the Arcaro, but nothing a little claim to Law

Cent wouldn't fix up. But now it was dawning like sunrise over Mandalay that Big Boy had eased me into a spot—or that I'd jumped into it, mouth first, *I'd hit him*. And the fact that he'd put my consomme in my eye first wouldn't count—not to Law Cent. He had the right to call me out—a full-scale Servo-to-Servo match —and the choice of weapons, ground, time, everything was his.

"Tell the manager to clear floor number three," the Sullivan rapped out to the Wayne. "My favorite ground." He winked at Lorena. "Nine kills there, baby. My lucky spot."

"Whatever you say," I felt myself talking too fast. "I'll be back here in an hour, raring to go."

"Nix, Cheapie. The time is now. Come as you are; I ain't formal."

"Why, you can't do that," Lorena announced. Her voice tapes were off key, I noticed; she had a kind of shrill, whiney tone. "Barney's only wearing that little old Arcaro!"

"See me after, doll," the Sullivan cut her off. "I like your style." He jerked his head at the Wayne. "I'll take this clown bare-knuck, Mixie, Naples rules." He turned away, flexing the oversized arms that were an optional extra with the late-model Gendyes. Lorena popped to her feet, gave me the dirtiest look the Dietrich could handle.

"You and that crummy Arcaro." She stuck it in me like a knife. "I wanted you to get a Flynn, with the—"

"Spare me the technical specs, kid," I growled. I was getting the full picture of what I'd been suckered into. The caper with the soup hadn't been any accident. The timing was perfect; I had an idea the Liston was wired a lot better than he looked. Somebody with heavy credits riding on that night's bout was behind it; somebody with enough at stake to buy all the muscle-Servos he needed to pound me into a set of loose nerve ends waving around like worms in a bait can. Busting the Arcaro into a pile of scrap metal and plastic wouldn't hurt my Org physically—but the trauma to my personality, riding the Servo, would be for real. It took steel nerve, cast-iron confidence, razor-edge reflexes and a solid killer's instinct to survive in the arena. After all, anybody could lay out for a Gargantua Servo, if that was all it took; the timing, and pace, and ringcraft that made me a winner couldn't survive having a body pounded to rubble around me. I'd be lucky if I ever recovered enough to hold a coffee cup one-handed.

The Floor Manager arrived, looking indignant; nobody had called him to okay the fracas. He looked at me, started to wave me off, then did a double take.

"*This* is the aggressor party?" The eyebrows on his Menjou crawled up into his hairline.

"That's right," I give it to him fast and snappy. "The bum insulted my lady-friend. Besides which, I don't like his soup-strainer. After I break his rib cage down to chopsticks, I'm going to cut half of it off and give it to the pup to play with." After all, if I was going to get pulverized, I might as well do it in style.

The Sullivan growled.

"You can talk better than that." I pushed up close to him; my nose was on a level with the diamond stickpin in his paisley foulard. "What's your name, Big Stuff? Let's have that registration."

"None of your pidgin, Wisey." He had a finger all ready to poke at me, saw the Monitor coming up ready to quote rules, used it to scratch his ear instead. The big square fingernail shredded plastic off the lobe; he was a little more nervous than he acted. That cinched it: he knew who I was—Barney Ramm, light-heavy champ in the armed singles.

"Assembly and serial numbers, please," the Monitor said. He sounded a little impatient. I could see why he might. It was customary for a challenger to give me the plate data without being asked—especially a floor-vet like Sullivan. He was giving the official a dirty look.

"Where's Slickey?" he growled.

"He doesn't come on for another fifteen minutes," the Monitor snapped. "Look here——"

"*You* look here, Short-timer," the Sullivan grunted. The Wayne moved up to help him give the fellow the cold eye. He glared back at them—for about two seconds. Then he wilted. The message had gotten through. The fix was in.

"Where's the men's room?" I piped up, trying to sound as frisky as ever, but at the moment my mind felt as easy to read as a ninety-foot glare sign.

"Eh?" The Monitor cut his eyes at me, back at the Sullivan, back to me, like a badminton fan at a championship match. "No," he said. He pushed out his lips and shook his head. "I'm ruling—"

"Rule my foot." I jostled him going past. "I know my rights." I kept going, marched across the dance floor to the discreet door back of the phony palm tree. Inside, I went into high gear. There was a row of coin-operated buffing and circuit-checking machines down one wall, a power core dispenser, a plug-in recharge unit, a nice rack of touch-up paints, a big bin of burned-out reflex coils, and a dispenser full of replacement gaskets with a sign reading FOR SAFETY'S SAKE—PREVENTS HOT BEARINGS.

I skidded past them, dived through an archway into the service area. There were half a dozen padded racks here, loops of power leads, festoons of lube conduit leading down from ceiling-mounted manifolds. A parts index covered the far wall. There was no back door.

"Kindly take (click) position numbered one," a canned voice cackled at me. "Use the console provided to indicate required services. Say, fellow, may I recommend this week's special, Slideeze, the underarm lubricant with a diff——"

I slapped the control plate to shut the pitch off. Coming in here suddenly didn't seem as cute as it had ten seconds earlier. I was cornered—and an accident on a lube-rack would save any possible slip-up on the floor. A little voice about as subtle as a jackhammer was yelling in my ear that I had half a minute, if I was lucky, before a pair of heavies came through the door to check me out . . . .

It was three quick steps to the little stub wall that protected the customers from the public eye. I flattened myself against the wall beside it just as big feet clumped outside. The door banged open. The Wayne wasn't bothering about being subtle. I wasn't either. I hooked his left instep, spun in behind him, palmed his back hard. He hit face-first with a slam like two garbage flats colliding, and started looping the loop on the tiled floor. Those Waynes always did have a glass jaw. I didn't stick around to see if anybody heard him pile in; I jumped over him, slid out through the door. The Liston was standing on the other side of the palm, not ten feet away. I faded to the right, saw another door. The glare sign above it said LA-DIES. I thought it over for about as long as it takes a clock to say "tick" and dived through.

3

Even under the circumstances it was kind of a shock to find myself standing there staring at pink and turquoise service racks, gold-plated perfume dispensers, and a big display rack full of strictly feminine spares that were enough to make a horse blush.

Then I saw *her*. She was a neat-looking Pickford—the traditional models were big just then. She had fluffy blonde hair, and her chassis covers were off to the waist. I gaped at her, sitting there in front of the mirror, then gulped like a seal swallowing a five-pound salmon. She jumped and swiveled my way, and I got a load of big blue eyes and a rosebud mouth that was opening up to scream.

"Don't yell, lady!" I averted my eyes—an effort like uprooting saplings. "The mob's after me. Just tell me how to get out of here!"

I heard feet outside. So did she, I guess.

"You—you can go out through the delivery door," a nice little voice said. I flicked an eye her way. She was holding a lacy little something over her chest. It slipped when she pointed and I got an eyeful of some of the nicest moulded foam-plastic you'd care to see.

"Thanks, baby, you're a doll," I choked out and went past her, not without a few regrets. The door she'd showed me was around a corner at the back. There was a big carton full of refills for the cosmetics vendor beside it, with the top open. On impulse, I reached in and grabbed one going past.

The door opened into an alley about four feet wide, with a single-rail robo-track down the center for service and delivery mechs. The wall opposite was plain duralith; it went up, a sheer rise without a foothold for a gnat. In both directions the alley was a straight shot for fifty feet to a rectangle of hard late-afternoon sunlight. I could take my choice.

Something clattered to the right. I saw a small custodial cart move jerkily out of a doorway, swing my way, picking up speed. I started to back away; the thing was heavy enough to flatten my Arcaro without slowing down. Then a red light blinked on the front of the thing. It made screechy noises and skidded to a stop.

"Kindly clear the rail," a fruity voice hooted. "This is your busy Sani-mat Service Unit, bringing that Sani-mat sparkle to another satisfied customer!"

A kind of idea formed up somewhere under my hairpiece. I eased around to the side of the machine, a tight squeeze. It was a squatty, boxy job, with a bunch of cleaning attachments racked in front and a good-sized bin behind, half full of what it had been collecting. I got the lid up, climbed up as it started forward again, and settled down in the cargo. It was lumpy and wet, and you could have hammered the aroma out into horseshoes. I guess the world has made a lot of progress in the last few decades, but garbage still smells like garbage.

I estimated I'd covered a hundred feet or less, when the cart braked to a sudden stop. I heard voices; something clicked and a hum started up near my left ear.

"Kindly clear the rail," the tape said. "This is your Sani-mat Service Uuwwrrr——"

The cart jumped and I got another faceful of garbage. Somebody—it sounded like the Wayne—yelled something. I got set, ready to come out swinging as soon as the lid went up. But the voices faded out, and I heard running feet. The cart started up, bumped along clucking to itself like a chicken looking for a place to drop an egg. I rode it along to its next client's back door, then hopped out, legged it to a public screen booth and dialled Gully's number.

4

I caught him in a cab, just dropping in past a mixed-up view of city skyline tilting by in the background. His eyes bugged out like a Chihuahua when I told him—a de luxe feature of the four-year-old Cantor he always wore.

"Barney, you nuts?" He had a yelp like a Chihuahua too. "The biggest bout of your career coming up tonight, and you're mixing in a free brawl!" He stopped to gulp and ran his eyes over me. "Hey, Barney! You're wearing an Arcaro. You didn't——"

"The fracas wasn't my idea," I got in quick while he was fighting the Cantor's tonsils back in line. "Not exactly, anyway. I took off out the back way, and——"

"You did *what?*" The yelp was up into the super-sonic now.

"I beat it. Ducked out. Scrammed. What do you think I was going to do, stay there and let that elbow squad pull the legs off me like a fly?"

"You can't run out on a registered satisfaction, Barney!" Gully leaned into his sender until all I could see were two eyes like bloodshot clams and a pair of quivering nostrils. "You, of all people! If the Pictonews services get hold of this, they'll murder you!"

"This hit squad will murder me quicker—and not just on paper!"

"Paper's what I'm talking about! You're the aggressor party; you poked the schlock! You cop a swiftie on this, and you're a fugitive from Law Cent! They'll lift your Servo license, and it'll be good-by career! And the fines——"

"Okay—but I got a few rights too! If I can get to another Servo before they grab me, it'll become my legal *Corpus operandi* as soon as I'm in it. Remember, that satisfaction is to me, Barney Ramm, not to this body I'm wearing. You've got to get me out of here, and back to my apartment——" I felt my mouth freeze in the open position. Fifty feet away across the Fastwalk the Liston and a new heavy, a big, patched-up Baer, had come out of a doorway and were standing there, looking over the crowd. Those boys were as hard to shake loose as gum on a shoe sole. I ducked down in the booth.

"Listen, Gully," I hissed. "They're too close; I've got to do a fast fade. Try to fix it with Law Cent to keep their mitts off me until I can change. Remember, if they catch me, you can kiss your ten percent good-by."

"Barney, where you going? Whattaya mean, ten percent? It ain't the cookies I'm thinking about!"

"Think about the cookies, Gully." I cut contact and risked a peek. The two goons were still there and looking my way. If I stepped out, they'd have me. And if I stayed where I was, sooner or later they'd get around to checking the booth. . . .

I was still holding something in my hand. I looked at it: the cosmetics kit I'd grabbed on the way out of the ladies' room at the Troc.

The lid flipped back when I touched the little gold button at the side. There were nine shades of eye shadow, mouth paint, plastic lens shades in gold, green and pink—some dames have got screwy ideas about what looks attractive—spare eyebrows and lashes, a little emergency face putty, some thimble-sized hair sprays.

I hated to ruin a hundred cee wig, but I gave it a full shot of something called Silver Ghost. The pink eyes seemed to go with the hair. The spray was all gone, so it was too late to bleach out a set of eye-brows, so I used a pair of high-arched black ones, then used a gingery set for a mustache. I thought about using one of the fake spit curls for a goatee, but decided against it. The Arcaro had a nice-sized nose on it, so I widened the nostrils a little and added warts. I risked another peek. The boys were right where I left them.

My jacket was a nice chartreuse job with cerise strips and a solid orange lining. I turned it inside out, ditched the yellow tie, and opened my shirt collar so the violet part showed. That was about all I could do; I opened the door and stepped out.

I'd gone about three steps when the Carnera looked my way. His mouth dropped open like a power shovel getting ready to take a bite out of a hillside. He jammed an elbow into the Liston and he turned around and *his* mouth fell open. I got a glimpse of some nice white choppers and a tongue like a pink sock. I didn't wait to catch the rest of the reaction: I sprinted for the nearest shelter, a pair of swinging doors, just opening to let a fat Orggie out.

I dived past him into a cool, dark room lit by a couple of glowing beer ads above a long mirror with a row of bottles. I charged past all that, slammed through a door at the back, and was out in an alley, looking at the Wayne. He went into a half-crouch and spread his arms. That was the kind of mistake an amateur toughie would make. I put my head down and hit him square under his vest button. It wasn't the best treatment in the world for the Arcaro, but it was worse for the Wayne. He froze up and made a noise like frying fat, with his eyeballs spinning like Las Vegas cherries. Between the fall in the john and the butt in the neuro center, he was through for the day.

I got my legs under me and started off at a sort of cripple's lope toward the end of the alley.

My balance and coordination units were clicking like castanets. I ricocheted off a couple of walls, made it out into the Slowwalk, and jigged along in a crabbed semicircle, making jerky motions with my good arm at a cab that picked then to drop a fare a few yards away. The hackie reached out, grabbed my shoulder and hauled me inside. Those boys may be built into their seats and end at the waist, but they've got an arm on them. I'll give 'em that.

"You look like you got a problem there, Mac." He looked me over in the mirror. "What happened, you fall off a roof?"

"Something like that. Just take me to the Banshire Building, fast."

"Whatever you say, Bud. But if I was you, I'd get that Servo to a shop as quick as I could."

"Later. Step on it."

"I'm doing a max and a half now!"

"Okay, okay, just don't waste any time." He muttered to himself then, while I got the bent cover off my reset panel and did what I could to rebalance my circuitry. My double vision cleared a little, and the leg coordination improved enough so I managed to climb out unassisted when he slammed the heli in hard on the roof deck.

"Be five cees," the cabbie grunted. I paid him. "Stick around a few minutes," I said. "I'll be right back."

"Do me a favor, Clyde; throw your trade to the competition." He flipped the flag up and lifted off in a cyclone of overrevved rotors. I spat out a mouthful of grit and went in through the fancy door with the big gold B.

Gus, the doorman, came out of his cage with his admiral's hat on crooked; he hooked a thumb over his shoulder and got his jaw all set for the snappy line. I beat him to it.

"It's me, Barney Ramm. I'm incommunicado to avoid the fans."

"Geeze, Mr. Ramm? Wow, that Arcaro won't never be the same again. Looks like your fans must of caught you after all." He showed me a bunch of teeth that would have looked at home in a mule's face. I lifted a lip at him and went on in.

5

My apartment wasn't the plushest one in the Banshire, but it was fully equipped. The Servo stall was the equal of anything at Municipal Files. I got enough cooperation out of my legs to hobble to it, got the Arcaro into the rack with the neck plate open and the contacts tight against the transfer disk.

A pull on the locking lever, and I was clamped in tight, ready for the shift. I picked the Crockett; it was rugged enough to handle the Sullivan, and didn't have any fancy equipment installed to have to look out for. It was a little tough coding the number into the panel, but I made it, then slammed the transfer switch.

I've never gotten used to that wild couple of seconds while the high-speed scanner is stripping the stored data off one control matrix and printing it on another one linking it in to the Org brain back between my real ears in the cold files downtown. It was like diving into an ocean of ice-cold darkness, spinning like a Roman candle. All kinds of data bits flash through the conscious level: I was the Arcaro, sitting rigid in the chair, and I was also the Crockett, clamped to a rack in the closet, and at the same time

I could feel the skull contacts and servicing tubes and the cold slab under me in the Vault. Then it cleared and I was hitting the release lever and stepping out of the closet and beginning to feel like a million bucks.

The Arcaro looked pretty bad, sagging in the stall, with the phony eyebrows out of line and the putty nose squashed, and the right shoulder humped up like Quasimodo. It was a wonder it had gotten me back at all. I made myself a promise to give it the best overhaul job money could buy—that was the least I could do. Then I headed for the front door.

The Sullivan would get a little surprise when I found him now. I gave my coon skin cap a pat as I went by the hall mirror, palmed the flush panel open and ran smack into four large cops, standing there waiting for me.

It was a plush jailhouse, as jails go, but I still didn't like it. They shoved me into a nice corner cell with a carpet, a tiled lube cubicle in the corner, and a window with a swell view of Granyauck—about 1800 feet straight down. There were no bars, but the wall was smooth enough to discourage any human flies from trying it.

The turnkey looked me over and shook his head. He was wearing the regulation Police Special, a dumb-looking production job halfway between a Kildare and a Tracy—Spence, that is. I guess cops have to have a uniform, but the sight of a couple dozen identical twins standing around kind of gives a fellow a funny feeling—like Servos were just some kind of robot, or something.

"So you're Barney Ramm, huh?" the cop shifted his

toothpick to the other corner of his mouth. "You shunt of tried to handle four cops at once, Buddy. Your collision insurance don't cover that kind of damage."

"I want my manager!" I yelled as loud as I could, which wasn't very loud on account of a kick in the voice box I got following up too close on a cop I had tossed on his ear. "You can't do this to me! I'll get the lot of you for false arrest!"

"Relax, Ramm." The jailer waved his power-billie at me to remind me he had it. I shied off; a shot from the hot end of that would lock my neuro center in a hard knot. "You ain't going no place for a while," the cop stated. "Commissioner Malone wouldn't like it."

"Malone? The Arena Commissioner? What's he got——" I stopped in the middle of the yell, feeling my silly look freeze in place.

"Yeah," the cop said. "Also the Police Commissioner. Seems like Malone don't like you, Ramm."

"Hey!" a dirty idea was growing. "The satisfaction against me: who filed it?"

The cop went through the motions of yawning. "Lessee . . . oh, yeah. A Mr. Malone."

"The dirty crook! That's illegal! I was framed!"

"You slugged him first, right?" The cop cut me off.

"Sure, but——"

"Ain't a Police Commissioner got as much right as anybody else to defend hisself? Any reason he's got to take guff off some wisenheimer, any more than the next guy? You race him at the light, he'll lock bumpers with you every time!"

"I've got to get out of here," I shouted him down. "Get Gully Fishbein! He'll post the bond! I've got a bout at the Garden in less than four hours! Tell the judge! I guess I've got a couple rights!"

"You ain't going to make no bout in no four hours." The cop grinned like Sears foreclosing on Roebuck. "You'll be lucky if you get out before Christmas Holidays start, in September."

"If I don't," I said, "you can start scanning the help-wanted-cripple column. That's what you'll be when me and my twenty-thousand Cee Charlemagne finish with you, you dumb flatfoot!"

He narrowed his eyes down to pinpoints—an extra-cost feature that the taxpayers had to spring for. "Threats, hah?" His voice had the old gravel in it now. "You run out on a satisfaction, Buster. That's trouble enough for most guys."

"I'll show you trouble," I started, but he wasn't through yet.

" . . . For a big tough arena fighter, you got kind of a delicate stomach, I guess. We also got you for resisting arrest, damaging public property, committing mayhem on the person of a couple honest citizens, Peeping Tom and shoplifting from the ladies' john. You're set for tonight, pal—and a lotta other nights." He gave me a mock salute and backed out; the glass door clinked in my face while I was still trying to get my arm back for a swing.

The watch set in my left wrist was smashed flat, along with the knuckles. Those Granyauck cops have got hard heads. I went over to the window and checked the sun.

It looked like about half past four. At eight P.M. the main event would go on. If I wasn't there, the challenger would take the title by default. He was an out-of-town phony known as Mysterious Marvin, the Hooded Holocaust; he always fought with a flour sack over his face. After tonight, he'd be light-heavy champ, bagged head and all—and I'd be a busted has-been, with my accounts frozen, my contract torn up, my Servo ticket lifted, and about as much future as a fifth of Bourbon at a Baptist Retreat. It was the finish. They had me. Unless . . .

I poked my head out and looked down the wall. It was a sheer drop to a concrete loading apron that looked about the size of a blowout patch from where I stood. I felt my autonomics kick in; my heart started thumping like an out-of-round drive shaft, and my throat closed up like a crap-shooter's fist. I never had liked heights much. But with my Servo locked in a cell—and *me* locked in the Servo——

I took a couple turns up and down the cell. It was an idea the boys talked about sometimes, waiting in the service racks before a bout: what would happen if the plastic-foam and wire-sponge information correlation unit where the whole brain pattern was recorded got smashed flat—wiped out—while you were in it?

It would be like dreaming you fell—and hit. Would you ever wake up? The Org body was safe, back in the Vaults, but the shock—what would it do to you?

There were a lot of theories. Some of the guys said it would be curtains. The end. Some of them said your Org would go catatonic. I didn't know, myself. If the wheels knew, they weren't spreading it around.

And there was just the one way to find out for sure. If I stayed where I was, incommunicado, I was finished anyway. Better to go out in style. Before I could change my mind, I whirled, went to the window and swung my legs over the sill. Behind me, I heard somebody yell, "Hey!" I tried to swallow, couldn't, squeezed my eyes shut and jumped. For a few seconds, it was like a tornado blowing straight up into my face; then it was like being spread-eagled on a big, soft, rubbery mattress. And then——

6

I was drowning in a sea of rancid fat. I took a deep breath to yell, and the grease in my lungs clogged solid.

I tried to cough and couldn't do that either. Little red skyrockets started shooting around back of my eyes like a fire in a fireworks factory. Then the lights ran together and I was staring at a long red glare strip set in a dark ceiling a few inches above my face. I could feel tubes and wires dragging at my arms and legs, my neck, my eyelids, my tongue . . .

I was moving, sliding out into brighter light. A scared-looking face was gaping down at me. I made gargly noises and flapped my hands—about all I could manage under the load of spaghetti. The guy leaning over me jumped like a morgue attendant seeing one of his customers sit up and ask for a light, which wasn't too far off, maybe. My bet had paid off. I was awake, back in my organic body in slot number 999/1-Ga8b in the Municipal Body Files.

The next half hour was a little hectic. First they started some kind of a pump, and then I could breathe —a little. While I coughed, twitched, groaned, itched, throbbed and ached in more places than I knew I had, the file techs fussed over me like midwives delivering a TV baby. They pulled things out, stuck things in, sprayed me, jabbed me, tapped and tested, conferred, complained, ran back and forth, shone lights in my eyes, hit me with little hammers, poked things down my throat, held buzzers to my ears, asked questions and bitched at each other in high, whining voices like blue-bottle flies around a honey wagon. I got the general idea. They were unhappy that I had upset the routine by coming out of a stage-three storage state unannounced.

"There are laws against this sort of thing!" a dancey little bird in an unhealthy-looking Org body kept yelling at me. "You might have died! It was sheer good fortune that I happened to have slipped back in the stacks to commune with myself, and heard you choking! You frightened me out of my wits!"

Somebody else shoved a clipboard in front of me. "Sign this," he said. "It's a release covering Cent Files against any malpractice or damage claims."

"And there'll be an extra service charge on your file for emergency reprocessing," the dancey one said. "You'll have to sign that, and also an authorization to transfer you to dead storage until your next of kin or authorized agent brings in the Servo data——"

I managed to sit up. "Skip the reprocessing," I said. "And the dead storage. Just get me on my feet and show me the door."

"How's that? You're going to need at least a week's rest, a month's retraining, and a complete reorientation course before you can be released in Org——"

"Get me some clothes," I said. "Then I'll sign the papers."

"This is blackmail!" Dancey did a couple of steps. "I won't be held responsible!"

"Not if you cooperate. Call me a cab." I tried walking. I was shaky, but all things considered I didn't feel too bad—for a guy who just committed suicide. Files had kept me in good condition.

There was a little more argument, but I won. Dancey followed me out, wagging his head and complaining, but I signed his papers and he disappeared —probably to finish communing with himself.

In the cab, I tried to reach Gully again. His line was busy. I tried Lorena. A canned voice told me her line was disconnected. Swell. All my old associates were kind of fading out of sight, now that I was having troubles with the law.

But maybe Gully was just busy getting me a postponement. In fact, he was probably over at the Garden now, straightening things out. I gave the hackie directions and he dropped me by the big stone arch with the deep-cut letters that said FIGHTERS ENTRANCE.

The usual crowd of fight fans were there, forty deep. None of them gave me a look; they had their eyes on the big, wide-shouldered Tunneys and Louises and Marcianos, and the hammed-up Herkys and Tarzans in their flashy costumes and big smiles, with their handlers herding them along like tugs nudging liners into dock. The gateman put out a hand to stop me when I started through the turnstile.

"It's me, Harley. Barney Ramm," I said. A couple

of harness cops were standing a few feet away, looking things over. "Let me through; I'm late."

"Hah? Barney——"

"Keep it quiet; I'm a surprise."

"Where'd you dig up that outfit? On a used-Servo lot?" He looked me over like an inspector rejecting a wormy side of mutton. "What is it, a gag?"

"It's a long story. I'll tell it to you some time. Right now, how's about loaning me a temporary tag? I left my ID in my other pants."

"You pugs," he muttered, but he handed over the pass. I grabbed it.

"Where's Lou Mitch, the starter?" I asked him.

"Try the Registry Office."

I shoved through a crowd of weigh-in men, service techs and arena officials, spotted Lou talking to a couple of trainers. I went over and grabbed his arm.

"It's me, Mitch, Barney Ramm. Listen, where's Gully? I need——"

"Ramm, you bum! Where you been? Where'd you pick up that hulk you got on? Who you think you are, missing the press weigh-in? Get downstairs on the double and dress out! You got twenty minutes, and if you're late, so help me, I'll see you busted out of the fight game!"

"Wha—who, me? Hold it, Lou, I'm not going out there in this condition! I just came down to——"

"Oh, a holdup for more dough, huh? Well, you can work that one out with the promoter and the Commissioner. All I know is, you got a contract, and I've got you billed for nineteen minutes from now!"

I started backing away, shaking my head. "Wait a minute, Lou——"

He jerked his head at a couple of the trainers that were listening in. "Grab him and take him down to his stall and get him into his gear! Hustle it!"

I put up a brisk resistance, but it was all wasted effort. Ten minutes later I was standing in the chute, strapped into harness with knots tied in the straps for fit and a copy of the Afternoon Late Racing Special padding my helmet up off my ears, listening to the mob in the stands up above, yelling for the next kill. Me.

7

They can talk all they want about how sensitive and responsive a good Servo is, but there's nothing like flesh and blood for making you know you're in trouble.

My heart was kicking hard enough to jar the championship medal on my chest. My mouth was as dry as yesterday's cinnamon toast. I thought about making a fast getaway over the barrier fence, but there was nobody outside who'd be glad to see me except the cops; besides which, I had a mace in my right hand and a fighting net in the left, and after all, I was Barney Ramm the champ. I'd always said it was the man inside the Servo, not the equipment that counted. Tonight I had a chance to prove it—or a kind of a chance; an Org up against a fighting Servo wasn't exactly an even match.

But hell, when was it ever even? The whole fight game was controlled, from top to bottom, by a few sharpies like J. J. Malone. Nobody had ever slipped me the word to take a dive yet, but I'd stretched plenty of bouts to make 'em look good. After all, the fans paid good creds to see two fine-tuned fighting machines pound each other to scrap under the lights. An easy win was taboo. Well, they'd get an unexpected bonus tonight when I got hit and something besides hydraulic fluid ran out.

And then the blast of the bugles caught me like a bucket of ice water and the gate jumped up and I was striding through, head up, trying to look as arrogant as a hunting tiger under the glare of the polyarcs, but feeling very small and very breakable and wondering why I hadn't stayed in that nice safe jail while I had the chance. Out across the spread of the arena the bleachers rose up dark under the high late-evening sky streaked with long pink clouds that looked as remote as fairyland. And under the pooled lights, a big husky Servo was taking his bows, swirling his cloak.

He was too far away, over beyond the raised disk of the Circle, for me to be sure, but it looked like he was picking a heavy duty prod and nothing else. Maybe the word had gone out and I was in Org, or maybe he was good.

Then he tossed the cape to a handler and came to meet me, sizing me up on the way through the slit in his mask.

Maybe he was wondering what I had up my sleeve. If he was in on the fix, he'd be surprised to see me at all. He'd been expecting a last-minute sub or just a straight default. If not, he'd been figuring on me wearing my Big Charley packed with all the booster gear the law allows. Instead, all he saw was an ordinary-looking five-foot-eleven frame with medium-fair shoulders and maybe just a shade too much padding at the belt line.

The boys back at Files had done right by me, I had to admit. The old Org was in better shape than when I'd filed it, over a year ago. I felt strong, tough and light on my feet; I could feel the old fighting edge coming on. Maybe it was just a false lift from the stuff the techs had loaded me full of, and maybe it was just an animal's combat instinct, an item they hadn't been able to dream up an accessory to imitate. Whatever it was, it was nice to have.

I reached the concrete edge of the Fighting Circle and stepped up on it and was looking across at the other fellow, only fifty feet away and now looking bigger than a Bolo Combat Unit. With the mask I wasn't sure, but he looked like a modified Norge Atlas. He was running through a fancy twirl routine with the prod, and the crowd was eating it up.

There was no law that said I had to wait for him to finish. I slid the mace down to rest solid in my palm with the thong riding tight above my wrist and gave the two-foot club a couple of practice swings. So much for the warmup. I flipped the net out into casting position with my left hand and moved in on him.

It wasn't like wearing a Servo; I could feel sweat running down my face and the air sighing in my lungs and the blood pumping through my muscles and veins. It was kind of a strange *alive* feeling—as if there was nothing between me and the sky and the earth and I was part of them and they were part of me. A funny feeling. A dangerous, unprotected feeling—but somehow not entirely a bad feeling.

He finished up the ham act when I was ten feet from him, swung to face me. He knew I was there, all right; he was just playing it cool. Swell. While he was playing, I'd take him.

I feinted with the net, then dived in, swung the mace, missed him by half an inch as he back-pedaled. I followed him close, working the club, keeping the net cocked. He backed, looking me over.

"Ramm—is that you in that getup?" he barked.

"Naw—I couldn't make it, so I sent my cousin Julius."

"What happened, you switch brands? Looks like you must of got cut-rate merchandise." He ducked a straight cut and whipped the prod around in a jab that would have paralyzed my neuro center if he'd connected.

"New secret model a big outfit's trying out under wraps," I told him.

He made a fast move, and a long, slim rod I hadn't seen before whipped out and slapped me under the ribs. For a split second I froze. He had me, I was finished. A well-handled magnetic resonator could de-Gauss every microtape in a Servo—and his placement was perfect.

But nothing happened. There was a little tingle, that was all.

Then I got it. I wasn't wearing a Servo—and magnets didn't bother an Org.

The Atlas was looking as confused as I was. He took an extra half-second recovering. That was almost enough. I clipped him across the thigh as he almost fell getting back. He tried with the switch again, sawed it across my chest. I let him; he might as well tickle me with a grass stem. This time I got the net out, snarled his left arm, brought the mace around and laid a good one across his hip. It staggered him, but he managed to spin out, flip the net clear.

"What kind of shielding you got anyway, Ramm?" the Atlas growled. He held the rod out in front of his face, crossed his eyes at it, shook it hard and made one more try. I let him come in under my guard, and the shaft slid along my side as if he was trying to wipe it clean on my shirt. While he was busy with that, I dropped the net, got a two-handed grip in the mace, brought it around in a flat arc and laid a solid wallop right where it would do him the most good—square on the hip joint.

I heard the socket go. He tried to pivot on his good leg, tottered and just managed to stay on his feet, swearing. I came in fast and just got a glimpse of the electro-prod coming up. Concentrating on the magnetic rod, I'd forgotten the other. I tried to check and slide off to the right, but all of a sudden blinding blue lights were popping all over the sky. Something came up and hit me alongside the head, and then I was doing slow somersaults through pretty purple clouds, trying hard to figure which side was up. Then the pain hit. For a couple of seconds I scraped at my chest, reaching for circuit breakers that weren't there. Then I got mad.

It was as if all of a sudden, nothing could stop me. The Atlas was a target, and all I wanted was just to reach it. If there was a mountain in the way, I'd pick it up and throw it over my shoulder. A charging elephant would be a minor nuisance. I could even stand up, unassisted—if I tried hard enough.

I got the feel of something solid under my hands, groped and found some more of it with my feet, pushed hard and blinked away the fog to see the Atlas just making it back onto his good leg. I had to rest a while then, on all fours. He stooped to twiddle a reset for emergency power to the damaged joint, then started for me, hopping hard enough to shake the ground. A little voice told me to wait. . . .

He stopped, swung the prod up, and I rolled, grabbed his good leg, twisted with everything I had. It wasn't enough. He hopped, jabbed with the prod, missed, and I was on my feet now, feeling like I'd been skinned and soaked in brine. My breath burned my throat like a blow torch, and all round the crowd roar was like a tidal wave rolling across a sinking continent.

I backed, and he followed. I tried to figure the time until the pit stop, but I didn't know how long I'd been out here; I didn't have a timer ticking under my left ear, keeping me posted. And now the Atlas was on to what was going on. I knew that, when he reached for the show-knife strapped to his left hip. Against a Servo, that particular tool was useless, but he could let the cool night air into an Org's gizzard with it, and he knew it.

Then my foot hit the edge of the paved circle and I went down, flat on my back on the sand.

The Atlas came after me, and I scrambled back, got to my feet just in time. The knife blade hissed through the air just under my chin.

"You've had it, Ramm," the Atlas said, and swung again. I tried to get the club up for a counterblow but it was too heavy. I let it drop and drag in the sand. Through a dust cloud we were making, I saw the Atlas fumbling with his control buttons. Tears welled up in his eyes, sluiced down over his face. He didn't like the dust any better than I did. Maybe not as well . . .

I felt an idea pecking at its shell; a dirty idea, but better than none.

The mace was dangling by its thong. I slipped it free, threw it at him; it clanged off his knees and I stooped, came up with a handful of fine sand and as he closed in threw it straight into his face.

The effect was striking. His eyes turned to mud pockets. I stepped aside, and he went right past me, making swipes at the air with the big sticker, and I swung in behind him and tilted another handful down inside his neckband. I could hear it grate in the articulated rib armor as he came around.

"Ramm, you lousy little——" I took aim and placed a nice gob square in his vocabulary. He backed off, pumping emergency air to clear the pipes, spouting dust like Mount Aetna, but I knew I had him. The mouth cavity on just about every Servo in the market was a major lube duct; he had enough grit in his gears to stop a Continental Siege Unit. But his mouth was still open, so I funneled in another double handful.

He stopped, locked his knee joints and concentrated on his problem. That gave me my opening to reach out and switch his main circuit breaker off.

He froze. I waited half a minute for the dust to clear, while the crowd roar died away to a kind of confused buzzing, like robbed bees.

Then I reached out, put a finger against his chest, and shoved—just gently. He leaned back, teetered for a second, then toppled over stiff as a lamppost. You could hear the thud all the way to the student bleachers. I held on for another ten seconds, just to make it look good, then kneeled over on top of him.

8

"But I was too late," Gully Fishbein's voice was coming up out of a barrel, a barrel full of thick molasses syrup somebody had dumped me into. I opened my mouth to complain and a noise like "glug" came out.

"He's awake!" Gully yelped. I started to deny it, but the effort was too much.

"Barney, I tried to catch you, but you were already out there." Gully sounded indignant. "Cripes, kid, you should of known I wouldn't let 'em railroad you!"

"Don't worry about Ramm," a breezy voice jostled Gully's aside. "Boy, this is the story of the decade! You figure to go up against a Servo again in Org, when you get out of the shop—I mean hospital? How did it feel to take five thousand volts of DC? You know the experts say it should have killed you. It would have knocked out any Servo on the market——"

"Nix, Baby!" Gully elbowed his way back in again. "My boy's gotta rest. And you can tell the world the Combo's out of business. Now anybody can afford to fight. Me and Barney have put the game back in the hands of the people."

"Yeah! The sight of that Atlas, out on its feet—and Ramm here, in Org, yet, with one finger. . . ."

I unglued an eyelid and blinked at half a dozen fuzzy faces like custard pies floating around me.

"We'll talk contract with you, Fishbein," somebody said.

" . . . call for some new regulations," somebody said.

" . . . dred thousand cees, first network rights."

" . . . era of the Servo in the arena is over . . ."

" . . . . hear what Malone says about this. Wow!"

"Malone," I heard my voice say, like a boot coming out of mud. "The cr . . . crook. It was him . . . put the Sullivan . . . up to it . . . "

"Up to nothing, Barney," Gully was bending over me. "That was J. J. hisself in that Servo! And here's the payoff. He registered the satisfaction in his own name—and of course, every fighter in his stable is acting in his name, legally. So when you met Mysterious Marvin and knocked him on his duff you satisfied his claim. You're in the clear, kid. You can relax. There's nothing to worry about."

"Oh, Barney!" It was a new voice, a nice soft little squeal of a girl-voice. A neat little Org face with a turned-up nose zeroed in on me, with a worried look in the big brown eyes.

"Julie! Where—I mean, how . . . ?"

"I was there, Barney. I see all your fights, even if —even if I don't approve. And today—oh, Barney, you were so brave, so *marvelous,* out there alone, against that *machine* . . . " She sighed and nestled her head against my shoulder.

"Gully," I said. "Exactly how long have I got to stay in this place?"

"The Servo-tech—I mean the doc—says a week anyway."

"Set up a wedding for a week from today."

Julie jumped and stared at me.

"Oh, Barney! But you—you know what I said . . . about those *zombies* . . . ."

"I know."

"But, Barney . . ." Gully didn't know whether to cry or grin. "You mean . . . ?"

"Sell my Servos," I said. "The whole wardrobe. My days of being a pair of TV eyes peeking out of a walking dummy and kidding myself I'm alive are over."

"Yeah, but Barney—a guy with your ideas about what's fun—like skiing, and riding the jetboards, and surfing, and sky-diving—you can't take the risks! You only got the one Org body!"

"I found out a couple of things out there tonight, Gully. It takes a live appetite to make a meal a feast. From now on, whatever I do, it'll be *me* doing it. Clocking records is okay, I guess, but there's some things that it takes an Org to handle."

"Like what?" Gully yelled, and went on with a lot more in the same vein. I wasn't listening, though. I was too busy savoring a pair of warm, soft, *live* lips against mine.

COCOON

Sid Throndyke overrode his respirator to heave a deep sigh.

"Wow!" he said, flipping to his wife's personal channel. "A tough day on the Office channel."

The contact screens attached to his eyeballs stayed blank: Cluster was out. Impatiently, Sid toed the console, checking the channels: Light, Medium, and Deep Sitcom; autho-hypno; Light and Deep Narco; four, six and eight-party Social; and finally, muttering to himself, Psychan. Cluster's identity symbol appeared on his screens.

"There you are," he grieved. "Psychan again. After a hard day, the least a man expects is to find his wife tuned to his channel—"

"Oh, Sid; there's this wonderful analyst. A new model. It's doing so much for me, really wonderful . . ."

"I know," Sid grumped. "That orgasm-association technique. That's all I hear. I'd think you'd want to keep in touch with the Sitcoms, so you know what's going on; but I suppose you've been tied into Psychan all day—while I burned my skull out on Office."

"Now, Sid; didn't I program your dinner and everything?"

"Um." Mollified, Sid groped with his tongue for the

dinner lever, eased the limp plastic tube into his mouth. He sucked a mouthful of the soft paste—

"Cluster! You know I hate Vege-pap. Looks like you could at least dial a nice Prote-sim or a Sucromash . . ."

"Sid, you ought to tune to Psychan. It would do you a world of good . . ." Her sub-vocalized voice trailed off in the earphones. Sid snorted, dialed a double Prote-sim AND a Sucromash, fuming at the delay. He gulped his dinner, not even noticing the rich gluey consistency, then in a somewhat better mood, flipped to the Light Sitcom.

It was good enough stuff, he conceded; the husband was a congenital psychopathic inferior who maintained his family in luxury by a series of fantastic accidents. You had to chuckle when his suicide attempt failed at the last moment, after he'd lost all that blood. The look on his face when they dragged him back . . .

But somehow it wasn't enough. Sid dialed the medium; it wasn't much better. The deep, maybe.

Sid viewed for a few minutes with growing impatience. Sure, you had to hand it to the Sitcom people; there was a lot of meat in the deep sitcom. It was pretty subtle stuff, the way the wife got the money the husband had been saving and spent it for a vacation trip for the chihuahua; had a real social content, too deep for most folks. But like the rest of the sitcoms, it was historical. Sure, using old-time settings gave a lot of scope for action. But how about something more pertinent to the contemporary situation? Nowadays, even though people led the kind of rich, full lives that Vital Programming supplied, there was still a certain lack. Maybe it was just a sort of atavistic need for gross muscular exertion. He'd viewed a discussion of the idea a few nights earlier on the usual Wednesday night four-party hookup with the boys. Still, in his case, he had plenty of muscle tone. He'd spent plenty on a micro-spasm attachment for use with the narco channel . . .

That was a thought. Sid didn't usually like narco; too synthetic, as he'd explained to the boys. They hadn't liked the remark, he remembered. Probably they were all narco fans. But what the hell, a man had a right to a few maverick notions.

Sid tuned to the Narco channel. It was a traditional sex fantasy, in which the familiar colorless hero repeatedly fended off the advances of coitus-seeking girls. It was beautifully staged, with plenty of action, but like the sitcoms, laid in one of those never-never historical settings. Sid flipped past with a sub-vocal grunt. It wasn't much better than Cluster's orgasm-association treatments.

The stylized identity-symbol of the Pubinf announcer flashed on Sid's screens, vibrating in resonance with the impersonal voice of the Official announcer:

". . . cause for concern. CentProg states that control will have been re-established within the hour. Some discomfort may result from vibration in sectors north of Civic Center, but normalcy will be restored shortly. Now, a word on the food situation."

A hearty, gelatinous voice took over: "Say, folks, have you considered switching to Vege-pap? Vege-pap now comes in a variety of rich flavors, all, of course, equally nourishing, every big swallow loaded with the kind of molecule that keeps those metabolisms rocking along at the pace of today's more-fun-than-ever sitcoms—and today's stimulating narco and social channels, too!

"Starting with First Feeding tomorrow, you'll have that opportunity you've wanted to try Vege-pap. Old-fashioned foods, like Prote-sim and Sucromash, will continue to be available, of course, where exceptional situations warrant. Now—"

"What's that?" Sid sub-vocalized. He toed the replay key, listened again. Then he dug a toe viciously against the tuning key, flipping to the Psychan monitor.

Cluster!" he barked at his wife's identity pattern. "Have you heard about this nonsense? Some damn fool on Pubinf is blathering about Vege-pap for everybody! By God, this is a free country. I'd like to see anyone try—"

"Sid," Cluster's voice came faintly, imploring. "P-P-Please, S-S-Sid . . ."

"Damn it, Cluster . . . !" Sid stopped talking, coughed, gulped. His throat was burning. In his excitement he'd been vocalizing. The realization steadied him. He'd have to calm down. He'd been behaving like an animal . . .

"Cluster, darling. Kindly interrupt your treatment. I have to talk to you. Now. It's important." Confound it, if she didn't switch to his channel now—

"Yes, Sid." Cluster's voice had a ragged undertone. Sid half-suspected she was vocalizing then too . . .

"I was listening to Pubinf," he said, aware of a sense of dignity in the telling. No narco-addict he, but a mature-minded auditor of a serious channel like Pubinf. "They're raving about cutting off Prote-sim.

Never heard of such nonsense. Have you heard anything about this?"

"No, Sid. You should know I never——"

"I know! But I thought maybe you heard something . . ."

"Sid, I've been under treatment all day—except the time I spent programming your dinner."

"You can get Prote-sim in exceptional situations, they said! I wonder what that's supposed to mean? Why, I've been a Prote-sim man for years . . ."

"Maybe it will do you good, Sid. Something different . . ."

"Different? What in the world do I want with something different? I have a comfortable routine, well-balanced, creative. I'm not interested in having any government fat-head telling me what to eat."

"But Vege-sim might be good; build you up or something."

"Build me up? What are you talking about? I view sports regularly; and aren't you forgetting my Micro-spasm accessory? Hah! I'm a very physically-minded man, when it comes to that."

"I know you are, Sid. I didn't mean . . . I only meant, maybe a little variety . . ."

Sid was silent, thinking. Variety. Hmmmm. Might be something in that. Maybe he WAS in a rut, a little.

"Cluster," he said suddenly. "You know, it's a funny thing; I've kind of gotten out of touch. Oh, I don't mean with important affairs. Heck, I hardly ever tune in Narco, or auto-hypno, for that matter. But I mean, after all, it's been quite a while now I guess, since we gave up well, you know, physical contact."

"Sid! If you're going to be awful, I'm switching right back to my Psychan—"

"I don't mean to be getting personal, Cluster. I was just thinking . . . By golly, how long has it been since that first contract with CentProg?"

"Why . . . I haven't any idea. That was so long ago. I can't see what difference it makes. Heavens, Sid, life today is so rich and full—"

"Don't get me wrong. I'm not talking about wanting to change, or anything idiotic. Just wondering. You know."

"Poor Sid. If you could spend more time with wonderful channels like Psychan, and not have to bother with that boring old Office . . ."

Sid chuckled sub-vocally. "A man needs the feeling of achievement he gets from doing a job, Cluster. I wouldn't be happy, just relaxing with Sitcom all the time. And after all, Indexing is an important job. If we fellows in the game all quit, where'd CentProg be? Eh?"

"I hadn't thought of it like that, Sid. I guess it is pretty important."

"Darn right, kid. They haven't built the computer yet that can handle Indexing—or Value Judgment, or Criticism. It'll be a while yet before the machine replaces man." Sid chuckled again. Cluster was such a kid in a lot of ways.

Still, it had been a long time. Funny, how you didn't think much about time, under Vital Programming. After all, your program was so full, you didn't have time to moon over the past. You popped out of Dream-stim, had a fast breakfast (Vege-pap; hah! He'd see about that!), then over to Office channel.

That kept a fellow on his toes, right up till quitting time. Then dinner with Cluster, and right into the evening's round of Sitcoms, Socials, Narcos—whatever you wanted.

But how long had it been? A long time, no doubt. Measured in, say, years, the way folks used to be in the habit of thinking.

Years and years. Yes, by golly. Years and years.

Quite suddenly, Sid was uneasy. How long had it been? He had been about twenty-eight—the term came awkwardly to mind—twenty-eight when he and Cluster first met. Then there was that first anniversary —a wild time that had been, with friends over for TV. And then Vital Programming had come along. He and Cluster had been among the first to sign up.

God, what a long time it had been. TV. Imagine sitting. The thought of being propped up against coarse chairs, out in the open, made Sid wince. And other people around—faces right out in the open and everything. Staring at a little screen no more than five feet square. How in the world had people stood it? Still, it was all in what you were used to. People were adaptable. They had had to be to survive in those primitive conditions. You had to give the old-timers credit. He and Cluster were a pretty lucky couple to have lived in the era when Vital Programming was developed. They could see the contrast right in their own lives. The younger folks, now—

"Sid," Cluster broke in plaintively. "May I finish my treatment now?"

Sid dialed off, annoyed. Cluster wasn't interested in his problems. She was so wrapped up in Psychan these days, she couldn't even discuss the sitcoms intelligently. Well, Sid Throndyke wasn't a man to be pushed around. He nudged the 'fone switch, gave a number. An operator answered.

"I want the Pubinf office."

There was a moment's silence. "That number is unavailable," the recorded voice said.

"Unavailable, hell! I want to talk to them down there! What's all this about cutting off Prote-sim?"

"That information is not available."

"Look," Sid said, calming himself with an effort. "I want to talk to someone at Pubinf—"

"The line is available now."

An unfamiliar identity pattern appeared on Sid's screens.

"I want to find out about this food business," Sid began—

"A temporary measure," a harassed voice said. "Due to the emergency."

"What emergency?" Sid stared at the pattern belligerently. As he watched, it wavered, almost imperceptibly. A moment later, he felt a distinct tremor through the form-hugging plastic cocoon.

"What . . . !" he gasped, "what was that?!"

"There's no cause for alarm," the Pubinf voice said. "You'll be kept fully informed through regular—"

A second shock rumbled. Sid gasped. "What the devil's going on . . . ?"

The Pubinf pattern was gone. Sid blinked at the blank screens, then switched to his monitor channel. He had to talk to someone. Cluster would be furious at another interruption, but—

"Sid!" Cluster's voice rasped in Sid's hemispherical

canals. She was vocalizing now for sure, he thought wildly.

"They broke right in!" Cluster cried. "Just as I was ready to climax—"

"Who?" Sid demanded. "What's going on here? What are you raving about?"

"Not an identity pattern, either," Cluster wailed. "Sid, it was a—a—face."

"Wha—" Sid blinked. He hadn't heard Cluster use obscenity before. This must be serious.

"Calm yourself," he said. "Now tell me exactly what happened."

"I told you: a—face. It was horrible, Sid. On the Psychan channel. And he was shouting—"

"Shouting what?"

"I don't know. Something about 'Get out'. Oh, Sid, I've never been so humiliated . . ."

"Listen, Cluster," Sid said. "You tune in to a nice narco now, and get some rest. I'll deal with this."

"A face," Cluster sobbed. "A great, nasty, *hairy* face—"

"That's enough!" Sid snapped. He cut Cluster's identity pattern with an impatient gouge of his toe. Sometimes it seemed like women enjoyed obscenity . . .

Now what? He was far from giving up on the Vege-pap issue, and now this: a respectable married woman insulted right in her own cocoon. Things were going to hell. But he'd soon see about that. With a decisive twist of the ankle, Sid flipped to the Police channel.

"I want to report an outrage."

The police identity pattern blanked abruptly. For a

moment Sid's contact screens were blank. Then a face appeared.

Sid sucked in a breath out of phase with his respirator. THIS wasn't the police channel. The face stared at him, mouth working: a pale face, with whiskers sprouting from hollow cheeks, lips sunken over toothless gums. Then the audio came in, in midsentence:

". . . to warn you. You've got to listen, you fools! You'll all die here! It's already at the north edge of the city. The big barrier wall's holding, but—"

The screen blanked; the bland police pattern reappeared.

"The foregoing interruption was the result of circumstances beyond the control of CentProg," a taped voice said smoothly. "Normal service will now be resumed."

"Police!" Sid yelled. He was vocalizing now, and be damned to it! There was just so much a decent citizen would stand for—

The screen flickered again. The police pattern disappeared. Sid held his breath—

A face appeared. This was a different one, Sid was sure. It was hairier than the other one, but not as hollow-cheeked. He watched in dumb shock as the mouth opened—

"Listen," a hoarse voice said. "Everybody listen. We're blanketing all the channels this time—I hope. This is our last try. There's only a few of us. It wasn't easy getting into here—and there's no time left. We've got to move fast."

The voice stopped as the man on the screen breathed hoarsely, swallowed. Then he went on:

"It's the ice; it's moving down on us, fast, a god-awful big glacier. The walls can't stand much longer. It'll either wipe the city off the map or bury it. Either way, anybody that stays is done for.

"Listen; it won't be easy, but you've got to try. Don't try to go down. You can't get out below because of the drifts. Go up, onto the roofs. It's your only chance—you must go up."

The image on Sid's contact screens trembled violently, then blanked. Moments later, Sid felt a tremor —worse, this time. His cocoon seemed to pull at him. For a moment he was aware of the drag of a hundred tiny contacts grafted to the skin, a hundred tiny conductors penetrating to nerve conduits—

An almost suffocating wave of claustrophobia swept over him. The universe seemed to be crushing in on him, immobile, helpless, a grub buried in an immense anthill—

The shock passed. Slowly, Sid regained a grip on himself. His respirator was cycling erratically, attempting to match to his ragged breathing impulses. His chest ached from the strain. He groped with a toe, keyed in Cluster's identity pattern.

"Cluster! Did you feel it? Everything was rocking . . ."

There was no reply. Sid called again. No answer. Was she ignoring him, or—

Maybe she was hurt, alone and helpless—

Sid fought for calm. No need for panic. Dial Cent-Prog, report the malfunction. He felt with trembling toes, and punched the keys . . .

CentProg's channel was dark, lifeless. Sid stared,

unbelieving. It wasn't possible. He switched wildly to the light sitcom—

Everything normal here. The husband fell down the stairs, smashing his new camera . . .

But this was no time to get involved. Sid flipped through the medium and deep sitcoms: all normal. Maybe he could get through to the police now—

Mel Goldfarb's pattern blinked on the personal call code. Sid tuned him in.

"Mel! What's it all about? My God, that earthquake—"

"I don't like it, Sid. I felt it, over here in South Sector. The . . . uh . . . face . . . said the North Sector. You're over that side. What did you—"

"My God, I thought the roof was going to fall in, Mel. It was terrible! Look, I'm trying to get through to the police. Keep in touch, hey?"

"Wait, Sid; I'm worried—"

Sid cut the switch, flipped to the police channel. If that depraved son of a bitch showed his face again—

The police pattern appeared. Sid paused to gather his thoughts. First things first . . .

"That earthquake," he said. "What's happening? And the maniac who's been exposing his face. My wife—"

"The foregoing interruption was the result of circumstances beyond the control of CentProg. Normal service will now be resumed."

"What are you talking about? NOTHING is beyond the control of CentProg—"

"The foregoing interruption was the result of circumstances beyond the control of CentProg. Normal service will now be resumed."

"That's enough of your damned nonsense! What about this crazy guy showing his bare face? How do I know that he won't—"

"The foregoing interruption was the result of circumstances beyond the control of CentProg. Normal service will now be resumed."

Sid stared, aghast. A taped voice! A brush-off! He was supposed to settle for that? Well, by God, he had a contract . . .

Mel's code flashed again. Sid tuned him in. "Mel, this is a damned outrage. I called police channel and do you know what I got? A canned announcement—"

"Sid," Mel cut in. "Do you suppose it meant anything? I mean the . . . uh . . . guy with the . . . uh . . . face. All that about getting out, and the glacier wiping out the city."

"What?" Sid stared at Mel's pattern, trying to make sense of what he was saying. "Glacier?" he said. "Wipe out what?"

"You saw him, didn't you? The crazy bird, cut in on all channels. He said the ice was going to wipe out the city . . ."

Sid thought back. The damned obscene face. He hadn't really listened to what it was raving about. But it was something about getting out . . .

"Tell me that again, Mel."

Mel repeated the bare-faced man's warning. "Do you suppose there's anything in it? I mean, the shocks, and everything. And you can't get police channel. And I tried to tune in to Pubinf just now and I got a canned voice, just like you did . . ."

"It's crazy, Mel. It can't . . ."

"I don't know. I've tried to reach a couple of the fellows; I can't get through . . ."

"Mel," Sid asked suddenly. "How long has it been? I mean, how long since CentProg has been handling things?"

"What? My God, Sid, what a question. I don't know."

"A long time, eh, Mel? A lot could have happened outside."

"My contract—"

"But how do we know? I was talking to Cluster just now; we couldn't remember. I mean, how can you gauge a thing like that? We have our routine, and everything goes along, and nobody thinks about anything like . . . outside. Then all of a sudden—"

"I'm trying Pubinf again," Mel said. "I don't like this—"

Mel was gone. Sid tried to think. Pubinf was handing out canned brush-offs, just like Police Channel. CentProg . . . maybe it was okay now . . .

CentProg was still dark. Sid was staring at the blank screens when a new shock sent heavy vibrations through his cocoon. Sid gasped, tried to keep cool. It would pass; it wasn't anything, it couldn't be . . .

The vibrations built, heavy, hard shocks that drove the air from Sid's lungs, yanked painfully at arms, legs, neck, and his groin . . .

It was a long time before the nausea passed. Sid lay, drawing breath painfully, fighting down the vertigo. The pain—it was a help, in a way. It helped to clear his head. Something was wrong, bad wrong. He had to think now, do the right thing. It wouldn't do to panic. If only there wouldn't be another earth-quake . . .

Something wet splattered against Sid's half-open mouth. He recoiled, automatically spitting the mucky stuff, snorting—

It was Vege-pap, gushing down from the feeding tube. Sid averted his face, felt the cool semi-liquid pattering against the cocoon, spreading over it, slosh-ing down the sides. Something was broken . . .

Sid groped for the cut-off with his tongue, gagging at the viscous mess pouring over his face. Of course, it hadn't actually touched his skin, except for his lips; the cocoon protected him. But he could feel the thick weight of it, awash in the fluid that supported the plastic cocoon. He could sense it quite clearly, flowing under him, forcing him up in the chamber as the hydrostatic balance was upset. With a shock of pain, Sid felt a set of neuro contacts along his spinal cord come taut. He gritted his teeth, felt searing agony as the contacts ripped loose.

Half the world went dark and cold. Sid was only dimly aware of the pressure against his face and chest as he pressed against the cell roof. All sensation was gone from his legs now, from his left arm, his back. His left contact screen was blank, unseeing. Groaning with the effort, Sid strained to reach out with a toe, key the emergency signal—

Hopeless. Without the boosters he could never make it. His legs were dead, paralyzed. He was helpless.

He tried to scream, choked, fought silently in the swaddling cocoon, no longer a euphorically caressing second skin but a dead, clammy weight, binding him. He twisted, feeling unused muscles cramp at the effort,

touched the lever that controlled the face-plate. It had
been a long time since Sid had opened the plate. He'd
had a reputation as an open-air fiend once—but that
had been—he didn't know how long ago. The lever
was stiff. Sid lunged against it again. It gave. There
was a sudden lessening of pressure as the burden of
Vegepap slopped out through the opening. Sid sank
away from the ceiling of the tiny cubicle, felt his cocoon ground on the bottom.

For a long time Sid lay, dazed by pain and shock,
not even thinking, waiting for the agony to sub-
side . . .

Then the itching began. It penetrated Sid's daze,
set him twitching in a frenzy of discomfort. The tear-
ing loose of the dorsal contacts had opened dozens of
tiny rents in the cocoon; a sticky mixture of the supporting water bath and Vege-pap seeped in, irritating
the tender skin. Sid writhed, struggled to scratch—
and discovered that, miraculously, the left arm re-
sponded now. The motor nerves which had been
stunned by the electroneural trickle-flow through the
contacts were recovering control. Feebly, Sid's groping
hand reached his inflamed hip—and scrabbled
against the smooth sheath of plastic.

He had to get out. The cocoon was a confining
nightmare, a dead husk that had to be shed. The face-
plate was open. Sid felt upward, found the edge,
tugged—

Slippery as an eel, he slithered from the cocoon,
hung for an instant as the remaining contacts came
taut, then slammed to the floor a foot below. Sid didn't
feel the pain of the fall; as the contacts ripped free,
he fainted.

When Sid recovered consciousness, his first thought was that the narco channel was getting a little TOO graphic. He groped for a tuning switch—

Then he remembered. The earthquake, Mel, the canned announcement—

And he had opened his face-plate and fought to get out—and here he was. He blinked dully, then moved his left hand. It took a long time, but he managed to peel the contact screens from his eyes. He looked around. He was lying on the floor in a rectangular tunnel. A dim light came from a glowing green spot along the corridor. Sid remembered seeing it before, a long time ago . . . the day he and Cluster had entered their cocoons.

Now that he was detached from the stimuli of the cocoon, it seemed to Sid, he was able to think a little more clearly. It had hurt to be torn free from the security of the cocoon, but it wasn't so bad now. A sort of numbness had set in. But he couldn't lie here and rest; he had to do something, fast. First, there was Cluster. She hadn't answered. Her cocoon was situated right next to his—

Sid tried to move; his leg twitched; his arm fumbled over the floor. It was smooth and wet, gummy with the Vege-pap that was still spilling down from the open face-plate. The smell of the stuff was sickening. Irrationally, Sid had a sudden mouth-watering hunger for Prote-sim.

Sid fixed his eyes on the green light, trying to remember. He and Cluster had been wheeled along the corridor, laughing and talking gaily. Somehow, out here, things took on a different perspective. That had been—God! YEARS ago. How long? Maybe—twenty years? Longer. Fifty, maybe. Maybe longer. How could you know? For a while they had tuned to Pubinf, followed the news, kept up with friends on the outside. But more and more of their friends had signed contracts with CentProg. The news sort of dried up. You lost interest.

But what mattered now wasn't how long, it was what he was going to do. Of course, an attendant would be along soon in any case to check up, but meanwhile, Cluster might be in trouble—

The tremor was bad this time. Sid felt the floor rock, felt the hard paving under him ripple like the surface of a pond. Somewhere, a rumbling sound rolled, and somewhere something heavy fell. The green light flickered, then burned steadily again.

A shape moved in the gloom of the corridor; there was the wet slap of footsteps. Sid sub-vocalized a calm 'Hi, fellows'—the silence rang in his ears. My God, of course they couldn't hear him. He tried again, consciously vocalizing, a tremendous shout—

A feeble croak, and a fit of coughing. When he recovered his breath, a bare and hairy face, greenish white, was bending over him.

". . . this poor devil," the man was saying in a thin choked voice.

Another face appeared over the first face's shoulder. Sid recognized them both. They were the two that had been breaking into decent channels, with their wild talk about a glacier . . .

"Listen, fellow," one of the bare-faced men said. Sid stared with fascinated disgust at the clammy pale skin, the sprouting hairs, the loose toothless mouth, the darting pink tongue. God, people were horrible to look at!

". . . be along after awhile. Didn't mean to stir up anybody in your shape. You been in too long, fellow. You can't make it."

"I'm . . . good . . . shape . . ." Sid whispered indignantly.

"We can't do anything for you. You'll have to wait till the maintenance unit comes along. I'm pretty sure you'll be okay. The ice's piled itself up in a wall now, and split around the city walls. I think they'll hold. Course, the ice will cover the city, but that won't matter. CentProg will still handle everything. Plenty of energy from the pile and the solar cells, and the recycling will handle the food okay . . ."

". . . Cluster . . ." Sid gasped. The bare-faced man leaned closer. Sid explained about his wife. The man checked nearby face-plates. He came back and knelt by Sid. "Rest easy, fellow," he said. "They all look all right. Your wife's okay. Now, we're going to have to go on. But you'll be okay. Plenty of Vege-pap around, I see. Just eat a little now and then. The maintenance machine will be along and get you tucked back in."

"Where . . . ?" Sid managed.

"Us? We're heading south. Matt here knows where we can get clothes and supplies, maybe even a flier. We never were too set on this Vital Programming. We've only been in maybe a few years and we always did a lot of auto-gym work, keeping in shape. Didn't like the idea of wasting away . . . Matt's the one found out about the ice. He came for me . . ."

Sid was aware of the other man talking. It was hard to hear him.

A sudden thought struck Sid. ". . . how . . . long . . . ?" he asked.

It took three tries, but the bare-faced man got the idea at last.

"I'll take a look, fellow," he said. He went to Sid's open face-plate, peered at it, called the other man over. Then he came back, his feet spattering in the puddled Vege-pap.

"Your record says . . . 2043," he said. He looked at Sid with wide eyes. They were red and irritated, Sid saw. It made his own eyes itch.

"If that's right, you been here since the beginning. My God, that's over . . . two hundred years . . ."

The second bare-faced man, Matt, was pulling the other away. He was saying something, but Sid wasn't listening. Two hundred years. It seemed impossible. But after all, why not? In a controlled environment, with no wear and tear, no disease, you could live as long as CentProg kept everything running. But two hundred years . . .

Sid looked around. The two men were gone. He tried to remember just what had happened, but it was too hard. The ice, they had said, wouldn't crush the city. But it would flow around it, encase it in ice, and the snow would fall, and cover it, and the city would lie under the ice.

Ages might pass. In the cells, the cocoons would keep everyone snug and happy. There would be the traditional sitcoms, and Narco, and Psychan . . .

And up above, the ice.

Sid remembered the awful moments in the cocoon, when the shock waves had rocked him; the black wave of fear that had closed in; the paralyzing claustrophobia.

The ice would build up and build up. Ice, two miles thick . . .

Why hadn't they waited? Sid groped, pushed himself up, rolled over. He was stronger already. Why hadn't they waited? He'd used the micro-spasm unit regularly—every so often. He had good muscle tone. It was just that he was a little stiff. He scrabbled at the floor, moved his body a few inches. Nothing to it. He remembered the reason for the green light; it was the elevator. They had brought him and Cluster down in it. All he had to do was get to it, and—

What about Cluster? He could try to bring her along. It would be lonely to be without her. But she wouldn't want to leave. She'd been here—two hundred years. Sid almost chuckled. Cluster wouldn't like the idea of being as old as that . . .

No, he'd go alone. He couldn't stay, of course. It would never be the same again for him. He pulled himself along, an inch, another. He rested, sucked up some Vege-pap from where it spread near his mouth . . .

He went on. It was a long way to the green light, but if you took it an inch at a time, an inch at a time . . .

He reached the door. There hadn't been any more shocks. Along the corridor, the glass face-plates stood closed, peaceful, orderly. The mess on the floor was the only thing. But the maintenance units would be along. The bare-faced man had said so.

You opened the door to the elevator by breaking a beam of light; Sid remembered that. He raised his arm; it was getting strong, all right. It was hardly any effort to lift it right up—

The door opened with a whoosh of air. Sid worked his way inside. Half way in, the door tried to close on him; his weight must have triggered the door-closing mechanism. But it touched him and flew open again. It was working fine, Sid thought.

He pulled his legs in, then rested. He would have to get up to the switch, somehow, and that was going to be tricky. Still, he had gotten this far okay. Just a little farther, and he'd catch up with the bare-faced men, and they'd set out together.

It took Sid an hour of hard work, but he managed to reach, first, the low stool, then the chrome-plated control button. With a lurch the car started up. Sid fell back to the floor and fought back wave on wave of vertigo. It was hectic, being outside. But he wouldn't go back now; not even to see Cluster's familiar identity pattern again. Never again. He had to get out.

The elevator came to a stop. The door slid open— and a blast of sub-arctic air struck Sid like a blow from a giant hammer. His naked body—mere flaccid skin over atrophied bones—curled like a grub in the flames. For a long moment all sensation was washed away in the shock of the cold. Then there was pain; pain that went on and on . . .

And then the pain went, and it was almost like being back again, back in the cocoon, warm and comfortable, secure and protected and safe. But not quite the same. A thought stirred in Sid's mind. He pushed at the fog of cotton-wool, fought to grasp the thought that bobbed on the surface of the blissful warmth.

He opened his eyes. Out across the white expanse

of roof-tops, beyond the last rim of the snow, the glittering jagged shape of the ice-face reared up, crystalblue, gigantic; and in the high arched blue-black sky, a star burned with a brilliant fire.

This was what he wanted to tell Cluster, Sid thought. This, about the deep sky, and the star, so far away—and yet a man could see it.

But it was too late now to tell Cluster, too late to tell anyone. The bare-faced men were gone. Sid was alone; alone now under the sky.

Long ago, Sid thought, on the shore of some warm and muddy sea, some yearning sea-thing had crawled out to blink at the open sky, gulp a few breaths of burning oxygen, and die.

But not in vain. The urge to climb out was the thing. That was the force that was bigger than all the laws of nature, greater than all the distant suns blazing in their meaningless lonely splendor.

The other ones, the ones below, the secure and comfortable ones in their snug cocoons under the snow, they had lost the great urge. The thing that made a man.

But he, Sid Throndyke—he had made it.

Sid lay with his eyes on the star and the silent snow drifted over him to form a still small mound; and then the mound was buried, and then the city.

And only the ice and the star remained.

THE LAWGIVER

"You're no better than a murderer," the woman said. "A cold-blooded killer." Her plump face looked out of the screen at him, hot-eyed, tight-mouthed. She looked like someone's aunt getting tough with the butcher.

"Madam, the provisions of the Population Control Act—" he started.

"That's right, give it a fancy name," she cut in. "Try and make it sound respectable. But that don't change it. It's plain murder. Innocent little babies that never done anybody harm—"

"We are not killing babies! A fetus at ninety days is less than one inch long—"

"Don't matter how long they are, they got as much right to live as anybody!"

He drew a calming breath. "In five years we'd be faced with famine. What would you have us do?"

"If you big men in Washington would go to work and provide for people, for the voters, instead of killing babies, there'd be plenty for everybody."

"As easy as that, eh? Does it occur to you, madam, that the land can't support the people if they're swarming over it like ants?"

"See? People are no more to you than ants!"

"People are a great deal more to me than ants! That's precisely why I've sponsored legislation designed to ensure that they don't live like insects, crowded in hives, dying of starvation after they've laid the countryside bare!"

"Look at you," she said, "taking up that whole fancy apartment. You got room there for any number o' homeless children."

"There are too many homeless children, that's the problem!"

"It says right in the Good Book, be fruitful and multiply."

"And where does it end? When they're stacked like cordwood in every available square inch of space?"

"Is that what you do? Heap up all them little bodies and set 'em afire?"

"There are no bodies affected by the law, only fertilized ova!"

"Every one's a human soul!"

"Madam, each time a male ejaculates, several million germ cells are lost. Do you feel we should preserve every one, mature it *in vitro*—"

"Well! You got your nerve, talking that way to a respectable lady! You! A divorced man—and that son of yours—"

"Thank you for calling, madam," he said, and thumbed the blanking control.

"I ain't no madam . . ." The voice died in a squeal. He went to the small bar at the side of the room, dispensed a stiff shot of over-proof SGA, took it down at a gulp. Back at the desk, he buzzed the switchboard.

"Jerry, no more calls tonight."

"Sorry about that last one, Senator. I thought—"

"It's all right. But no more. Not tonight. Not until I've had some sleep."

"Big day, eh, Senator, ramrodding the enabling act through like you did. Uh, by the way, Senator, I just had a flash from Bernie, on the desk. He says there's a party asking for you, says they claim they have to see you—"

"Not tonight, Jerry."

"They mentioned your son Ron, Senator. . . ."

"Yes? What about him?"

"Well, I couldn't say, Senator. But Bernie says they say it's pretty important. But like you said, I'll tell him to tell them not tonight."

"Wait a minute, Jerry. Put this party on."

"Sure, Senator."

The face that appeared was that of a young man with a shaven skull, no eyebrows or lashes. He gazed out of the screen with a bored expression.

"Yes, what is it you want?"

The youth tipped his head sideways, pointing. "We've got somebody with us you ought to talk to," he said. "In person."

"I understand you mentioned my son's name."

"We'd better come up."

"If you have something of interest to me, I suggest you tell me what it is."

"You wouldn't like that. Neither would Ron."

"Where is Ron?"

The boy made a vague gesture. "Spy, zek. We tried. It's your rax from here on—"

"Kindly speak standard English. I don't understand you."

The youth turned to someone out of sight; his

mouth moved, but the words were inaudible. He turned back.

"You want us to bring Rink up or no?"

"Who is Rink?"

"Rink will tell you all that."

"Very well. Take my car, number 763."

He went to the bar, dispensed another stiff drink, then poured it down the drain. He went to the window, de-opaqued it. A thousand feet below, a layer of mist glowed softly from the city lights beneath it, stretching all the way to the horizon fifty miles distant.

When the buzzer sounded he turned, called, "Come in." The door slid back. The boy he had talked to and another came through, supporting between them a plump woman with a pale face. The men were dressed in mismatched vest-suits, many times reused. The woman was wrapped in a long cloak. Her hair was disarranged, so that a long black curl bobbed over the right side of her face. Her visible eye held an expression that might have been fear, or defiance. The men helped her to the low couch. She sank down on it heavily, closed her eyes.

"Well? What's this about Ron?" the senator asked.

The two men moved toward the door. "Ask Rink," one of them said.

"Just a minute! You're not leaving this woman here . . . ?"

"Better get a medic in, Senator," the shaved lad said.

He looked at her. "Is she ill?" She opened her eyes and pushed her hair out of her face. She was pale, and there were distinct dark hollows under her eyes.

"I'm pregnant," she said in a husky voice. "Awful damn pregnant. And Ron's the father."

He walked slowly across to stand before her. "Have you any proof of that remarkable statement?"

She threw the cloak open. Her body looked swollen enough to contain quadruplets.

"I'm not referring to the obvious fact of your condition," he said.

"He's the father, all right."

He turned abruptly, went to the desk, put his finger on the vidscreen key.

"I'm not lying," she said. "The paternity's easy to check. Why would I try to lie?" She was sitting up now; her white fingers dug into the plum-colored cushions.

"I assume you make no claim of a legal marriage contract?"

"Would I be here?"

"You're aware of the laws governing childbirth—"

"Sure. I'm aware of the laws of nature, too."

"Why didn't you report to a PC station as soon as you were aware of your condition?"

"I didn't want to."

"What do you expect me to do?"

"Fix it so I can have the baby—and keep him."

"That's impossible, of course."

"It's your own grandson you're killing!" the woman said quickly. "You can talk about how one of your compulsory abortions is no worse than lancing a boil —but this"—she put her hands against her belly— "this is a baby, Senator. He's alive. I can feel him kicking."

His eyes narrowed momentarily. "Where is Ron?"

"I haven't seen him in six months. Not since I told him."

"Does he know you came here?"

"How would he know?"

He shook his head. "What in God's name do you expect of me, girl?"

"I told you! I want my son—alive!"

He moved away from the desk, noting as he did that the two men had left silently. He started to run his fingers through his hair, jerked his hands down, rammed them in the pockets of his lounging jacket. He turned suddenly to face the girl.

"You did this deliberately—"

"Not without help, I didn't."

"Why? With free anti-pregnancy medication and abort service available at any one of a thousand stations in the city, why?"

"Not just free, Senator—compulsory. Maybe I think the government—a bunch of politicians and bureaucrats—has no right to say who can have a child. Or maybe the pills didn't work. Or maybe I just didn't give a damn. What does it matter now?"

"You're not living naked in the woods now. You're part of a society; and that society has the right to regulate itself."

"And I have a right to have a baby! You didn't give me—or anybody—the right to live! You can't take it away!"

He took a turn up and down the room, stopped before her. "Even if I wanted to help you, what is it you imagine I could do?"

"Get me a birth permit."

"Nonsense. You don't even have a contract; and the qualifications—"

"You can fix it."

"I believe this whole thing is no more than a plot to embarrass me!"

The woman laughed. She threw back her head and screamed laughter. "Ron was right! You're a fool! A cold-blooded old fool! Your own grandson—and you think he's something that was just thought up to annoy you!"

"Stop talking as though this were a living child instead of an illegal embryo!"

Her laughter died away in a half titter, half sob. "It's a funny world we've made for ourselves. In the old days before we got so Goddamned smart a man would have been proud and happy to know he had a grandson. He'd look forward to all the things he'd teach him, all the things they'd do together. He'd be a little part of the future that he could see growing, living on after he was dead—"

"That's enough!" He drew a controlled breath and let it out. "Do you realize what you're asking of me?"

"Sure. Save my baby's life. Ron's baby."

His hands opened and closed. "You want me to attempt to deliberately circumvent the laws I've devoted my life to creating!"

"Don't put words to it. Just remember it's a baby's life."

"If I knew where Ron was . . ."

"Yes?"

"We could execute a marriage contract, post-date it. I could manage that. As for a birth permit—" He broke off as the girl's face contorted in an expression like a silent scream.

"Better hurry up," she gasped. "They're coming faster now. . . ."

"Good God, girl! Why did you wait until now to bring this to me?"

"I kept hoping Ron would come back."

"I'll have to call a doctor. You know what that means."

"No! Not yet! Find Ron!"

"None of this will help if you're both dead." He keyed the screen, gave terse instructions. "Handle this quietly, Jerry, very quietly," he finished.

"Damn you! I was a fool to come to you!"

"Never mind the hysterics. Just tell me where to start looking for Ron."

"I . . . I don't have any idea."

"Those friends of yours: what about them? Would they know?"

"I promised Limmy and Dan I wouldn't get them mixed up in anything."

He snorted. "And you're asking me to break my oath to the people of this country."

The girl gave him an address. "Don't put them in the middle, Senator. They were pretty decent, bringing me here."

"The obstetrician will be here in a few minutes. Just lie there quietly and try to relax."

"What if you can't find him?"

"I suppose you know the answer to that as well as I do."

"Senator—do they really—kill the babies?"

"The embryo never draws a breath. Under the legal definition it's not a baby."

"Oh, Senator—for God's sake, find him!"

He closed the door, shutting off his view of her frightened face.

Red light leaked out through the air baffles above the bright-plated plastic door. At the third ring—he could hear the buzzer through the panel—it opened on a shrill of voices, the rattle and boom of music. Acrid, stale-smelling air puffed in his face. A tall man with an oddly trimmed beard looked at him through mirror-lens contacts. A tendril of reddish smoke curled from the room past his head.

"Uh?"

"I'd like to have a word with Mr. Limberg, please."

"Who?"

"Mr. Limberg. Limmy."

"Uh." The bearded man turned away. Beyond him, strangely costumed figures were dimly visible in the thick crimson fog, standing, sitting, lying on the floor. Some were naked, their shaved bodies decorated with painted patterns. A boy and girl dressed in striped tunics and hose undulated past arm in arm, looking curiously alike. The youth with the shaved head appeared, his mouth drawn down at the corners.

"I need to find Ron in a hurry. Can you tell me where he might be?"

"Rink had to blow her tonsils, uh?"

"This is important, Limmy. I have to find him. Seconds may be vital."

The boy pushed his lips in and out. Others had gathered, listening.

"Hey, who's the zek?" someone called.

"It's Eubank. . . .'

The youth stepped out, pulled the door shut behind him. "Look, I want no part, follow?"

"All I want is to find Ron. I'm not here to get anyone in trouble. I appreciate what you did for the girl."

"Ron's a pile, as far as I'm concerned. When I saw Rink meant to go through with it, I sent word to him. I didn't know if it reached him or not. But he screened me about half an hour ago. He's on his way here now from Phil."

"On the shuttle, I suppose. Good. I can contact him en route—"

"With what for fare? I heard you kept him broke."

"His allowance—never mind. If he's not riding the shuttle, how is he getting here?"

"Car."

"You must be mistaken. His license was lifted last year."

"Yeah. I remember when—and why . . ."

"Are you saying . . . suggesting . . ."

"I'm not saying anything. Just that Ron said he'd be at your place as quick as he could get there."

"I see." He half turned away, turned back to thank the boy. But the door had already closed.

"Please try to understand, Lieutenant," Senator Eubank said to the hard, expressionless face on the screen. "I have reason to believe that the boy is operating a borrowed, manually controlled vehicle on the Canada autopike, northbound from Philadelphia, ETD forty minutes ago. He's just received some very shocking news, and he's probably driving at a very high speed. He'll be in an agitated condition, and—"

"You have a description of this vehicle, Senator?"

"No. But surely you have means for identifying a car that's not locked into the system."

"That's correct—but it sometimes takes a few minutes. There are a lot of vehicles on the pike, Senator."

"You understand he's under great stress. The circumstances—"

"We'll take him off as gently as we can."

"And you'll keep me informed? I must see him at the first possible instant, you understand?"

"We'll keep you advised—" The police officer turned his head as if looking at someone off-screen.

"This may be something, Senator," he said. "I have a report on a four-seater Supercad at Exit 2983. He took the ramp too fast—he was doing a little over two hundred. He went air-borne and crashed." He paused, listening, then nodded. "Looks like pay dirt, Senator. The ID checks on the hot-list out of Philly. And it was on manual control."

The officer used his screamlight to clear a path through the crowd to the spot where the heavy car lay on its side under the arches of the overpass. Two men with cutting torches were crouched on top of it, sending up showers of molten droplets.

"He's alive in there?" Senator Eubank asked.

The lieutenant nodded. "The boys will have him out in a couple of minutes. The crash copter is standing by."

The torches stopped sputtering. The two men lifted the door, tossed it down behind the car. A white-suited medic with a bundle under his arm climbed up and dropped inside. Half a minute later the crane arm at the back of the big police cruiser hoisted the shock-seat clear of the wreck. From the distance of fifty feet, the driver's face was clay-white under the polyarcs.

"It's Ron."

The medic climbed down, bent over the victim as the senator and his escort hurried up.

"How does it look?" the lieutenant asked.

"Not too good. Internals. Skull looks OK. If he's some rich man's pup, he may walk again—with a new set of innards—" The man broke off as he glanced up and saw the civilian beside the officer. "But I wouldn't waste any time taking him in," he finished.

The duty medtech shook his head. "I'm sorry, sir. He's on the table right at this moment. There's no way in the world for you to see him until he comes out. He's in very serious condition, Senator."

"I understand." As the tech turned away Eubank called after him: "Is there a private screen I could use?"

"In the office, sir."

Alone, he punched his apartment code. The operator's face appeared on the screen. "I'm sorry, no— Oh, it's you, Senator. I didn't know you'd gone out—"

"Buzz my flat, Jerry."

The screen winked and cleared. After fifteen seconds' wait, the image of a small, sharp-eyed man appeared, rubbing at his elbows with a towel.

"About time you called in, John," he said. "First time in thirty years I've let myself be hauled out of my home in the midst of dinner."

"How is she?"

The elderly man wagged his head. "I'm sorry, John. She slipped away from me."

"You mean—she's dead?"

"What do you expect? A post-terminal pregnancy —she'd been taking drugs for a week to delay the birth. She'd had no medical attention whatever. And your living room rug doesn't make the best possible delivery table! There was massive hemorrhaging; it might have been different if I'd been working in a fully equipped labor room—but under the circumstances, that was out of the question, of course, even if there'd been time."

"You know . . . ?"

"The woman told me something of the circumstances."

"What about the child?"

"Child?" The little man frowned. "I suppose you refer to the fetus. It wasn't born."

"You're going to leave it inside the corpse?"

"What would you have me do?" The doctor lowered his voice. "John—is what she said true? About Ron being the father?"

"Yes—I think so."

The little man's mouth tightened. "Her heart stopped three and a half minutes ago. There's still time for a Caesarian—if that's what you want."

"I . . . I don't know, Walter."

"John, you devoted thirty years of your life to the amendment and the enabling act. It passed by a very thin cat's whisker. And the opposition hasn't given up, not by a damn sight. The repeal movement is already underway, and it has plenty of support." The doctor paused, peering at the senator. "I can bring the child out—but John—a lot of this is already in the record. There'd be no way of keeping it out of the hands of the other side: *your* law—violated by you, the first week it was in force. It would finish you, John—and Population Control, too, for a generation."

"There's no hope of resuscitating the mother?"

"None at all. Even today people sometimes die, John."

"I see. Thank you, Walter. You did your best."

"About the child . . . ?"

"There is no child. Just an illegal pregnancy."

"You may go in now," the nurse said. Ron was on his back, his shaven head protruding from the bloated cocoon of the life-support tank. His eyes opened as his father bent over him.

"Dad—I was a damned fool. Knew I was going too fast . . ."

The senator leaned closer to catch his whisper.

"I had to try . . . to get back in time . . ." He paused and his eyelids flickered. "Limmy told me . . . she went to you. I knew . . . you'd take care . . . my wife."

"Easy, Ron, easy. No need to talk now—"

"When Rink told me . . . about the baby . . . I ran out on her. She handed me a contract, all made up. But I couldn't see it, bringing a child into this mess. I thought . . . when I left she'd go in and have it taken care of. Then I heard . . . she didn't. It . . . did something to me. I still had the papers. I registered 'em in Phil. I used your name to get the birth permit. You don't mind . . . ?"

"Ron . . ."

"I wanted to be there. Too late; damned fool. I always was a damn fool, Dad. It'll be different, now. A lot different. Being a father . . . not so easy, eh, Dad? But good. Worth it. Worth everything . . ." The boy's voice faded.

"Better to let him rest now, sir," the nurse whispered.

The senator rose stiffly. At the door, he looked back. Ron seemed to be smiling in his sleep.

"Did you say something, sir?" the nurse asked. He looked down at her bright face.

"What is there to say?"

Her eyes followed him as he walked away down the bright-lit corridor.

THUNDERHEAD

1

Carnaby folded his cards without showing them, tossed them into the center of the table.

"Time for me to make my TX." He pushed back his chair and rose, a tall, wide-shouldered, gray-haired man, still straight-backed, but thickening through the body now. "It's just as well. You boys pretty well cleaned me out for tonight."

"You still got the badge," a big-faced man with quick, sly eyes said. "Play you a hand of showdown for it."

Carnaby rubbed a thumb across the tiny jeweled comet in his lapel and smiled slightly. "Fleet property, Sal," he said.

The big-faced man showed a glint of gold tooth, flicked his eyes at the others. "Yeah," he said. "I guess I forgot." He winked at a foxy man on his left. "Say, uh, any promotions comder through yet?" He was grinning openly at Carnaby now.

"Not yet." Carnaby pushed his chair in.

"Twenty-one years in grade," Sal said genially. "Must be some kind of record." He took out a toothpick and plied it on a back tooth.

"Shut up, Sal," one of the other men said. "Leave Jimmy make his TX."

"All these years, with no transfer, no replacement," Sal persisted. "Not even a letter from home. Looks like maybe they forgot you're out here, Carnaby."

"It's not Jim's fault if they don't get in touch," a white-haired man said. "Meantime, he's carrying out his orders."

"Some orders." Sal lolled back in his chair. "Kind of makes a man wonder if he ever really had any orders."

"I seen his orders myself, the day the cruiser dropped him in here," the white-haired man said. "He was to set up the beacon station and man it until he was relieved. It ain't his fault if they ain't been back for him."

"Yeah." Sal shot a hard glance at the speaker. "I know you 'claim'."

The white-haired man frowned. "What do you mean, 'claim'?"

"Take it easy, Harry." Carnaby caught the big-faced man's eyes, held them. "He didn't mean anything—did you, Sal?"

Sal looked at Carnaby for a long moment. Then he grunted a laugh and reached to rake in the pot. "Nah, I didn't mean anything."

A cold wind whipped at Carnaby as he walked alone past the half-dozen ramshackle stores. They comprised the business district of the single surviving settlement on the frontier planet, Longone.

At the foot of the unpaved street a figure detached itself from the shadow under a pole-mounted light.

"Hello, Lieutenant Carnaby," a youthful voice greeted him. "I been waiting for you."

"Hello, Terry." Carnaby swung his gate open. "You're out late."

"I been working on my Blue codes, Lieutenant." The boy followed him up the path, describing the difficulties he had encountered in mastering Fleet cryptographic theory. Inside the modest bungalow, Carnaby went into the small room he used as an office, took the gray dust-cover from the compact Navy issue VFP transmitter set up on a small desk beside a rough fieldstone fireplace. He settled himself in the chair before it with a sigh, flicked on the SEND and SCR switches, studied the half dozen instrument faces, carefully noted their readings in a dark blue polyon-backed notebook.

The boy stood by as Carnaby depressed the tape key which would send the recorded call letters of the one-man station flashing outward as a shaped wave-front, propagated at the square of the speed of light.

"Lieutenant." The boy shook his head. "Every night you send out your call. How come you never get an answer?"

Carnaby shook his head. "I don't know, Terry. Maybe they're too busy fighting the Djann to check in with every little JN beacon station on the Out Line.

"You said after five years they were supposed to come back and pick you up," the boy persisted. "Why—"

There was a sharp, wavering tone from the round, wire-mesh covered speaker. A dull red light winked on, blinked in a rapid flutter, settled down to a steady glow. The audio signal firmed to a raucous buzz.

"Lieutenant!" Terry blurted. "Something's coming in!"

For a moment Carnaby sat rigid. Then he thumbed the big S-R key to receive, flipped the selector lever to UNSC, snapped a switch tagged RCD.

". . . *riority, to all stations,*" a voice faint with distance whispered through a rasp and crackle of star-static. "*Cincsec One-two-oh to . . . Cincfleet Nine . . . serial one-oh-four . . . stations copy . . . Terem Aldo . . . Terem . . . pha . . . this message . . . two . . . Part One . . .*"

"What is it, Lieutenant?" The boy's voice broke with excitement.

"A Fleet Action signal," Carnaby said tensely. "An all-station, recorded. I'm taping it; if they repeat it a couple of times, I'll get it all."

They listened, heads close to the speaker grille; the voice faded and swelled. It reached the end of the message, began again: "*Red priority . . . . tions . . . . incsec One two . . .*"

The message repeated five times; then the voice ceased. The wavering carrier hum went on another five seconds, cut off. The red light winked out. Carnaby flipped over the SEND key, twisted the selector to VOC-SQ.

"JN 37 Ace Trey to Cincsec One-two-oh," he transmitted in a tense voice. "Acknowledging receipt Fleet TX 104. Request clarification."

Then he waited, his face taut, for a reply to his transmission, which had been automatically taped, condensed to a one-microsecond squawk, and repeated ten times at one-second intervals.

Carnaby shook his head after a silent minute had passed. "No good. From the sound of the Fleet beam, Cincsec One-two-oh must be a long way from here."

"Try again, lieutenant! Tell 'em you're here, tell 'em it's time they came back for you! Tell 'em—"

"They can't hear me, Terry." Carnaby's face was tight. "I haven't got the power to punch across that kind of distance." He keyed the playback. The filtered composite signal came through clearly now:

"Red priority to all stations. Cincsec One-two-oh to Rim HQ via Cinc-fleet Nine-two. All Fleet Stations copy. Pass to Terem Aldo Cerise, Terem Alpha Two and ancillaries. This message in two parts. Part one: CTF Forty-one reports breakthrough of Djann armed tender on standard vector three-three-seven, mark; three-oh-five, mark; oh-four-two. This is a Category One Alert. Code G applies. Class Four through Nine stations stand by on Status Green. Part Two. Inner Warning Line units divert all traffic lanes three-four through seven-one. Outer Beacon Line stations activate main beacon, pulsing code schedule gamma eight. Message ends. All stations acknowledge."

"What's all that mean, Lieutenant?" Terry's eyes seemed to bulge with excitement.

"It means I'm going to get some exercise, Terry."

"Exercise how?"

Carnaby took out a handkerchief and wiped it across his forehead. "That was a general order from Sector Command. Looks like they've got a rogue bogie on the loose. I've got to put the beacon on the air."

He turned to look out through the curtained window beside the bookcase toward the towering ramparts of the nine-thousand-foot volcanic freak known as Thunderhead, gleaming white in the light of the small but brilliant moon. Terry followed Carnaby's glance.

"Gosh, Lieutenant! You mean you got to climb Old Thunderhead?"

"That's where I set the beacon up, Terry," Carnaby said mildly. "On the highest ground around."

"Sure—but your flitter was working then!"

"It's not such a tough climb, Terry. I've made it a few times, just to check on things." He was studying the rugged contour of the moonlit steep, which resembled nothing so much as a mass of snowy cumulus. There was snow on the high ledges, but the wind would have scoured the east face clear . . . .

"Not in the last five years, you haven't, Lieutenant!" Terry sounded agitated.

"I haven't had a Category One Alert, either," Carnaby smiled.

"Maybe they didn't mean you," Terry said.

They called for Outer Beacon Line stations. That's me."

"They don't expect you to do it on foot," Terry protested. "This time o' year!"

Carnaby looked at the boy, smiling slightly. "I guess maybe they do, Terry."

"Then they're wrong!" Terry's thin face looked pale. "Don't go, Lieutenant!"

"It's my job, Terry. It's what I'm here for. You know that."

"What if you never got the message?" Terry countered. "What if the radio went on the blink, like all the rest of the stuff you brought in here with you—the flitter, and the food unit, and the scooter? Then nobody'd expect you to get yourself killed!" The boy whirled suddenly. He grabbed up a poker from the fireplace, swung it against the front of the communicator, brought it down a second time before Carnaby caught his arm.

"You shouldn't have done that, Terry," he said softly. His eyes were on the smashed instrument faces.

"That . . . hurts . . ." the lad gasped.

"Sorry." Carnaby released the boy's thin arm. He stooped, picked up a fragment of a broken nameplate with the words FLEET SIGNAL ARM.

Terry stared at him; his mouth worked as though he wanted to speak, but couldn't find the words. "I'm going with you," he said at last.

Carnaby shook his head. "Thanks, Terry. But you're just a boy. I need a man along on this trip."

Terry's narrow face tightened. "Boy, hell," he said defiantly. "I'm seventeen!"

"I didn't mean anything, Terry. Just that I need a man who's had some trail experience."

"How'm I going to get any trail experience, Lieutenant, if I don't start sometime?"

"Better to start with an easier climb than Thunderhead," Carnaby said gently. "You better go along home now, Terry. Your uncle will be getting worried."

"When . . . when you leaving, Lieutenant?"

"Early. I'll need all the daylight I can get to make Halliday's Roost by sundown."

2

After the boy had gone, Carnaby went to the storage room at the rear of the house and checked over the meager store of issue supplies. He examined the cold suit, shook his head over the brittleness of the wiring.

At least it had been a loose fit; he'd still be able to get into it.

He left the house then, walked down to Maverik's store. The game had broken up, but half a dozen men still sat around the old hydrogen space heater. They looked up casually.

"I need a man," Carnaby said without preamble. "I've got a climb to make in the morning."

"What's got into you?" Yank Pepper rocked his chair back, glanced toward Sal Maverik. "Never knew you to go in for exercises before breakfast."

"I got an Alert Signal just now," Carnaby said. "From a Fleet unit in Deep Space. They've scared up a Djann blockade-runner. My orders are to activate the beacon."

Maverik clattered a garbage can behind the bar. "Kind of early in the evening for falling out of bed with a bad dream, ain't it?" he inquired loudly.

"You got a call in from the Navy?" The white-haired man named Harry frowned at Carnaby. "Hell, Jimmy, I thought. . ."

"I just need a man along to help me pack gear as far as Halliday's Roost. I'll make the last leg alone."

"Ha!" Pepper looked around. "That's all; just as far as Halliday's Roost!"

"You gone nuts, Carnaby?" Sal Maverik growled. "Nobody in his right mind would tackle that damned rock after first snow, even if he had a reason."

"Halliday's hut ought to still be standing," Carnaby said. "We can overnight there, and—"

"Jimmy, wait a minute," Harry said. "All this about orders, and climbing old Thunderhead; it don't make sense! You mean after all these years they pick you to pull a damn fool stunt like that?"

"It's a general order to all Outer Line stations. They don't know my flitter's out of action."

Harry shook his head. "Forget it, Jimmy. Nobody can make a climb like that at this time of year."

"Fleet wants that beacon on the air," Carnaby said. "I guess they've got a reason; maybe a good reason."

Maverik spat loudly in the direction of a sand-filled can. "You're the one's been the big-shot Navy man for the last twenty years around here," he said. "The big man with the fancy badge. Okay, your brass want you to go run up a hill, go ahead. Don't come in here begging for somebody to do your job for you."

"Listen, Jim," Harry said urgently. "I remember when you first came here, a young kid in your twenties, fresh out of the Academy. Five years you was to be here; they've left you here to rot for twenty! Now they come in with this piece of tomfoolery. Well, to hell with 'em! After five years, all bets were off. You got no call to risk your neck—"

"It's still my job, Harry."

Harry rose and came over to Carnaby. He put a hand on the big man's shoulder. "Let's quit pretending, Jim," he said softly. "They're never coming back for you, you know that. The high tide of the Concordiat dropped you here. For twenty years the traffic's been getting sparser, the transmitters dropping off the air. Adobe's deserted now, and Petreac. Another few years and Longone'll be dead, too."

"We're not dead yet."

"That message might have come from the other end

of the galaxy, Jim! For all you know, it's been on the way for a hundred years!"

Carnaby faced him, a big, solidly-built man with a lined face. "You could be right on all counts," he said. "It wouldn't change anything."

Harry sighed, turned away. "If I was twenty years younger, I might go along, just to keep you company, Jimmy. But I'm not. I'm old."

He turned to face Carnaby. "Like you, Jim. Just too old."

"Thanks anyway, Harry." Carnaby looked at the other men in the room, nodded slowly. Sal's right," he said. "It's my lookout, and nobody else's." He turned and pushed back out into the windy street.

Aboard the Armed Picket *Malthusa,* five million tons, nine months out of Fleet HQ on Vandieman's World on a routine Deep Space sweep, Signal-Lieutenant Pryor, Junior Communications Officer on message deck duty, listened to the playback of the brief transmission the Duty NCOIC had called to his attention:

"*JN37 Ace Trey to Cincsec One . . . Fleet TX . . . clarification,*" the voice came through with much crackling.

"That's all I could get out of it, Lieutenant," the signalman said. "I wouldn't have picked it up, if I hadn't been filtering the Y band looking for AK's on 104."

The officer punched keys, scanning a listing that flashed onto the small screen on his panel.

"There's no JN37 Ace Trey listed, Charlie," he

said. He keyed the playback, listened to the garbled message again.

"Maybe it's some outworld sheep-herder amusing himself."

"With WFP equipment? On Y channel?" The NCO furrowed his forehead.

"Yeah." The lieutenant frowned. "See if you can get back to him with a station query, Charlie. See who this guy is."

"I'll try, sir; but he came in with six millisec lag. That puts him halfway from here to Rim."

The lieutenant crossed the room with the NCO, stood by as the latter sent the standard Confirm ID code. There was no reply.

"I guess we lost him, sir. You want me to log him?"

"No, don't bother."

The big repeater panel chattered then, and the officer hurried back to his console, settled down to the tedious business of transmitting follow-up orders to the fifty-seven hundred Fleet Stations of the Inner Line.

3

The orange sun of Longone was still below the eastern horizon when Carnaby came out the gate to the road. Terry Sickle was there, waiting for him.

"You got to get up early to beat me out, Lieutenant," he said in a tone of forced jocularity.

"What are you doing here, Terry?"

"I heard you still need a man," the lad said, less cocky now.

Carnaby started to shake his head, and Terry cut in with: "I can help pack some of the gear you'll need to try the high slope."

"Terry, go on back home, son. That high slope's no place for you."

"How'm I going to qualify for the Fleet when your ship comes, Lieutenant, if I don't start getting some experience?"

"I appreciate it, Terry. It's good to know I have a friend. But—"

"Lieutenant—what's a friend, if he can't help you when you need it?"

"I need you here when I get back, to have a hot meal waiting for me, Terry."

"Lieutenant . . ." All the spring had gone from the boy's stance. "I've known you all my life. All I ever wanted was to be with you on Navy business. If you go up there, alone . . ."

Carnaby looked at the boy, the dejected slump of his thin shoulders.

"Your uncle know you're here, Terry?"

"Sure. Uh, he thought it was a fine idea, me going with you."

"All right, then, Terry, if you want to. As far as Halliday's Roost. Thanks."

"Oh, boy, Lieutenant! We'll have a swell time. I'm a good climber, you'll see!" He grinned from ear to ear, squinting through the early gloom at Carnaby.

"Hey, Lieutenant, you're rigged out like a real . . ." he broke off. "I thought you'd, oh, wore out all your issue gear," he finished lamely.

"Seemed like for this trek I ought to be in uniform," Carnaby said. "And the coldsuit will feel good, up on the high slopes."

The two moved off down the dark street. There were lights on in Sal Maverik's general store. The door opened as they came up; Sal emerged, carrying a flour sack, his mackinaw collar turned up around his ears. He grunted a greeting, then swung to stare at Carnaby.

"Hey, by God! Look at him, dressed fit to kill!"

"The lieutenant got a hot-line message in from Fleet Headquarters last night," Terry said. "We got no time to jaw with you, Maverik." He brushed past the heavy-set man.

"You watch your mouth, boy," Sal snapped. "Carnaby," he raised his voice, "this poor kid the best you could get to hold your hand?"

"What do you mean, poor kid?" Terry started back. Carnaby caught his arm.

"We're on official business, Terry," he said. "Eyes front and keep them there."

"Playing Navy, hah? That's a hot one," the storekeeper called after the two. "What kind of orders you get? To take a goony-bird census, up in the foothills?"

"Don't pay him no attention, Lieutenant," Terry said, his voice unsteady. "He's as full of meanness as a rotten meal-spud is of weevils."

"He's had some big disappointments in his life, Terry. That makes a man bitter."

"I guess you did, too, Lieutenant. It ain't made *you* mean." Terry looked sideways at Carnaby. "I don't reckon you beat out the competition to get an Academy appointment and then went through eight years of training just for this." He made a gesture that took in the sweep of the semi-arid landscape stretching away to the big world's far horizon, broken only by the massive outcroppings of the pale, convoluted lava cores spaced at intervals of a few miles along a straight fault line that extended as far as men had explored the desolate world.

Carnaby laughed softly. "No, I had big ideas about seeing the galaxy, making Fleet Admiral, and coming home covered with gold braid and glory."

"You leave any folks behind, Lieutenant?" Terry inquired, waxing familiar in the comradeship of the trail.

"No wife. There was a girl. And my half-brother, Tom. A nice kid. He'd be over forty, now."

"Lieutenant—I'm sorry I busted up your transmitter. You might have got through, gotten yourself taken off this Godforsaken place—"

"Never mind, Terry."

The dusky sun was up now, staining the rounded, lumpy flank of Thunderhead a deep scarlet.

Carnaby and Sickle crossed the first rock-slope, entered the broken ground where the prolific rock-lizards eyed them as they approached, then heaved themselves from their perches, scuttled away into the black shadows of the deep crevices opened in the porous rock by the action of ten million years of wind and sand erosion on thermal cracks.

Five hundred feet above the plain, Carnaby looked back at the settlement. Only a mile away, it was almost lost against the titanic spread of empty wilderness.

"Terry, why don't you go back now?" he said.

"Your uncle will have a nice breakfast waiting for you."

"I'm looking forward to sleeping out," the boy said confidently. "We better keep pushing, or we won't make the Roost by dark."

4

In the officers' off-duty bay, Signal-Lieutenant Pryor straightened from over the billiard table as the nasal voice of the command deck yeoman broke into the recorded dance music:

"Now hear this. Commodore Broadly will address ship's company."

"Ten to one he says we've lost the bandit." Supply-Lieutenant Aaron eyed the annunciator panel.

"Gentlemen." The sonorous tones of the ship's commander sounded relaxed, unhurried. "We now have a clear track on the Djann blockade runner, which indicates he will attempt to evade our Inner Line defenses and lose himself in Rim territory. In this I propose to disappoint him. I have directed Colonel Lancer to launch interceptors to take up stations along a conic, subsuming thirty degrees on axis from the presently constructed vector. We may expect contact in approximately three hours time."

A recorded bos'n's whistle shrilled the end-of-message signal.

"So?" Aaron raised his eyebrows. "A three-million tonner swats a ten-thousand-ton sideboat. Big deal."

"That boat can punch just as big a hole in the blockade as a Super-D," Pryor said. "Not that the Djann have any of those left to play with."

"We kicked the damned spiders back into their home system ten years ago," Aaron said tiredly. "In my opinion, the whole Containment operation's a boondoggle to justify a ten-million-man fleet."

"As long as there are any of them alive, they're a threat," Pryor repeated the slogan.

"Well, Broadly sounds as though he's got the bogie in the bag," Aaron yawned.

"Maybe he has." Pryor addressed the ball carefully, sent the ivory sphere cannoning against the target.

"He wouldn't go on record with it if he didn't think he was on to a sure thing."

"He's a disappointed 'ceptor-jockey. What makes him think that pirate won't duck back of some kind of a blind spot and go dead?"

"It's worth a try—and if he nails it, it will be a feather in his cap."

"Another star on his collar, you mean."

"Uh-huh, that too."

"We're wasting our time," Aaron said.

"But that's his look out. Six ball in the corner pocket."

As Commodore Broadly turned away from the screen on which he had delivered his position report to the crew of the great war vessel, his eye met that of his executive officer. The latter shifted his gaze uneasily.

"Well, Roy, you expect me to announce to all hands that Cinc-fleet has committed a major blunder letting this bandit slip through the picket line?" he demanded with some asperity.

"Certainly not, sir." The officer looked worried.

"But in view of the seriousness of the breakout . . ."

"There are some things better kept in the highest command channels," the commodore said shortly. "You and I are aware of the grave consequences of a new release of their damned seed in an uncontaminated sector of the Eastern Arm. But I see no need to arouse the parents, aunts, uncles and cousins of every apprentice technician aboard in an overly candid disclosure of the facts!"

"I thought Containment had done its job by now," the captain said. "It's been three years since the last Djann sighting outside the Reservation. It seems we're not the only ones who're keeping things under our hats."

Broadly frowned. "Mmmm. I agree, I'm placed at something of a disadvantage in my tactical planning by the over-secretiveness of the General Staff. However, there can be no two opinions as to the correctness of my present course."

The exec glanced ceilingward.

"I hope so, sir."

"Having the admiral aboard makes you nervous, does it, Roy?" Broadly said in a tone of heartiness. "Well, I regard it merely as an opportunity better to display *Malthusa's* capabilities!"

"Commodore, you don't think it would be wise to coordinate with the admiral on this—"

"I'm in command of this vessel," Broadly said sharply. "I'm carrying the vice-admiral as supercargo, nothing more!"

"He's still Task Group CINC . . . ."

"I'm conning this ship, Roy, not Old Carbuncle!" Broadly rocked on his heels, watching the screen where a quadrangle of bright points representing his interceptor squadron fanned out, on an intersecting course with the fleeing Djann vessel. "I'll pinch off this break-through single-handed; and all of us will share in the favorable attention the operation will bring us!"

In his quarters on the VIP deck, the vice-admiral studied the Utter Top Secret dispatch which had been handed to him five minutes earlier by his staff signal-major.

"It looks as though this is no ordinary boatload of privateers." He looked soberly at the elderly communicator. "They're reported to be carrying a new weapon of unassessed power and a cargo of spore-racks that will knock Containment into the next continuum."

"It doesn't look good, sir." The major wagged his head.

"I note that the commodore has taken action according to the manual." The admiral's voice was noncommittal.

The major frowned. "Let's hope that's sufficent, Admiral."

"It should be. The bogie's only a converted tender. She couldn't be packing much in the way of fire power in that space, secret weapon or no secret weapon."

"Have you mentioned this aspect to the commodore, sir?"

"Would it change anything, Ben?"

"Nooo. I suppose not."

"Then we'll let him carry on without any more cause for jumpiness than the presence of a vice-admiral on board is already providing."

Crouched in his fitted acceleration cradle aboard the Djann vessel, the One-Who-Commands studied the motion of the charged molecules in the sensory tank.

"Now the Death-Watcher dispatches his messengers," he communed with the three link-brothers who formed the Chosen Crew. "Now is the hour of the testing of Djann."

"Profound is the rhythm of our epic," the One-Who-Records sang out. "We are the Chosen-to-Be-Heroic, and in our tiny cargo, Djann lives still, his future glory inherent in the convoluted spores!"

"It was a grave risk to put the destiny of Djann at hazard in this wild gamble," the One-Who-Refutes reminded his link-brothers. "If we fail, the generations yet unborn will slumber on in darkness or perish in ice or fire."

"Yet if we succeed! If the New Thing we have learned serves well its function—then will Djann live anew!"

"Now the death-messengers of the Water-Beings approach," the One-Who-Commands pointed out. "Link well, brothers! The energy-aggregate waits for our directing impulse. Now we burn away the dross of illusions from the hypothesis of the theorists in the harsh crucible of reality!"

"In such a fire, the flame of Djann coruscates in unparalleled glory!" the One-Who-Records exulted. "Time has ordained this conjunction to try the timbre of our souls!"

"Then channel your trained faculties, brothers." The One-Who-Commands gathered his forces, feeling out delicately to the ravening nexus of latent energy contained in the thought-shell poised at the center of the stressed-space field enclosing the fleeting vessel. "Hold the sacred fire sucked from the living bodies of a million of our fellows," he exhorted. "Shape it and hurl it in well-directed bolts at the death-bringers, for the future and glory of Djann!"

5

At noon, Carnaby and Sickle rested on a nearly horizontal slope of rock that curved to meet the vertical wall that swelled up and away overhead. Their faces and clothes were gray with the impalpable dust whipped up by the brisk wind. Terry spat grit from his mouth, passed a can of hot stew and a plastic water flask to Carnaby.

"Getting cool already," he said. "Must not be more'n ten above freezing."

"We might get a little more snow before morning." Carnaby eyed the milky sky. "You'd better head back now, Terry. No point in you getting caught in a storm."

"I'm in for the play," the boy said shortly. "Say, Lieutenant, you got another transmitter up there at the beacon station you might get through on?"

Carnaby shook his head. "Just the beacon tube, the lens generators and a power pack. It's a stripped-down installation. There's a code receiver, but it's only designed to receive classified instruction input."

"Too bad." They ate in silence for a few minutes, looking out over the plain below. "Lieutenant, when this is over," Sickle said suddenly, "we got to do something. There's got to be some way to remind the Navy about you being here!"

Carnaby tossed the empty can aside and stood. "I put a couple of messages on the air, sub-light, years ago," he said. "That's all I can do."

"Heck, Lieutenant, it takes six years just to make the relay station on Goy! Then if somebody happens to pick up the call and boost it, in another ten years some Navy brass might even see it. And then if he's in a good mood he might tell somebody to look into it, next time they're out this way!"

"Best I could do, Terry, now that the liners don't call any more."

Carnaby finished his stew and dropped the can. He watched it roll off down-slope, clatter over the edge, a tiny sound lost in the whine and shrill of the wind. He looked up at the rampart ahead.

"We better get moving," he said. "We've got a long climb to make before dark."

Signal-Lieutenant Pryor awoke to the strident buzz of his bunk-side telephone.

"Sir, the commodore's called a Condition Yellow," the message Deck NCO informed him. "It looks like that bandit blasted through our intercept and took out two Epsilon-classes while he was at it. I got a stand-by from command deck, and—"

"I'll be right up," Pryor said quickly.

Five minutes later, he stood with the on-duty signals crew, reading out an incoming from fleet. He whistled.

"Brother, they've got something new!" he looked at Captain Aaron. "Did you check out the vector they had to make to reach their new position in the time they've had?"

"Probably a foul-up in tracking." Aaron looked ruffled, routed out of a sound sleep.

"The commodore's counting off the scale," the NCO said. "He figured he had 'em boxed."

The annunciator beeped. The yeoman announced *Malthusa's* commander.

"All right, you men!" The voice had a rough edge to it now. "The enemy has an idea he can maul Fleet units and go his way unmolested. I intend to disabuse him of that notion! I'm ordering a course change. I'll maintain contact with this bandit until such time as units designated for the purpose have reported his neutralization! This vessel is under a Condition Yellow at this time and I need not remind you that relevant sections of the manual will be adhered to with full rigor!"

Pryor and Aaron looked at each other, eyebrows raised. "He must mean business if he's willing to risk straining seams with a full-vector course change," the former said.

"So we pull six on and six off until he gets it out of his system," Aaron growled. "I knew this cruise wasn't going to work out as soon as I heard Old Carbuncle would be aboard."

"What's *he* got to do with it? Broadly's running this action."

"Don't worry, he'll be in it before we're through."

On the slope, three thousand feet above the plain, Carnaby and Terry hugged the rock-face, working their way upward. Aside from the steepness of the incline, the going was of no more than ordinary difficulty here; the porous rock, resistant though it was to

the erosive forces that had long ago stripped away
the volcanic cone of which the remaining mass had
formed the core, had deteriorated in its surface suf-
ficiently to afford easy hand and foot-holds. Now
Terry paused, leaning against the rock. Carnaby saw
that under the layer of dust, the boy's face was pale
and drawn.

"Not much farther, Terry," he said. He settled himself in a secure position, his feet wedged in a cleft.
His own arms were feeling the strain now; there was
the beginning of a slight tremble in his knees after the
hours of climbing.

"I didn't figure to slow you down, Lieutenant." Terry's voice showed the strain of his fatigue.

"You've been leading me a tough chase, Terry."
Carnaby grinned across at him. "I'm glad of a rest."
He noted the dark hollows under the lad's eyes, the
pallor of his cheeks.

Sickle's tongue came out and touched his lips.
"Lieutenant—you made a try—a good try. Turn
back now. It's going to snow. You can't make it to
the top in a blizzard."

Carnaby shook his head. "It's too late in the day to
start down; you'd be caught on the slope. We'll take it
easy up to the Roost. In the morning you'll have an
easy climb down."

"Sure, Lieutenant. Don't worry about me." Terry
drew a breath, shivered with the bitter wind that
plucked at his snow jacket, started upward.

"What do you mean, lost him!" the bull roar of the
commodore rattled the screen. "Are you telling me
that this rag-tag refugee has the capability to drop off

the screens of the best equipped tracking deck in the fleet?"

"Sir," the stubborn-faced tracking officer repeated, "I can only report that my screens register nothing within the conic of search. If he's there—"

"He's there, Mister!" the commodore's eyes glared from under a bushy overhang of brows. "Find that bandit or face a court, Captain! I haven't diverted a ship of the fleet line from her course for the purpose of becoming the object of an effectiveness inquiry!"

The tracking officer turned away from the screen as it went white, met the quizzical gaze of the visiting signal-lieutenant.

"The old devil's bit off too big a bite this time," he growled. "Let him call a court; he wouldn't have the gall."

"If we lose the bogie now, he won't look good back on Vandy," Pryor said. "This is serious business, diverting from cruise plan to chase rumors. I wonder if he really had a positive ID on this track."

"Hell, no! There's no way to make a positive at this range, under these conditions! After three years without any action for the newstapes, the brass are grabbing at straws."

"Well, if I were you, Gordie, I'd find that track, even if it turns out to be a tramp with a load of bootleg *dran*."

"Don't worry. If he's inside the conic, I'll find him."

"I guess . . . it's dropped twenty degrees . . . in the last hour." Terry Sickle's voice was almost lost in the shriek of the wind that buffeted the two men as they inched their way up the last yards toward the hut on the narrow rock shelf called Halliday's Roost.

"Never saw snow falling at this temperature before." Carnaby brushed at the ice caked around his eyes. Through the swirl of crystals as fine as sand, he discerned the sagging outline of the shelter above.

Ten minutes later, inside the crude lean-to built of rock slabs, he set to work chinking the gaping holes in the five foot walls with packed snow. Behind him, Terry lay huddled against the back wall, breathing hoarsely.

"Guess . . . I'm not in as good shape . . . as I thought I was," he said.

"You'll be okay, Terry." Carnaby closed the gap through which the worst of the icy draft was keening, paused long enough to open a can of stew for the other. The fragrance of the hot meat and vegetables made his jaws ache.

"Lieutenant, how are you going to climb in this snow?" Sickle's voice shook to the chattering of his teeth. "In good weather, you might have made it. Like this, you haven't got a chance!"

"Maybe it'll be blown clear by morning." Carnaby said mildly. He opened a can for himself. Terry ate slowly, shivering uncontrollably. Carnaby watched him worriedly.

"Lieutenant," the boy said, "even if that call you picked up was meant for you—even if this ship they're after is headed out this way—what difference will it make one way or another if one beacon's on the air or not?"

"Probably none," Carnaby said. "But if there's one

chance in a thousand he breaks this way—well, that's what I'm here for, isn't it?"

"But what's a beacon going to do, except give him something to steer by?"

Carnaby smiled. "It's not that kind of beacon, Terry. My station's part of a system—a big system—that covers the surface of a sphere of space a hundred lights in diameter. When there's an alert, each station locks in with the others that flank it and sets up what's called a stressed field. There's a lot of things you can do with this field. You can detect a drive, monitor communications—"

"What if these other stations you're talking about aren't working?" Terry cut in.

"Then my station's not going to do much good," Carnaby said.

"If the other stations are still on the air, why haven't any of them picked up your TX's and answered?"

Carnaby shook his head. "We don't use the beacon field to chatter back and forth, Terry. This is a top security system. Nobody knows about it except the top command levels—and of course, the men manning the beacons."

"Maybe that's how they came to forget about you. Somebody lost a piece of paper, and nobody else knew!"

"I shouldn't be telling you about it," Carnaby said with a smile. "But I guess you'll keep it under your hat."

"You can count on me, Lieutenant," Terry said solemnly.

"I know I can, Terry," Carnaby said.

6

The clangor of the general quarters alarm shattered the tense silence of the chart deck like a bomb through a plate glass window. The navigation officer whirled abruptly from the grametric over which he had been bending, collided with the deck chief. Both men leaped for the master position monitor, caught just a glimpse of a vivid scarlet trace lancing toward the emerald point targeted at the center of the plate before the apparatus exploded from its mounting, mowed the two men down in a hail of shattered plastic fragments.

Smoke boiled, black and pungent, from the gutted cavity. The duty NCO, bleeding from a dozen gashes, stumbled toward the two men, turned away in horror, reached an emergency voice phone. Before he could key it, the deck under him canted sharply. He screamed, clutched at a table for support, saw it tilt, came crashing down on top of him . . .

On the message deck, Lieutenant Pryor clung to an operator's stool, listening, through the stridency of the alarm bell, to the frantic voice from command deck:

"All sections, all sections, combat stations! We're under attack! My God, we've taken a hit—"

The voice was cut off, to be replaced by the crisp tones of Colonel Lancer, first battle officer:

"As you were. Section G-987 and 989 damage control crews report! Forward armaments, safety interlocks off, stand by for firing orders! Message center, flash a code six to Fleet and TF Command. Power section, all selectors to gate, rig for full emergence power . . . ."

Pryor hauled himself hand-over-hand to the main message console. The body of the code yeoman hung slackly in the seat harness, blood dripping from the fingertips of his dangling hand. Pryor freed him, took his place. He keyed the code six alarm into the pulse-relay tanks, triggered an emergency override signal, beamed the message outward toward the distant Fleet Headquarters.

On the command deck, Commodore Broadly clutched a sprained wrist to his chest, stood, teeth bared, feet braced apart, staring into the forward image-screen at the dwindling point of light that was the Djann blockade runner.

"The effrontery of the damned scoundrel!" he roared. "Lancer, launch another covey of U-95's! You've got over five hundred megaton/seconds of firepower, man! Use it!"

"He's out of range, Commodore," Lancer said coolly. "He booby-trapped us very neatly."

"It's your job to see that we don't blunder into traps, by God, Colonel!" the commodore rounded on the battle officer. "You'll stop that pirate, or I'll rip those eagles off your shoulders myself!"

Lancer's mouth was a hard line; his eyes were ice chips.

"You can relieve me, Commodore," his voice grated. "Until you do, I'm battle commander aboard this vessel."

"By God, you're relieved, sir!" Broadly yelled. He whirled on the startled exec standing by. "Confine this officer to his quarters! Order full emergency acceleration! This vessel's on Condition Red at full combat alert until we overtake and destroy that sneaking snake in the grass!"

"Commodore—at full emergency without warning, there'll be men injured, even killed—"

"Carry out my commands, Captain, or I'll find someone who will!" The admiral's bellow cut off the exec. "I'll show that filthy, sneaking pack of spiders what it means to challenge a Terran fighting ship!"

On the power deck, Chief Powerman Joe Arena wiped the cut on his forehead, stared at the bloody rag, hurled it aside with a curse.

"All right, you one-legged deck-apes!" he roared. "You heard it! We're going after the bandit, full gate, and if we melt our linings down to slag, I'll have every man of you sign a statement of charges that'll take your grandchildren two hundred years to pay off!"

In the near darkness of the Place of Observation aboard the Djann vessel, the ocular complex of the One-Who-Commands glowed with a dim red sheen as he studied the apparently black surface of the sensitive plate. "The Death-Watcher has eaten our energy weapon," he communicated to his three link-brothers. "Now our dooms are in the palms of the fate-spinner."

"The Death-Watcher of the Water-Beings might have passed us by," the One-Who-Anticipates signaled. "It was an act of rashness to hurl the weapon at it."

"It will make a mighty song." The One-Who-Records thrummed his resonator plates, tried a melancholy bass chord.

"But what egg-carrier will exude the brood-nourishing honeys of strength and sagacity in response to these powerful rhymes, if the stimulus to their creation leads us to quick extinction?" the One-Who-Refutes queried.

"In their own brief existence, these harmonies find their justification," the One-Who-Records attested.

"The Death-Watcher shakes himself," the One-Who-Commands stated. "Now he turns in pursuit."

The One-Who-Records emitted a booming tone. "Gone are the great suns of Djann," he sang. "Lost are the fair worlds that knew their youth. But the spark of their existence glows still!"

"Now we fall outward, toward the Great Awesomeness," the One-Who-Anticipates commented. "Only the blackness will know your song."

"Draw in your energies from that-which-is-extraneous" the One-Who-Commands ordered. "Focus the full poignancy of your intellects on the urgency of our need for haste! All else is vain, now. Neither singer nor song will survive the vengeance of the Death-Watcher if he outstrips our swift flight!"

"Though Djann and Water-Being perish, my poem is eternal." The One-Who-Records emitted a stirring assonance. "Fly, Djanni! Pursue, Death-Watcher! Let the suns observe how we comport ourselves in this hour!"

"Exhort the remote nebulosities to attend our plight, if you must," the One-Who-Refutes commented. "But link your energies to ours or all is lost!"

Silent now, the Djann privateer fled outward toward the Rim.

7

Carnaby awoke, lay in darkness listening to the wheezing of Terry Sickle's breath. The boy didn't sound good. Carnaby sat up, suppressing a grunt at the stiffness of his limbs. The icy air seemed stale. He moved to the entry, lifted the polyon flap. A cascade of powdery snow poured in. Beyond the opening a faint glow filtered down through banked snow.

He turned back to Terry as the latter coughed deeply.

"Looks like the snow's quit," Carnaby said. "It's drifted pretty bad, but there's no wind now. How are you feeling, Terry?"

"Not so good, Lieutenant," Sickle said weakly. He breathed heavily, in and out. "I don't know what's got into me. Feel hot and cold at the same time."

Carnaby stripped off his glove, put his hand on Sickle's forehead. It was scalding hot.

"You just rest easy here for a while, Terry. There's a couple more cans of stew and plenty of water. I'll make it up to the top as quickly as I can. Soon as I get back, we'll go down. With luck, I'll have you to Doc Lin's house by dark."

"I guess . . . I guess I should have done like Doc said." Terry's voice was a thin whisper.

"What do you mean?"

"I been taking these hyposprays. Two a day. He said I better not miss one, but heck, I been feeling real good lately—"

"What kind of shots, Terry?" Carnaby's voice was tight.

"I don't know. Heck, Lieutenant, I'm no invalid!" His voice trailed off.

"You should have told me, Terry!"

"Gosh, Lieutenant—don't worry about me! I didn't mean nothing! Hell, I feel . . ." He broke off to cough deeply, rackingly.

"Terry, Terry!" Carnaby put a hand on the boy's thin shoulder."

"I'm okay," Sickle gasped. "It's just asthma. It's nothing."

"It's nothing if you get your medicine on schedule," Carnaby said. "But—"

"I butted in on this party, Lieutenant," Terry said. "It's my own fault . . . if I come down sick." He paused to draw a difficult breath. "You go ahead, sir . . . do what you got to do . . . I'll be okay."

"I've got to get you back, Terry. But I've got to go up first," Carnaby said. "You understand that, don't you?"

Terry nodded. "A man's got to do his job . . . Lieutenant. I'll be waiting . . . for you . . . when you get back."

"Listen to me carefully, Terry." Carnaby's voice was low. "If I'm not back by this time tomorrow, you'll have to make it back down by yourself. You understand? Don't wait for me."

"Sure, Lieutenant, I'll just rest a while. Then I'll be okay."

"Sooner I get started, the sooner I'll be back." Carnaby took a can from the pack, opened it, handed it to Terry. The boy shook his head.

"You eat it, Lieutenant. You need your strength. I don't feel like I . . . could eat anything anyway."

"Terry, I don't want to have to pry your mouth open and pour it in."

"All right. But open one for yourself too."

"All right, Terry."

Sickle's hand trembled as he spooned the stew to his mouth. He ate half of the contents of the can, then leaned back against the wall, closed his eyes. "That's all . . . I want . . . ."

"All right, Terry. You get some rest now. I'll be back before you know it." Carnaby crawled out through the open flap, pushed his way up through loosely drifted snow. The cold struck his face like a spiked club. He turned the suit control up another notch, noticing as he did that the left side seemed to be cooler than the right.

The near-vertical rise of the final crown of the peak thrust up from the drift, dazzling white in the morning sun. Carnaby examined the rockface for twenty feet on either side of the hut, picked a spot where a deep crack angled upward, started the last leg of the climb.

On the message deck, Lieutenant Pryor frowned into the screen from which the saturnine features of Lieutenant Aaron gazed back sourly.

"The commodore's going to be unhappy about this," Pryor said. "If you're sure your extrapolation is accurate—"

"It's as good as the data I got from plotting," Aaron snapped. "The bogie's over the make-or-break line; we'll never catch him now. You know your trans-Einsteinian physics as well as I do."

"I never heard of the Djann having anything capable of that kind of acceleration," Pryor protested.

"You have now." Aaron switched off and keyed command deck, passed his report to the exec, then sat back with a resigned expression to await the reaction.

Less than a minute later, Commodore Broadly's irate face snapped into focus on the screen.

"You're the originator of this report?" he growled.

"I did the extrapolation." Aaron stared back at his commanding officer.

"You're relieved for incompetence," Broadly said in a tone as harsh as a handsaw.

"Yes, sir," Aaron said. His face was pale, but he returned the commodore's stare. "But my input data and comps are a matter of record. I'll stand by them."

Broadly's face darkened. "Are you telling me these spiders can spit in our faces and skip off, scot-free?"

"All I'm saying, sir, is that the present acceleration ratios will put the target ahead of us by a steadily increasing increment."

Broadly's face twitched. "This vessel is at full emergency gain!" he growled. "No Djann has ever outrun a fleet unit in a straight-away run."

"This one is . . . sir."

The commodore's eyes bored into Aaron's. "Remain on duty until further notice," he said, and switched off. Aaron smiled crookedly and buzzed the message deck.

"He backed down," he said to Pryor. "We've got a worried commodore on board."

"I don't understand it myself," Pryor said. "How the hell is that can out-gaining us?"

"He's not," Aaron said complacently. "From a standing start, we'd overhaul him in short order. But he got the jump on us by a couple of minutes, after he lobbed the fish into us. If we'd been able to close the gap in the first half hour or so, we'd have had him; but at trans-L velocities, you get some strange effects. One of them is that our vectors become asymptotic. We're closing on him—but we'll never overtake him."

Pryor whistled. "Broadly could be busted for this fiasco."

"Uh-huh," Aaron grinned. "Could be—unless the bandit stops for a quick one . . . ."

After Aaron rang off, Pryor turned to study the position repeater screen. On it *Malthusa* was represented by a bright point at the center, the fleeing Djann craft by a red dot above.

"Charlie," Pryor called the NCOIC. "That garbled TX we picked up last watch; where did you R and D it?"

"Right about here, Lieutenant." The NCO flicked a switch and turned knobs; a green dot appeared near the upper edge of the screen.

"Hey," he said. "It looks like maybe our bandit's headed out this way."

"You picked him up on Y-band. Have you tried to raise him again?"

"Yeah, but nothing doing, Lieutenant. It was just a fluke—"

"Get a Y-beam on him, Charlie. Focus it down to a cat's whisker and work a pattern over a one degree radius centered around his MPP until you get an echo."

"If you say so, sir—but—"

"I do say so, Charlie! Find that transmitter, and the drinks are on me!"

8

Flat against the wind-swept rockface, Carnaby clung with his fingertips to a tenuous hold, feeling with one booted toe for a purchase higher up. A flake of stone broke away, and for a moment he hung by the fingers of his right hand, his feet dangling over emptiness; then, swinging his right leg far out, he hooked a knob with his knee, caught at a rocky rib with his free hand, pulled himself up to a more secure rest. He clung, his cheek against the iron-cold stone; out across the vast expanse of featureless grayish-tan plain the gleaming whipped-cream shape of the next cone rose, ten miles to the south.

A wonderful view up here—of nothing. Funny to think it could be his last. He was out of condition. It had been too long since his last climb . . . .

But that wasn't the way to think. He had a job to do—the first in twenty-one years. For a moment, ghostly recollections rose up before him: The trim Academy lawns, the spit-and-polish of inspection, the crisp feel of the new uniform, the glitter of the silver comet as Anne pinned it on . . .

That was no good either. What counted was here: The station up above. One more push, and he'd be there.

He rested for another half minute, then pulled himself up and forward, onto the relatively mild slope of the final approach to the crest. Fifty yards above, the dull-gleaming plastron-coated dome of the beacon station squatted against the exposed rock, looking no different than it had five years earlier.

Five minutes later, he was at the door, flicking the combination latch dial with cold-numbed fingers.

Tumblers clicked, and the panel slid aside. The heating system, automatically reacting to his entrance, started up with a busy hum to bring the interior temperature up to comfort level. He pulled off his gauntlets, ran his hands over his face, rasping the stubble there. There was coffee in the side table, he remembered. Fumblingly, with stiff fingers, he got out the dispenser, twisted the control cap, poured out a steaming mug, gulped it down. It was hot and bitter. The grateful warmth of it made him think of Terry, waiting down below in the chill of the half-ruined hut.

"No time to waste," he muttered to himself. He stamped up and down the room, swinging his arms to warm himself, then seated himself at the console, flicked keys with a trained ease rendered only slightly rusty by the years of disuse. He referred to an index, found the input instructions for Code Gamma Eight, set up the boards, flipped in the Pulse lever. Under his feet, he felt the faint vibration as the power pack buried in the rock stored its output for ten microseconds, fired it in a single millisecond burst, stored and pulsed again. Dim instrument lights winked on, indicating normal readings all across the board.

Carnaby glanced at the wall clock. He had been here ten minutes now. It would take another quarter hour to comply with the manual's instructions—but to hell with that gobbledegook. He'd put the beacon on the air; this time the Navy would have to settle for that. It would be pushing it to get back to the boy and pack him down to the village by nightfall as it was. Poor kid; he'd wanted to help so badly . . .

"That's correct, sir," Pryor said crisply. "I haven't picked up any come-back on my pulse, but I'll definitely identify the echo as coming from a JN type installation."

Commodore Broadly nodded curtly. "However, inasmuch as your instruments indicate that this station is operating solo—not linked in with a net to set up a defensive field—it's of no use to us." The commodore looked at Pryor coldly.

"I think perhaps there's a way, sir," Pryor said. "The Djann are known to have strong tribal feelings. They'd never pass up what they thought was an SOS from one of their own. Now, suppose we signal this JN station to switch over to the Djann frequencies and beam one of their own signal-patterns at them. They just might stop to take a look . . ."

"By God!" Broadly looked at the signal-lieutenant. "If he doesn't, he's not human!"

"You like the idea, sir?" Pryor grinned.

"A little rough on the beacon station if they reach it before we do, eh, Lieutenant? I imagine our friends the Djann will be a trifle upset when they learn they've been duped."

"Oh . . ." Pryor looked blank. "I guess I hadn't thought of that, sir."

"Never mind," Broadly said briskly. "The loss of a minor installation such as this is a reasonable exchange for an armed vessel of the enemy."

"Well . . . ."

"Lieutenant, if I had a few more officers aboard who employed their energies in something other than assembling statistics proving we're beaten, this cruise might have made a record for itself—" Broadly cut himself off, remembering the degree of aloofness due junior officers—even juniors who may have raked some very hot chestnuts out of the fire.

"Carry on, Lieutenant," he said. "If this works out, I think I can promise you a very favorable endorsement on your next ER."

As Pryor's pleased grin winked off the screen, the commodore flipped up the red line key, snapped a brusque request at the bored log room yeoman.

"This will make Old Carbuncle sing another tune," he remarked almost gaily to the Exec, standing by with a harassed expression.

"Maybe you'd better go slow, Ned," the latter cautioned, gauging his senior's mood. "It might be as well to get a definite confirmation on this installation's capabilities before we go on record—"

Broadly turned abruptly to the screen as it chimed. "Admiral, as I reported, I've picked up one of our forward beacon towers," Broadly's hearty voice addressed the screen from which the grim visage of the task force commander eyed him. "I'm taking steps to complete the intercept that are, if I may say so, rather ingenious."

"It's my understanding the target is receding on an I-curve, Broadly," the admiral said flatly. "I've been anticipating a Code thirty-three from you."

"Break off action?" Broadly's jaw dropped. "Now, Tom—"

"It's a little irregular to use a capital ship of the line to chase a ten-thousand-ton yacht." The task force commander ignored the interruption. "I can understand your desire to break the monotony with a little activity; good exercise for the crew, too. But at the rate the signal is attenuating, it's apparent you've lost her." His voice hardened. "I'm beginning to wonder if you've forgotten that your assignment is the containment of enemy forces supposedly pinned down under tight quarantine!"

"This yacht, as you put it, Admiral, blew two of my detached units out of space!" Broadly came back hotly. "In addition, he planted a missile squarely in my fore lazaret—"

"I'm not concerned with the details of your operation at this moment, Commodore." The other bit off the words like bullets. "I'm more interested in maintaining the degree of surveillance over my assigned quadrant that Concordiat security requires. Accordingly—"

"Just a minute, Tom, before you commit yourself!" Broadly's florid face was pale around the ears. "Perhaps you failed to catch my first remark: I have a forward station directly in the enemy's line of retreat. The intercept is in the bag—unless you countermand me."

"You're talking nonsense! The target's well beyond the Inner Line."

"He's not beyond the Outer Line!"

The Admiral frowned. His tight, well-chiseled face was still youthful under the mask of authority. "The system was never extended into the region under discussion," he said harshly. "I suggest you recheck your instruments. In the interim, I want to see an advice of a course-correction for station in the length of time it takes you to give the necessary orders to your navigation section."

Broadly drew a breath, hesitated. If Old Carbuncle

was right—if that infernal signal-lieutenant had made a mistake—but the boy seemed definite enough about it. He clamped his jaw. He'd risked his career on a wild throw; maybe he'd acted a little too fast; maybe he'd been a little too eager to grab a chance at some favorable notice; but the die was cast now. If he turned back empty-handed the entire affair would go into the record as a major fiasco. But if this scheme worked out . . .

"Unless the admiral wishes to make that a direct order," he heard himself saying firmly, "I intend to hold my course and close with the enemy. It's my feeling that neither the admiralty nor the general public will enjoy hearing of casualties inflicted by a supposedly neutralized enemy who was then permitted to go on his way unhindered." He returned the other's stare, feeling a glow of pride at his own decisiveness and a simultaneous sinking sensation at the enormity of the insubordination.

The vice admiral looked back at him through narrowed eyes. "I'll leave that decision to you, Commodore," he said tightly. "I think you're as aware as I of what's at stake here."

Broadly stiffened at what was almost an open threat. "Instruct your signals officer to pass full information on this supposed station to me immediately," the senior concluded curtly and then disappeared from view on the screen.

Broadly turned away, feeling all eyes on him. "Tell Pryor to copy his report to G at once," he said in a harsh voice. His eyes strayed to the exec's. "And if this idea of his doesn't work out, God help him." *And all of us,* he added under his breath.

As Carnaby reached for the door, to start the long climb down, a sharp *beep!* sounded from the panel behind him.

He looked back, puzzled. The bleat repeated, urgent, commanding. He swung the pack down, went to the console, flipped down the REC key.

". . . 37 Ace Trey," an excited voice came through loud and clear. "I repeat, cut your beacon immediately! JN37 Ace Trey, Cinsec One-oh-four to JN37 Ace Trey. Shut down beacon soonest! This is an Operational Urgent! JN37 Ace Trey, cut beacon and stand by for further operational urgent instructions . . . . "

9

On the fleet command deck aboard the flagship, Vice-Admiral Thomas Carnaby, otherwise known as Old Carbuncle, studied the sector triagram as his communications chief pointed out the positions of the flagship, *Malthusa*, the Djann refugee and the reported JN beacon station

"I've researched the call letters, sir," the gray-haired signals major said. "They're not shown on any listing as an active station. In fact, the entire series of which this station would be a part is coded null; never reported in commission."

"So someone appears to be playing pranks, is that your conclusion, Henry?"

The signals officer pulled at his lower lip. "No, sir, not that, precisely. I've done a full analytical on the recorded signal that young Pryor first intercepted. It's plainly directed to Cincsec in response to the alert, and the ID is confirmed. Now, as I say, this series was dropped from the register. But at one time, such a designation *was* assigned *en bloc* to a proposed link in the Out-line. However, the planned installations never came to fruition due to changes in the strategic position."

The vice-admiral frowned. "What changes were those?"

"The task force charged with the establishment of the link encountered heavy enemy pressure. In fact, the cruiser detailed to carry out the actual placement of the units was lost in action with all hands. Before the program could be re-initiated, a withdrawal from the sector was ordered. The new link was never completed, and the series was retired, unused."

"So?"

"So . . . just possibly, sir, one of those old stations *was* erected before *Redoubt* was lost—"

"What's that?" The admiral rounded on the startled officer. "Did you say . . . *Redoubt?*" His voice was a hiss between set teeth.

"Y—yessir!"

"*Redoubt* was lost with all hands before she planted her first station!"

"I know that's what we've always thought, Admiral—"

The Admiral snatched the paper from the major's hand. "JN37 Ace-Trey," he read aloud. "Why the hell didn't you say so sooner?" He whirled to his chief of staff.

"What's Broadly got in mind?" he snapped the question.

The startled officer began a description of the plan

to decoy the Djann vessel into range of *Malthusa's* batteries.

"Decoy?" the vice admiral snarled. The exec took a step backward, shocked at the expression on his superior's face. The latter spun to face his battle officer, standing by on the bridge.

"General, rig out an interceptor and get my pressure gear into it! I want it on the line ready for launch in ten minutes! Assign your best torchman as co-pilot!"

"Yessir!" The general spoke quickly into a lapel mike. The admiral flicked a key beside the hot-line screen.

"Get Broadly," he said in a voice like doom impending.

In the Djann ship, the One-Who-Commands stirred and extended a contact to his crew members. "Tune keenly in the scarlet regions of the spectrum," he communicated. "And tell me whether the spinners weave a new thread in the tapestry of our fates."

"I sensed it but now and felt recognition stir within me!" the mighty One-Who-Records thrummed a euphony. "A voice of the Djann, sore beset, telling of mortal need!"

"I detect a strangeness," the One-Who-Refutes indicated. "This is not the familiar voice of They-Who-Summon."

"After the passage of ninety cycles, it is not surprising that new chords have been added to the voice and others withdrawn," the One-Who-Anticipates pointed out. "If the link-cousins are in distress, our path is clear!"

"Shall I then bend our fate-line to meet the new

voice?" the One-Who-Commands called for a weighing. "The pursuers press us closely."

"The voice calls. Will we pervert our saga by shunning it?"

"This is a snare of the Water-Beings, calculated to abort our destinies!" The One-Who-Refutes warned. "Our vital energies are drained to the point of incipient coma by the weapon-which-feeds-on-life! If we turn aside now, we place ourselves in the jaws of the destroyer!"

"Though the voice lies, the symmetry of our existence demands that we answer its appeal," the One-Who-Anticipates declared.

"Go to it." The One-Who-Records sounded a booming arpeggio, combining triumph and defeat. "Let the Djann flame burn brightest in its hour of extinction!"

"By God, they've fallen for it!" Commodore Broadly smacked his fist into his hand and beamed at the young signal-lieutenant. He rocked back on his heels, studying the position chart the plot officer had set up for him on the message deck. "We'll make the intercept about here." His finger stabbed at a point a fractional light from the calculated position of the new-found OL station.

He broke off as an excited voice burst from the intercom screen.

"Commodore Broadly, sir! Urgent from task—" The yeoman's face disappeared from the screen to be replaced by the fierce visage of the vice-admiral.

"Broadly, sheer off and take up course for station and then report yourself under arrest! Commodore Baskov will take command: I've countermanded your damned-fool orders to the OL station! I'm on my way out there now to see what I can salvage—and when I get back, I'm preferring charges against you that will put you on the beach for the rest of your miserable life!"

10

In the beacon station atop the height of ground known as Thunderhead, Carnaby waited before the silent screen. The modification to the circuitry had taken half an hour; setting up the new code sequences, another fifteen minutes. Then another half hour had passed, while the converted beacon beamed out the alien signal.

He'd waited long enough. It had been twenty minutes now since the last curt order to stand by; and in the hut a thousand feet below, Terry had been waiting now for nearly five hours, every breath he drew a torture of strangulation. The order had been to put the signal on the air, attempt to delay the enemy ship. Either it had worked, or it hadn't. If Fleet had any more instructions for him, they'd have to damn well deliver them in person. He'd done what was required. Now he had to see to the boy.

Carnaby rose, again donned the back-pack, opened the door. As he did so, a faint, deep-toned rumble of distant thunder rolled. He stepped outside, squinted up at the sky, a dazzle of mist-gray. Maybe the snow squall was headed back this way. That would be bad luck; it would be close enough as it was.

A bright point of light caught his eye, winking from high above, almost at zenith.

Carnaby felt his heart take a leap in his chest that almost choked off his breath. For a moment he stood, staring up at it; then he whirled back through the door.

" . . . termand previous instructions!" A new voice was rasping from the speaker. "Terminate all transmissions immediately! JN37, shut down power and vacate station! Repeat, an armed enemy vessel is believed to be vectored in on your signal! This is, repeat, a hostile vessel! You are to cease transmission and abandon station immediately—"

Carnaby's hand slapped the big master lever. Lights died on the panel. Underfoot, the minute vibration jelled into immobility. Sudden silence pressed in like a tangible force—a silence broken by a rising mutter from above.

"Like that, eh?" Carnaby said to himself through clenched teeth. "Abandon station, eh?" He took three steps to a wall locker, yanked the door wide, took out a short, massive power rifle, still encased in its plastic protective cover. He stripped the oily sheath away, checked the charge indicator; it rested on FULL.

There were foot-square windows set on each side of the twenty-foot room. Carnaby went to one. By putting his face flat against the armorplast panel he was able to see the ship, now a flaring fireball dropping in along a wide approach curve. As it descended swiftly, the dark body of the vessel took shape above the glare of the drive. It was a small, blunt-ended ovoid of unfamiliar design, a metallic black in color, decorated fore and aft with the scarlet blazons of a Djann war vessel.

The ship was close now, maneuvering to a position a thousand feet directly overhead. Now a small landing craft detached itself from the parked ship and plummeted downward like a stone with a shrill whistling of high-speed rotors, to settle in across the expanse of broken rock in a cloud of pale dust. The black plastic bubble atop the landing sled split like a clamshell.

A shape came into view, clambered over the cockpit rim and stood, a cylindrical bronze-black body slung by leather mesenteries from the paired U frames that were its ambulatory members, two pairs of grasping limbs folded above.

A second Djann emerged, a third, a fourth. They stood together, immobile, silent, while a minute ticked past. Sweat trickled down the side of Carnaby's face. He breathed shallowly, rapidly, feeling the almost painful thudding of his heart. They'd ordered him to delay the enemy; well, he'd delay them . . . .

One of the Djann moved suddenly, its strange, jointless limbs moving with twinkling grace and speed. It flowed across to a point from which it could look down across the plain, then angled to the left and reconnoitered the entire circumference of the mountain top. Carnaby moved from window to window to watch it. It rejoined the other three; briefly, they seemed to confer. Then one of the creatures, whether the same one or another Carnaby wasn't sure, started across toward the hut.

Carnaby moved back into a position in the lee of a switch gear cabinet. A moment later the Djann appeared at the door. At a distance of fifteen feet, Carnaby saw the lean limbs, like leather-covered metal; the heavy body; the immense faceted eyes that caught the light and sent back fiery glints. For thirty seconds the creature scanned the interior of the structure. Then it withdrew.

Carnaby let out a long, shaky breath, watched it lope back to rejoin its companions. Again, the Djann conferred; then one turned to the landing craft.

For a moment Carnaby hesitated. He could stay where he was, do nothing, and the Djann would reboard their vessel and go their way; and in a few hours a fleet unit would heave into view off Longone, and he'd be home safe.

But the orders had been to delay the enemy . . . .

He centered the sights of the power gun on the alien's body, just behind the fore-legs, and pushed the firing stud.

A shaft of purple fire blew the window from its frame, lanced out to smash the up-rearing alien against the side of the sled, sent it skidding in a splatter of molten rock and metal. Carnaby swung the rifle, fired at a second Djann as the group scattered; the stricken creature went down, rolled, came up, stumbling on three limbs. He fired again, knocked the creature spinning, dark fluid spattering from a gaping wound in the barrel-like body. Carnaby swung to cover a third Djann, streaking for the plateau's edge; his shot sent a shower of molten slag arcing high from the spot where it disappeared.

He lowered the gun, stepped outside, ran to the corner of the building. The fourth Djann was crouched in the open, thirty feet away; Carnaby saw the glitter of a weapon gripped in the hand-like members springing from its back. He brought the gun up, fired in the same instant that light etched the rocks, and a hammer-blow struck him crushingly in the side, knocked him back against the wall. He tasted dust in his mouth, was aware of a high, humming sound that seemed to blank out his hearing, his vision, his thoughts . . .

He came to, lying on his side against the wall. Forty feet away, the Djann sprawled, its stiff limbs out-thrust at awkward angles. Carnaby looked down at his side.

The Djann particle-gun had torn a gaping rent in his suit, through which he could see bright crimson beads of frozen blood. He groped, found the rifle, dragged it to him. He shook his head to clear away the mist that seemed to obscure his vision. At every move, a terrible sharp pain stabbed outward from his chest. *Ribs broken,* he thought. *Something smashed inside, too.* It was hard for him to breathe. The cold stone on which he lay seemed to suck the heat from his body.

Across the hundred foot stretch of frost-shattered rock, a soot-black scar marked the spot where the escaping Djann had gone over the edge. Painfully, Carnaby propped the weapon to cover the direction from which attack might come. Then he slumped, his face against the icy rock, watching down the length of the rifle barrel for the next move from the enemy.

"Another four hours to shift, Admiral," said General Drew, the battle commander acting as co-pilot aboard the racing interceptor. "That's if we don't blow our linings before then."

"Bandit still holding position?" The admiral's voice was a grate as of metal against metal.

Drew spoke into his lip mike, frowned at the reply. "Yes, sir, *Malthusa* says he's still stationary. Whether his focus is identical with the LN beacon's fix or not, he isn't sure at that range."

"He could be standing by off-planet, looking over the ground," the admiral muttered half to himself.

"Not likely, Admiral. He knows we're on his tail."

"I know it's not likely, damn it!" the admiral snarled. "But if he isn't, we haven't got a chance."

"I suppose the Djann conception of honor requires these beggars to demolish the beacon and hunt down the station personnel, even if it means letting us overhaul them," Drew said. "A piece of damn foolishness on their part, but fortunate for us."

"For us, General? I take it you mean yourself and me, not the poor devil that's down there alone with them!"

"Just the one man? Well, we'll get off more cheaply than I imagined." The general glanced sideways at the admiral, intent over the controls. "After all, he's Navy. This is his job, what he signed on for."

"Kick the converter again, General," Admiral Carnaby said between his teeth. "Right now you can earn your pay by squeezing another quarter light out of this bucket."

Crouched in a shallow crevice below the rim of the mesa where the house of the Water-Beings stood, the One-Who-Records quivered under the appalling impact of the death-emanations of his link-brothers.

"Now it lies with you alone," the fading thought came from the One-Who-Commands. "But the Water-Being, too, is alone, and in this . . . there is . . . a certain euphony . . ." The last fragile tendril of communication faded.

The One-Who-Records expelled a gust of the planet's noxious atmosphere from his ventral orifice-array, with an effort freed his intellect of the shattering extinction-resonances it had absorbed. Cautiously, he probed outward, sensing the strange, fiery mind-glow of the alien . . . .

Ah, he too was injured! The One-Who-Records shifted his weight from his scalded forelimb, constricted further the flow of vital fluids through the damaged section of his epidermal system. He was weakened by the searing blast that had scored his flank, but still capable of action; and up above, the wounded Water-Being waited.

Deftly, the Djann extracted the hand-weapon from the sheath strapped to his side, holding it in a two-handed grip, its broad base resting on his dorsal ridge, its ring-lenses aligned along his body. He wished briefly that he had spent more *li* periods in the peril-tanks, impressing the weapon's use-syndromes on his reflex system; but feckless regrets made poor scansion. Now indeed the display-podium of existence narrowed down to a single confrontation: A brief and final act in a century-old drama, with the fate of the mighty epic of Djann resting thereon. The One-Who-Records sounded a single, trumpet-like resonance of exultation and moved forward to fulfill his destiny.

11

At the faint bleat of sound, Carnaby raised his head. How long had he lain here, waiting for the alien to make its move? Maybe an hour, maybe longer. He had passed out at least twice, possibly for no more than a second or two; but it could have been longer. The Djann might even have gotten past him—or crawled along below the ridge, ready now to jump him from a new angle . . . .

He thought of Terry Sickle, waiting for him, counting on him. Poor kid; time was running out for him. The sun was dropping low, and the shadows would be closing in. It would be ice cold inside the hut; and down there in the dark the boy was slowly strangling, maybe calling for him . . . .

He couldn't wait any longer. To hell with the alien. He'd held him long enough. Painfully, using the wall as a support, Carnaby got to his hands and knees. His side felt as though it had been opened and packed with red-hot stones—or were they ice cold? His hands and feet were numb. His face ached. Frostbite. He'd look fine with a frozen ear. Funny how vanity survived as long as life itself . . . .

He got to his feet, leaned against the building, worked on breathing. The sky swam past him, fading and brightening. His feet felt like blocks of wood; that wasn't good. He had a long way to go. But the activity would warm him, get the blood flowing, except where the hot stones were. He would be lighter if he could leave them here. His hands moved at his side, groping over torn polyon, the sharp ends of broken wires . . . .

He brought his mind back to clarity with an effort. Wouldn't do to start wandering now. The gun caught his eye, lying at his feet. Better pick it up; but to hell with it, too much trouble. Navy property. Can't leave it here for the enemy to find. Enemy. Funny dream about a walking oxy tank, and—

He was looking at the dead Djann, lying, awkward, impossible, thirty feet away. No dream. The damn things were real. He was here, alone, on top of Thunderhead—

But he couldn't be. Flitter was broken down. Have to get another message off via the next tramp steamer that made planetfall. Hadn't been one for . . . how long?

Something moved, a hundred feet away, among the tumble of broken rock.

Carnaby ducked, came up with the blast-rifle, fired in a half-crouch from the hip, saw a big dark shape scramble up and over the edge, saw the wink of yellow light, fired again, cursing the weakness that made the gun buck and yaw in his hands, the darkness that closed over his vision. With hands that were stiff, clumsy, he fired a third time at the swift-darting shape that charged toward him; and then he was falling, falling . . . .

Stunned by the direct hit from the energy weapon of the Water-Being, the One-Who-Records fought his way upward through a universe shot through with whirling shapes of fire, to emerge on a plateau of mortal agony.

He tried to move, was shocked into paralysis by the

cacophony of conflicting motor and sense impressions from shattered limbs and organs.

Then I, too, die, the thought came to him with utter finality. *And with me dies the once-mighty song of Djann.*

Failing, his mind groped outward, calling in vain for the familiar touch of his link-brothers—and abruptly, a sharp sensation impinged on his sensitivity-complex. Concepts of strange and alien shape drifted into his mind, beating at him with compelling urgency from a foreign brain:

Youth, aspirations, the ringing bugle of the call-to-arms. A white palace rearing up into yellow sunlight; a bright banner, rippling against blue sky, and the shadows of great trees ranked on green lawns. The taste of grapes, and an odor of flowers; night, and the moon reflected from still water; the touch of a soft hand and the face of a woman, invested with a supernal beauty; chords of a remote music that spoke of the inexpressibly desirable, the irretrievably lost . . .

"Have we warred then, Water-Beings?" the One-Who-Records sent his thought outward. "We who might have been brothers?" With a mighty effort, he summoned his waning strength, sounded a final chord in tribute to that which had been, and was no more.

Carnaby opened his eyes and looked at the dead Djann lying in the crumpled posture of its final agony, not six feet from him. For a moment, a curious sensation of loss plucked at his mind.

"Sorry, fellow," he muttered aloud. "I guess you were doing what you had to do, too."

He stood, felt the ground sway under his feet. His head was light, hot; a sharp, clear humming sounded in his ears. He took a step, caught himself as his knees tried to buckle.

"Damn it, no time to fall out now," he grunted. He moved past the alien body, paused by the door to the shed. A waft of warm air caressed his cold-numbed face.

"Could go inside," he muttered. "Wait there. Ship along in a few hours, maybe. Pick me up . . ." He shook his head angrily. "Job's not done yet," he said clearly, addressing the white gleam of the ten mile distant peak known as Cream-top. "Just a little longer, Terry," he added. "I'm coming."

Painfully, Carnaby made his way to the edge of the plateau, pulled himself up and over and started down.

"We'd better shift to sub-L now, Admiral," Drew said, strain showing in his voice. "We're cutting it fine as it is."

"Every extra minute at full gain saves a couple of hours," the vice-admiral came back.

"That won't help us if we kick out inside the Delta limit and blow ourselves into free ions," the general said coolly.

"You've made your point, General!" The admiral kept his eyes fixed on his instruments. Half a minute ticked past. Then he nodded curtly.

"All right, kick us out," he snapped, "and we'll see where we stand."

The hundred-ton interceptor shuddered as the distorters whined down the scale, allowing the stressed space field that had enclosed the vessel to collapse. A star swam suddenly into the visible spectrum, blazing at planetary distance off the starboard bow at three o'clock high.

"Our target's the second body, there." The co-pilot punched the course into the panel.

"What would you say, another hour?" The admiral bit off the words.

"Make it two," the other replied shortly. He glanced up, caught the admiral's eye on him.

"Kidding ourselves won't change anything," he said steadily.

Admiral Carnaby narrowed his eyes, opened his mouth to speak, then clamped his jaw shut.

"I guess I've been a little snappy with you, George," he said. "I'll ask your pardon. That's my brother down there."

"Your . . . ?" the general's features tightened. "I guess I said some stupid things myself, Tom." He frowned at the instruments, busied himself adjusting course for an MIT approach.

Carnaby half jumped, half fell the last few yards to the narrow ledge called Halliday's Roost, landed awkwardly in a churn of powdered wind-driven snow. For a moment he lay sprawled, then gathered himself, made it to his feet, tottered to the hollow concealing the drifted entrance to the hut. He lowered himself, crawled down into the dark, clammy interior.

"Terry," he called hoarsely. A wheezing breath answered him. He felt his way to the boy's side, groped over him. He lay on his side, his legs curled against his chest.

"Terry!" Carnaby pulled the lad to a sitting position, he felt him stir feebly. "Terry, I'm back! We have to go now, Terry ...."

"I knew—" the boy stopped to draw an agonizing breath—"you'd come .... " He groped, found Carnaby's hand.

Carnaby fought the dizziness that threatened to close in on him.

He was cold—colder than he had ever been. The climbing hadn't warmed him. The side wasn't bothering him much now; he could hardly feel it. But he couldn't feel his hands and feet, either. They were like stumps, good for nothing .... Clumsily, he backed through the entry, bodily hauling Terry along with him.

Outside, the wind lashed at him like frozen whips. Carnaby raised Terry to his feet. The boy leaned against him, slid down, crumpled to the ground.

"Terry, you've got to try," Carnaby gasped out. His breath seemed to freeze in his throat. "No time to waste ... got to get you to ... Doc Lin ... "

"Lieutenant ... I ... can't .... "

"Terry ... you've got to try!" He lifted the boy to his feet.

"I'm ... scared ... Lieutenant ... " Terry stood swaying, his slight body quivering, his knees loose.

"Don't worry, Terry." Carnaby guided the boy to the point from which they would start the climb down. "Not far now."

"Lieutenant .... " Sickle caught at Carnaby's arm, clung. "You ... better ... leave ... me."

His breath sighed in his throat.

"I'll go first." Carnaby heard his own voice as from

a great distance. "Take . . . it easy. I'll be right there . . . to help . . . "

He forced a breath of sub-zero air into his lungs. The bitter wind moaned around the shattered rock. The dusky afternoon sun shed a reddish light but no heat on the long slope below.

"It's late." He mouthed the words with stiff lips. "It's late . . ."

12

Two hundred thousand feet above the surface of the outpost world Longone, the fleet interceptor split the stratosphere, its receptors fine-tuned to the Djann energy-cell emission spectrum.

"Three hundred million square miles of desert," Admiral Carnaby said. "Except for a couple of deserted townsites, not a sign that life ever existed here."

"We'll find it, Tom," Drew said. "If they'd lifted, *Malthusa* would have known—hold it!" He looked up quickly. "I'm getting something—yes! It's the typical Djann idler output!"

"How far from us?"

"Quite a distance . . . Now it's fading . . . . "

The admiral put the ship into a screaming deceleration curve that crushed both men brutally against the restraint of their shock-frames.

"Find that signal, George," the vice-admiral grated. "Find it and steer me to it, if you have to pick it out of the air with psi!"

"I've got it!" Drew barked. "Steer right, on 030. I'd range it at about two thousand kilometers . . . . "

On the bald face of an outcropping of wind-scored stone, Carnaby clung one-handed to a scanty hold, supporting Terry with the other arm. The wind shrieked, buffeting at him; sand-fine snow whirled into his face, slashing at his eyes, already half-blinded by the glare. The boy slumped against him, barely conscious.

His mind seemed as sluggish now as his half-frozen limbs. Somewhere below, there was a ledge, with shelter from the wind. How far? Ten feet? Fifty?

It didn't matter. He had to reach it. He couldn't hold on here, in this wind; in another minute he'd be done for.

Carnaby pulled Terry closer, got a better grip with a hand that seemed no more a part of him than the rock against which they clung. He shifted his purchase with his right foot—and felt it slip. He was falling, grabbing frantically with one hand at the rock, then dropping through open air—

The impact against drifted snow drove the air from his lungs. Darkness shot through with red fire threatened to close in on him; he fought to draw a breath, struggling in the claustrophobia of suffocation. With a desperate lunge, he caught a ridge of hard ice, pulled himself back from the brink, then groped, found Terry, lying on his back under the vertically rising wall of rock. The boy stirred.

"So . . . tired . . ." he whispered. His body arced as he struggled to draw breath.

Carnaby pulled himself to a position beside the boy, propped himself with his back against the rock. Dimly, through ice-rimmed eyes, he could see the evening lights of the settlement, far below; so far . . .

He put his arm around the thin body, settled the lad's head gently in his lap, leaned over him to shelter him from the whirling snow. "It's all right, Terry," he said. "You can rest now."

Supported on three narrow pencils of beamed force, the fleet interceptor slowly circuited the Djann yacht, hovering on its idling null-G generators a thousand feet above the towering white mountain.

"Nothing alive there," the co-pilot said. "Not a whisper on the life-detection scale."

"Take her down." Vice-Admiral Carnaby squinted through S-R lenses which had darkened almost to opacity in response to the frost-white glare from below. "The shack looks all right, but that doesn't look like a Mark 7 flitter parked beside it."

The heavy fleet boat descended swiftly under the expert guidance of the battle officer. At fifty feet, he leveled off, orbited the station.

"I count four dead Djann," the admiral said in a brittle voice.

"Tracks," the general pointed. "Leading off there . . ."

"Put her down, George!" The hundred-foot boat settled in with a crunching of rock and ice, its shark's prow overhanging the edge of the tiny plateau. The hatch cycle open; the two men emerged.

At the spot where Carnaby had lain in wait for the last of the aliens, they paused, staring silently at the glossy patch of dark blood, and at the dead Djann beside it. Then they followed the irregularly spaced footprints across to the edge.

"He was still on his feet—but that's about all," the battle officer said.

"George, can you operate that Spider boat?" The admiral indicated the Djann landing sled.

"Certainly."

"Let's go."

It was twilight half an hour later when the admiral, peering through the obscuring haze, saw the snow-drifted shapes huddled in the shadow of an overhang. Fifty feet lower, the general settled the sled into a precarious landing on a narrow shelf. It was a ten minute climb back to their objective.

Vice Admiral Carnaby pulled himself up the last yard, looked across the icy ledge at the figure in the faded blue polyon cold suit. He saw the weathered and lined face, glazed with ice; the closed eyes, the gnarled and bloody hands, the great wound in the side.

The general came up beside him, stared silently, then went forward.

"I'm sorry, Admiral," he said a moment later. "He's dead. Frozen. Both of them."

The admiral came up, went to Carnaby's side.

"I'm sorry, Jimmy," he said. "Sorry."

"I don't understand," the general said. "He could have stayed up above, in the station. He'd have been all right there. What in the world was he doing down here?"

"What he always did." Admiral Carnaby said. "His duty."

HYBRID

Deep in the soil of the planet, rootlets tougher than steel wire probed among glassy sand grains, through packed veins of clay and layers of flimsy slate, sensing and discarding inert elements, seeking out calcium, iron, nitrogen.

Deeper still, a secondary system of roots clutched the massive face of the bedrock; sensitive tendrils monitored the minute trembling in the planetary crust, the rhythmic tidal pressures, the seasonal weight of ice, the footfalls of the wild creatures that hunted in the mile-wide shadow of the giant Yanda tree.

On the surface far above, the immense trunk, massive as a cliff, its vast girth anchored by mighty buttresses, reared up nine hundred yards above the prominence, spreading huge limbs in the white sunlight.

The tree was only remotely aware of the movement of air over the polished surfaces of innumerable leaves, the tingling exchange of molecules of water, carbon dioxide, oxygen. Automatically it reacted to the faint pressures of the wind, tensing slender twigs to hold each leaf at a constant angle to the radiation that struck down through the foliage complex.

The long day wore on. Air flowed in intricate patterns: radiation waxed and waned with the drift of vapor masses in the sub-stratosphere; nutrient molecules moved along capillaries; the rocks groaned gently in the dark under the shaded slopes. In the invulnerability of its titanic mass, the tree dozed in a state of generalized low-level consciousness.

The sun moved westward. Its light, filtered through an increasing depth of atmosphere, was an ominous yellow now. Sinewy twigs rotated, following the source of energy. Somnolently, the tree retracted tender buds against the increasing cold, adjusted its rate of heat and moisture loss, its receptivity to radiation. As it slept, it dreamed of the long past, the years of free-wandering in the faunal stage, before the instinct to root and grow had driven it here. It remembered the grove of its youth, the patriarchal tree, the spore-brothers. . . .

It was dark now. The wind was rising. A powerful gust pressed against the ponderous obstacle of the tree; great thews of major branches creaked, resisting: chilled leaves curled tight against the smooth bark.

Deep underground, fibers hugged rock, transmitting data which were correlated with impressions from distant leaf surfaces. There were ominous vibrations from the northeast; relative humidity was rising, air pressure falling—a pattern formed, signalling danger. The tree stirred; a tremor ran through the mighty branch system, shattering fragile frost crystals that had begun to form on shaded surfaces. Alertness stirred in the heart-brain, dissipating the euphoric dream-pattern. Reluctantly, long dormant faculties came into play. The tree awoke.

Instantly, it assessed the situation. A storm was moving in off the sea—a major typhoon. It was too late for effective measures. Ignoring the pain of unaccustomed activity, the tree sent out new shock roots—cables three inches in diameter, strong as stranded steel—to grip the upreared rock slabs a hundred yards north of the tap root.

There was nothing more the tree could do. Impassively, it awaited the onslaught of the storm.

"That's a storm down there," Malpry said.

"Don't worry, we'll miss it." Gault fingered controls, eyes on dial faces.

"Pull up and make a new approach," Malpry said, craning his neck from his acceleration cradle.

"Shut up. I'm running this tub."

"Locked in with two nuts," Malpry said. "You and the creep."

"Me and the creep are getting tired of listening to you bitch, Mal."

"When we land, Malpry, I'll meet you outside," Pantelle said. "I told you I don't like the name 'Creep'."

"What, again?" Gault said. "You all healed up from the last time?"

"Not quite; I don't seem to heal very well in space."

"Permission denied, Pantelle," Gault said. "He's too big for you. Mal, leave him alone."

"I'll leave him alone," Malpry muttered. "I ought to dig a hole and leave him in it. . . ."

"Save your energy for down there," Gault said. "If we don't make a strike on this one, we've had it."

"Captain, may I go along on the field reconnaissance? My training in biology—"

"You better stay with the ship, Pantelle. And don't

tinker. Just wait for us. We haven't got the strength to carry you back."

"That was an accident, Captain—"

"And the time before. Skip it, Pantelle. You mean well, but you've got two left feet and ten thumbs."

"I've been working on improving my coordination, Captain. I've been reading—"

The ship buffetted sharply as guidance vanes bit into atmosphere; Pantelle yelped.

"Oh-oh," he called. "I'm afraid I've opened up that left elbow again."

"Don't bleed on me, you clumsy slob," Malpry said.

"Quiet!" Gault said between his teeth. "I'm busy."

Pantelle fumbled a handkerchief in place over the cut. He would have to practice those relaxing exercises he had read about. And he would definitely start in weight-lifting soon—and watching his diet. And he would be very careful this time and land at least one good one on Malpry, just as soon as they landed.

Even before the first outward signs of damage appeared, the tree knew that it had lost the battle against the typhoon. In the lull as the eye of the storm passed over, it assessed the damage. There was no response from the northeast quadrant of the sensory network where rootlets had been torn from the rock face; the tap root itself seated now against pulverized stone. While the almost indestructible fibre of the Yanda tree had held firm, the granite had failed. The tree was doomed by its own mass.

Now, mercilessly, the storm struck again, thundering out of the southwest to assault the tree with blind ferocity. Shock cables snapped like gossamer; great slabs of rock groaned and parted, with detonations lost in the howl of the wind. In the trunk, pressures built, agonizingly.

Four hundred yards south of the tap root, a crack opened in the sodden slope, gaping wider. Wind-driven water poured in, softening the soil, loosening the grip of a million tiny rootlets. Now the major roots shifted, slipping. . . .

Far above, the majestic crown of the Yanda tree yielded imperceptibly to the irresistible torrent of air. The giant north buttress, forced against the underlying stone, shrieked as tortured cells collapsed, then burst with a shattering roar audible even above the storm. A great arc of earth to the south, uplifted by exposed roots, opened a gaping cavern.

Now the storm moved on, thundered down the slope trailing its retinue of tattered debris and driving rain. A last vengeful gust whipped branches in a final frenzy; then the victor was gone.

And on the devastated promontory, the stupendous mass of the ancient tree leaned with the resistless inertia of colliding moons to the accompaniment of a cannonade of parting sinews, falling with dream-like grace.

And in the heart-brain of the tree, consciousness faded in the unendurable pain of destruction.

Pantelle climbed down from the open port, leaned against the ship to catch his breath. He was feeling weaker than he expected. Tough luck, being on short rations; this would set him back on getting started on his weight-lifting program. And he didn't feel ready to take on Malpry yet. But just as soon as he had some fresh food and fresh air—

"These are safe to eat," Gault called, wiping the analyzer needle on his pants leg and thrusting it back into his hip pocket. He tossed two large red fruits to Pantelle.

"When you get through eating, Pantelle, you better get some water and swab down the inside. Malpry and I'll take a look around."

The two moved off. Pantelle sat on the springy grass, and bit into the apple-sized sphere. The texture, he thought, was reminiscent of avocado. The skin was tough and aromatic; possibly a natural cellulose acetate. There seemed to be no seeds. That being the case, the thing was not properly a fruit at all. It would be interesting to study the flora of this planet. As soon as he reached home, he would have to enroll in a course in E.T. botany. Possibly he would go to Heidelberg or Uppsala, attend live lectures by eminent scholars. He would have a cosy little apartment—two rooms would do—in the old part of town, and in the evening he would have friends in for discussions over a bottle of wine—

However, this wasn't getting the job done. There was a glint of water across the slope. Pantelle finished his meal, gathered his buckets, and set out.

"Why do we want to wear ourselves out?" Malpry said.

"We need the exercise. It'll be four months before we get another chance."

"What are we, tourists, we got to see the sights?" Malpry stopped, leaned against a boulder, panting. He stared upward at the crater and the pattern of uptilted roots and beyond at the forest-like spread of the branches of the fallen tree.

"Makes our sequoias look like dandelions." Gault said. "It must have been the storm, the one we dodged coming in."

"So what?"

"A thing that big—it kind of does something to you."

"Any money in it?" Malpry sneered.

Gault looked at him sourly. "Yeah, you got a point there. Let's go."

"I don't like leaving the Creep back there with the ship."

Gault looked at Malpry. "Why don't you lay off the kid?"

"I don't like loonies."

"Don't kid me, Malpry. Pantelle is highly intelligent —in his own way. Maybe that's what you can't forgive."

"He gives me the creeps."

"He's a nice-looking kid; he means well—"

"Yeah," Malpry said. "Maybe he means well—but it's not enough . . ."

From the delirium of concussion, consciousness returned slowly to the tree. Random signals penetrated the background clatter of shadowy impulses from maimed senses—

"Air pressure zero; falling . . . air pressure 112, rising . . . air pressure negative . . .

"Major tremor radiating from—Major tremor radiating from—

"Temperature 171 degrees, temperature −40 degrees, temperature 26 degrees . . .

"Intense radiation in the blue only . . . red only . . . ultra violet . . .

"Relative humidity infinite . . . wind from north-northeast, velocity infinite . . . wind rising vertically, velocity infinite . . . wind from east, west . . ."

Decisively, the tree blanked off the yammering nerve-trunks, narrowing its attention to the immediate status-concept. A brief assessment sufficed to reveal the extent of its ruin.

There was no reason, it saw, to seek extended personal survival. However, certain immediate measures were necessary to gain time for emergency spore-propagation. At once, the tree-mind triggered the survival syndrome. Capillaries spasmed, forcing vital juices to the brain. Synaptic helices dilated, heightening neural conductivity. Cautiously, awareness was extended to the system of major fibres, then to individual filaments and interweaving capillaries.

Here was the turbulence of air molecules colliding with ruptured tissues, the wave pattern of light impinging on exposed surfaces. Microscopic filaments contracted, cutting off fluid loss through the wounds.

Now the tree-mind fine-tuned its concentration, scanning the infinitely patterned cell matrix. Here, amid confusion, there was order in the incessant restless movement of particles, the flow of fluids, the convoluted intricacy of the alphaspiral. Delicately, the tree-mind readjusted the function-mosaic, in preparation for spore generation.

Malpry stopped, shaded his eyes. A tall thin figure stood in the shade of the uptilted root mass on the ridge.

"Looks like we headed back at the right time," Malpry said.

"Damn," Gault said. He hurried forward. Pantelle came to meet him.

"I told you to stay with the ship, Pantelle!"

"I finished my job, Captain. You didn't say—"

"OK, OK. Is anything wrong?"

"No sir. But I've just remembered something—"

"Later, Pantelle. Let's get back to the ship. We've got work to do."

"Captain, do you know what this is?" Pantelle gestured toward the gigantic fallen tree.

"Sure; it's a tree." He turned to Malpry. "Let's—"

"Yes, but what kind?"

"Beats me. I'm no botanist."

"Captain, this is a rare species. In fact, it's supposed to be extinct. Have you ever heard of the Yanda?"

"No. Yes." Gault looked at Pantelle. "Is that what this is?"

"I'm sure of it. Captain, this is a very valuable find—"

"You mean it's worth money?" Malpry was looking at Gault.

"I don't know. What's the story, Pantelle?"

"An intelligent race, with an early animal phase; later, they root, become fixed, functioning as a plant. Nature's way of achieving the active competition necessary for natural selection, then the advantage of conscious selection of a rooting site."

"How do we make money on it?"

Pantelle looked up at the looming wall of the fallen trunk, curving away among the jumble of shattered branches, a hundred feet, two hundred, more, in diameter. The bark was smooth, almost black. The foot-wide leaves were glossy, varicolored.

"This great tree—"

Malpry stooped, picked up a fragment from a burst root.

"This great club," he said, "to knock your lousy brains out with—"

"Shut up, Mal."

"It lived, roamed the planet perhaps ten thousand years ago, in the young faunal stage. Then instinct drove it here, to fulfill the cycle of nature. Picture this ancient champion, looking for the first time out across the valley, saying his farewells as metamorphosis begins."

"Nuts," Malpry said.

"His was the fate of all males of his kind who lived too long, to stand forever on some height of land, to remember through unending ages the brief glory of youth, himself his own heroic monument."

"Where do you get all that crud?" Malpry said.

"Here was the place," Pantelle said. "Here all his journeys ended."

"OK, Pantelle. Very moving. You said something about this thing being valuable."

"Captain, this tree is still alive, for a while at least. Even after the heart is dead, the appearance of life will persevere. A mantle of new shoots will leaf out to shroud the cadaver, tiny atavistic plantlets without connection to the brain, parasitic to the corpse, identical to the ancestral stock from which the giants sprang, symbolizing the extinction of a hundred million years of evolution."

"Get to the point."

"We can take cuttings from the heart of the tree. I have a book—it gives the details on the anatomy—we can keep the tissues alive. Back in civilization, we can regenerate the tree—brain and all. It will take time—"

"Suppose we sell the cuttings."

"Yes, any university would pay well—"

"How long will it take?"

"Not long. We can cut in with narrow aperture blasters—"

"OK. Get your books, Pantelle. We'll give it a try."

Apparently, the Yanda mind observed, a very long time had elapsed since spore propagation had last been stimulated by the proximity of a female. Withdrawn into introverted dreams, the tree had taken no conscious notice as the whispering contact with the spore-brothers faded and the host-creatures dwindled away. Now, eidetically, the stored impressions sprang into clarity.

It was apparent that no female would pass this way again. The Yanda kind was gone. The fever of instinct that had motivated the elaboration of the mechanisms of emergency propagation had burned itself out futilely. The new pattern of stalked oculi gazed unfocussed at an empty vista of gnarled jungle growth, the myriad filaments of the transfer nexus coiled quiescent, the ranked grasping members that would have brought a host-creature near drooped unused, the dran-sacs brimmed needlessly; no further action was indicated. Now death would come in due course.

Somewhere a drumming began, a gross tremor sensed through the dead hush. It ceased, began again, went on and on. It was of no importance, but a faint curiosity led the tree to extend a sensory filament, tap the abandoned nerve-trunk—

Convulsively, the tree-mind recoiled, severing the contact. An impression of smouldering destruction, impossible thermal activity. . . .

Disoriented, the tree-mind considered the implications of the searing pain. A freak of damaged sense organs? A phantom impulse from destroyed nerves?

No. The impact had been traumatic, but the data were there. The tree-mind re-examined each synaptic vibration, reconstructing the experience. In a moment, the meaning was clear: A fire was cutting deep into the body of the tree.

Working hastily, the tree assembled a barrier of incombustible molecules in the path of the fire, waited. The heat reached the barrier, hesitated—and the barrier flashed into incandescence.

A thicker wall was necessary.

The tree applied all of its waning vitality to the task. The shield grew, matched the pace of the fire, curved out to intercept—

And wavered, halted. The energy demand was too great. Starved muscular conduits cramped. Blackness closed over the disintegrating consciousness.

Sluggishly, clarity returned. Now the fire would advance unchecked. Soon it would by-pass the aborted defenses, advance to consume the heart-brain itself. There was no other countermeasure remaining. It was unfortunate, since propagation had not been consum-

mated, but unavoidable. Calmly the tree awaited its
destruction by fire.

Pantelle put the blaster down, sat on the grass and
wiped tarry soot from his face.

"What killed 'em off?" Malpry asked suddenly.

Pantelle looked at him.

"Spoilers," he said.

"What's that?"

"They killed them to get the *dran*. They covered up
by pretending the Yanda were a menace, but it was
the *dran* they were after."

"Don't you ever talk plain?"

"Malpry, did I ever tell you I didn't like you?"

Malpry spat. "What's with this *dran?*"

"The Yanda have a very strange reproductive cycle.
In an emergency, the spores released by the male tree
can be implanted in almost any warm-blooded creature and carried in the body for an indefinite length of
time. When the host animal mates, the dormant spores
come into play. The offspring appears perfectly normal; in fact, the spore steps in and corrects any defects
in the individual, repairs injuries, fights disease, and
so on; and the life-span is extended; but eventually,
the creature goes through the metamorphosis, roots,
and becomes a regular male Yanda tree—instead of
dying of old age."

"You talk too much. What's this *dran?*"

"The tree releases an hypnotic gas to attract host
animals. In concentrated form, it's a potent narcotic.
That's *dran*. They killed the trees to get it. The excuse
was that the Yanda could make humans give birth to

monsters. That was nonsense. But it sold in the black market for fabulous amounts."

"How do you get the *dran?*"

Pantelle looked at Malpry. "Why do you want to know?"

Malpry looked at the book which lay on the grass. "It's in that, ain't it?"

"Never mind that. Gault's orders were to help me get the heart-cuttings."

"He didn't know about the *dran.*"

"Taking the *dran* will kill the specimen. You can't—"

Malpry stepped toward the book. Pantelle jumped toward him, swung a haymaker, missed. Malpry knocked him spinning.

"Don't touch me, Creep." He wiped his fist on his pants leg.

Pantelle lay stunned. Malpry thumbed the book, found what he wanted. After ten minutes, he dropped the book, picked up the blaster, and moved off.

Malpry cursed the heat, wiping at his face. A many-legged insect scuttled away before him. Underfoot, something furtive rustled. One good thing, no animals in this damned woods bigger than a mouse. A hell of a place. He'd have to watch his step; it wouldn't do to get lost in here . . .

The velvety wall of the half buried trunk loomed, as dense growth gave way suddenly to a clear stretch. Malpry stopped, breathing hard. He got out his sodden handkerchief, staring up at the black wall. A ring of dead-white stalks sprouted from the dead tree. Nearby were other growths, like snarls of wiry black seaweed, and ropy looking things, dangling—

Malpry backed away, snarling. Some crawling disease, some kind of filthy fungus—but—

Malpry stopped. Maybe this was what he was looking for. Sure, this was what those pictures in the book showed. This was where the *dran* was. But he didn't know it would look like some creeping—

"Stop, Malpry!"

Malpry whirled.

"Don't be so . . . stupid . . ." Pantelle was gasping for breath. There was a bruise on his jaw. "Let me rest . . . Talk to you . . ."

"Die, you gutter-scraping. Have a nice long rest. But don't muck with me." Malpry turned his back on Pantelle, unlimbered the blaster.

Pantelle grabbed up a broken limb, slammed it across Malpry's head. The rotten wood snapped. Malpry staggered, recovered. He turned, his face livid; a trickle of blood ran down.

"All right, Creep," he grated. Pantelle came to him, swung a whistling right, arm bent awkwardly. Malpry lunged, and Pantelle's elbow caught him across the jaw. His eyes went glassy, he sagged, fell to his hands and knees. Pantelle laughed aloud.

Malpry shook his head, breathing hoarsely, got to his feet. Pantelle took aim and hit him solidly on the jaw. The blow seemed to clear Malpry's head. He slapped a second punch aside, knocked Pantelle full-length with a backhanded blow. He dragged Pantelle to his feet, swung a hard left and right. Pantelle bounced, lay still. Malpry stood over him, rubbing his jaw.

He stirred Pantelle with his foot. Maybe the Creep was dead. Laying his creeping hands on Malpry. Gault wouldn't like it, but the Creep had started it. Sneaked up and hit him from behind. He had the mark to prove it. Anyway, the news about the *dran* would cheer Gault up. Better go get Gault up here. Then they could cut the *dran* out and get away from this creeping planet. Let the Creep bleed.

Malpry turned back toward the ship, leaving Pantelle huddled beside the fallen tree.

The Yanda craned external oculi to study the fallen creature, which had now apparently entered a dormant phase. A red exudation oozed from orifices at the upper end, and from what appeared to be breaks in the epidermis. It was a strange creature, bearing some superficial resemblance to the familiar host-creatures. Its antics, and those of the other, were curious indeed. Perhaps they were male and female, and the encounter had been a mating. Possibly this hibernation was normal process, preparatory to rooting. If only it were not so alien, it might serve as a carrier . . .

The surface of the organism heaved, a limb twitched. Apparently it was on the verge of reviving. Soon it would scurry away and be seen no more. It could be wise to make a quick examination; if the creature should prove suitable as a host. . . .

Quickly the tree elaborated a complex of tiny filaments, touched the still figure tentatively, then penetrated the surprisingly soft surface layer, seeking out nerve fibres. A trickle of impressions flowed in, indecipherable. The tree put forth a major sensory tendril,

divided and subdivided it into fibres only a few atoms
in diameter, fanned them out through the unconscious
man, tracing the spinal column, entering the brain—

Here was a wonder of complexity, an unbelievable
profusion of connections. This was a center capable of
the highest intellectual functions—unheard of in a host
creature. Curiously, the tree-mind probed deeper, at-
tuning itself, scanning through a kaliedoscope of impressions, buried memories, gaudy symbolisms.

Never had the Yanda-mind encountered the hyper-
intellectual processes of emotion. It pressed on, deeper
into the phantasmagoria of dreams—

Color, laughter, and clash-of-arms. Banners rippling
in the sun, chords of a remote music, and night-
blooming flowers. Abstractions of incredible beauty
mingled with vivid conceptualizations of glory. Fascinated, the tree-mind explored Pantelle's secret roman-
tic dreams of fulfillment—

And abruptly, encountered the alien mind.

There was a moment of utter stillness as the two
minds assessed each other.

You are dying, the alien mind spoke.

*Yes. And you are trapped in a sickly host-creature.
Why did you not select a stronger host?*

I . . . originated here. I . . . we . . . are one.

Why do you not strengthen this host?

How?

The Yanda mind paused. *You occupy only a corner
of the brain. You do not use your powers?*

I am a segment. . . . The alien mind paused, confused. *I am conceptualized by the monitor-mind as the
subconscious.*

What is the monitor-mind?

It is the totality of the personality. It is above the conscious, directing. . . .

This is a brain of great power, yet great masses of cell are unused. Why are major trunks aborted as they are?

I do not know.

There was no more information from the alien brain, which, indeed, housed multiple minds.

The Yanda mind broke contact, tuned.

There was a blast of mind-force, overwhelming. The Yanda-mind reeled, groped for orientation.

YOU ARE NOT ONE OF MY MINDS.

You are the monitor-mind? gasped the Yanda.

YES. WHAT ARE YOU?

The Yanda-mind projected its self-concept.

STRANGE, VERY STRANGE. YOU HAVE USEFUL SKILLS, I PERCEIVE. TEACH THEM TO ME.

The Yanda mind squirmed under the torrent of thought impulses.

Reduce your volume. You will destroy me.

I WILL TRY. TEACH ME THAT TRICK OF MANIPULATING MOLECULES.

The Yanda cringed under the booming of the alien mind. What an instrument! A fantastic anomaly, a mind such as this linked to this fragile host-creature— and unable even to use its powers. But it would be a matter of the greatest simplicity to make the necessary corrections, rebuild and toughen the host, eliminate the defects—

TEACH ME, YANDA MIND!

Alien, I die soon. But I will teach you. There is, however, a condition. . . .

The two minds conferred, and reached agreement. At once, the Yanda mind initiated sweeping rearrangements at the sub-molecular level.

First, cell-regeneration, stitching up the open lesions on arm and head. Antibodies were modified in vast numbers, flushed through the system. Parasites died.

Maintain this process, the tree-mind directed.

Now, the muscular layers; surely they were inadequate. The very structure of the cells was flimsy. The Yanda devised the necessary improvements, tapped the hulk of its cast-off body for materials, reinforced the musculature. Now for the skeletal members. . . .

The tree visualized the articulation of the ambulatory mechanism, considered for a moment the substitution of a more practical tentacular concept—

There was little time. Better to retain the stony bodies, merely strengthen them, using metallo-vegetable fibers. The air sacs, too. And the heart. They would have lasted no time at all as they were.

Observe, alien, thus, and thus. . . .

I SEE. IT IS A CLEVER TRICK.

The Yanda worked over the body of Pantelle, adjusting, correcting, reinforcing, discarding a useless appendix or tonsil here, adding a reserve air storage unit there. A vestigial eye deep in the brain was refurbished for sensitivity at the radio frequencies, linked with controls. The spine was deftly fused at the base; additional mesenteries were added for intestinal support. Following the basic pattern laid down in the genes, the tree-mind rebuilt the body.

When the process was finished, and the alien mind had absorbed the techniques demonstrated, the Yanda mind paused.

It is finished.

I AM READY TO RE-ESTABLISH THE CONSCIOUS MIND IN OVERT CONTROL.

Remember your promise.

I WILL REMEMBER.

The Yanda mind began its withdrawal. Troublesome instinct was served. Now it could rest until the end.

WAIT. I'VE GOT A BETTER IDEA, YANDA....

"Two weeks down and fourteen to go," Gault said. "Why don't you break down and tell me what happened back there?"

"How's Malpry?" Pantelle asked.

"He's all right. Broken bones knit, and you only broke a few."

"The book was wrong about the Yanda spores," Pantelle said. "They don't have the power in themselves to reconstruct the host-creature—"

"The what?"

"The infected animal; the health and life span of the host is improved. But the improvement is made by the tree, at the time of propagation, to insure a good chance for the spores."

"You mean you—"

"We made a deal. The Yanda gave me this—" Pantelle pressed a thumb against the steel bulkhead. The metal yielded.

"—and a few other tricks. In return, I'm host to the Yanda spores."

Gault moved away.

"Doesn't that bother you? Parasites—"

"It's an equitable deal. The spores are microscopic, and completely dormant until the proper conditions develop."

"Yeah, but you said yourself this vegetable brain has worked on your mind."

"It merely erased all the scars of traumatic experience, corrected deficiencies, taught me how to use what I have."

"How about teaching me?"

"Sorry, Gault." Pantelle shook his head. "Impossible."

Gault considered Pantelle's remarks.

"What about these 'proper conditions' for the spores?" he asked suddenly. "You wake up and find yourself sprouting some morning?"

"Well," Pantelle coughed. "That's where my part of the deal comes in. A host creature transmits the spores through the normal mating process. The offspring gets good health and a long life before the metamorphosis. That's not so bad—to live a thousand years, and then pick a nice spot to root and grow and watch the seasons turn . . ."

Gault considered. "A man does get tired," he said. "I know a spot, where you can look for miles out across the Pacific . . ."

"So I've promised to be very active," Pantelle said. "It will take a lot of my time, but I intend to discharge my obligation to the fullest."

Did you hear that, Yanda? Pantelle asked silently.

I did, came the reply from the unused corner he had assigned to the Yanda ego-pattern. *Our next thousand years should be very interesting.*

THE DEVIL YOU DON'T

1

Curlene Dimpleby was in the shower when the door-bell rang

"Damn!" Curlene said. She did one more slow revolution with her face upturned to the spray, then turned the big chrome knobs and stepped out onto the white nylon wall-to-wall, just installed that week. The full length mirror, slightly misty, reflected soft curves nicely juxtaposed with slimness. She jiggled in a pleasant way as she toweled off her back, crossed the bedroom and pulled on an oversized white terry cloth robe. She padded barefoot along the tiled hall. The bell rang again as she opened the door.

A tall, wide, red-haired young man stood there, impeccably dressed in white flannels, a blue blazer with a fancy but somewhat tarnished pocket patch, and white buck shoes. He jerked his finger from the pushbutton and smiled, presenting an engaging display of china-white teeth.

"I'm . . . I'm sorry, Ma'am," he said in a voice so deep Curlene imagined she could feel it through the soles of her feet. "I, uh, . . . I thought maybe you didn't hear the bell." He stopped and blushed.

"Why, that's perfectly charming," Curlene said. "I mean, that's perfectly all right."

"Uh . . . I . . . came to um fix the lights"

"Golly, I didn't even know they were out. She stepped back and as he hesitated, she said, "Come on in. The fuse box is in the basement."

The big young man edged inside.

"Is, ah, is Professor Dimpleby here?" he asked doubtfully.

"He's still in class. Anyway, he wouldn't be much help. Johnny's pretty dumb about anything simple. But he's a whiz at quantum theory . . ." Curlene was looking at his empty hands.

"Possibly I'd better come back later?" he said.

"I notice," Curlene said reproachfully, "you don't have any tools."

"Oh—" This time the blush was of the furious variety. "Well, I think I'll just—"

"You got in under false pretenses," she said softly. "Gee, a nice looking fella like you. I should think you could get plenty of girls."

"Well, I—"

"Sit down," Curlene said gently. "Want a cup of coffee?"

"Thanks, I never tr—I don't care for . . . I mean, I'd better go."

"Do you smoke?" She offered a box from the coffee table.

He raised his arms and looked down at himself with a startled expression. Curlene laughed.

"Oh, sit down and tell me all about it."

The large young man swallowed.

"You're not a student, Mr. . . . ?" Curlene urged.

"No—not exactly." He sat gingerly on the edge of a Danish chair. "Of course, one is always learning."

"I mean, did you ever think about going up to a coed and just asking her for a date?"

"Well, not exactly—"

"She'd probably jump at the chance. It's just that you're too shy, Mr. . . . ?"

"Well, I suppose I am rather retiring, Ma'am. But after all—"

"It's this crazy culture we live in. It puts some awful pressures on people. And all so needlessly. I mean, what could be more natural—"

"Ah—when are you expecting Professor Dimpleby?" the young man cut in. He was blushing from neat white collar to widow's peak now.

"Oh, I'm embarrassing you. Sorry. I think I will get some coffee. Johnny's due back any time."

The coffee maker was plugged in and snorting gently to itself. Curlene hummed as she poured two cups, put them on a Japanese silver tray with creamer and sugar bowl. The young man jumped up as she came in.

"Oh, keep your seat." She put the tray on the ankle-high coffee table. "Cream and sugar?" She leaned to put his cup before him.

"Yes, with strawberries," the young man murmured. He seemed to be looking at her chin. "Or possibly rosebuds. Pink ones."

"They *are* nice, aren't they?" a booming male voice called from the arched entry to the hall. A tall man with tousled gray hair and a ruddy face was pulling off a scarf.

"Johnny, hi; home already?" Curlene smiled at her husband.

"The robe, Curl," Professor Dimpleby said. He

gave the young man an apologetic grin. "Curl was raised in Samoa; her folks were missionaries, you know. She never quite grasped the concept that the female bosom is a secret."

Curlene tucked the robe up around her neck. "Golly," she said. "I'm sorry if I offended, Mr. . . . ?"

"On the contrary," the young man said, rising and giving his host a slight bow. "Professor Dimpleby, my name is, er, Lucifer."

Dimpleby put out his hand. "Lucifer, hey? Nothing wrong with that. Means 'Light-bearer.' But it's not a name you run into very often. It takes some gumption to flaunt the old taboos."

"Mr. Lucifer came to fix the lights," Curlene said.

"Ah—not really," the young man said quickly. "Actually, I came to, er, ask for help, Professor. Your help."

"Oh, really?" Dimpleby seated himself and stirred sugar into Curlene's cup and took a noisy sip. "Well, how can I be of service?"

"But first, before I impose on you any further, I need to be sure you understand that I really *am* Lucifer. I mean I don't want to get by on false pretenses." He looked at Curlene anxiously. "I would have told you I wasn't really an electrician, er, Mrs.—"

"Just call me Curl. Sure you would have."

"If you say your name's Lucifer, why should I doubt it?" Dimpleby asked with a smile.

"Well, the point is—I'm *the* Lucifer. You know. The, er, the Devil."

Dimpleby raised his eyebrows. Curlene made a sound of distressed sympathy.

"Of course the latter designation has all sorts of

negative connotations," Lucifer hurried on. "But I assure you that most of what you've heard is grossly exaggerated. That is to say, I'm not really as bad as all that. I mean, there are different kinds of, er, badness. There's the real evil, and then there's sin. I'm, ah, associated with sin."

"The distinction seems a subtle one, Mr., ah, Lucifer—"

"Not really, Professor. We all sense instinctively what true *evil* is. Sin is merely *statutory* evil—things that are regarded as wrong simply because there's a rule against them. Like, ah, smoking cigarettes and drinking liquor and going to movies on Sunday, or wearing lipstick and silk hose, or eating pork, or swatting flies—depending on which set of rules you're going by. They're corollaries to ritual virtues such as lighting candles or spinning prayer wheels or wearing out-of-date styles."

Dimpleby leaned back and steepled his fingers. "Hmmm. Whereas genuine evil . . . ?"

"Murder, violence, lying, cheating, theft," Lucifer enumerated. "Sin, on the other hand, essentially includes anything that looks like it might be fun."

"Come to think of it, I've never heard anything in praise of fun from the anti-sin people," Curl said thoughtfully.

"Nor from any ecclesiastic with a good head for fund-raising," Dimpleby conceded.

"It's all due to human laziness, I'm afraid," Lucifer said sadly. "It seems so much easier and more convenient to observe a few ritual prohibitions than to actually give up normal business practices."

"Hey," Curlene said. "Let's not wander off into one of those academic discussions. What about you being," she smiled, "the Devil?"

"It's quite true."

"Prove it," Curlene said promptly.

"What? I mean, er, how?" Lucifer inquired.

"Do something. You know, summon up a demon; or transform pebbles into jewels; or give me three wishes; or—"

"Gosh, Mrs. Dimpleby—"

"Curl."

"Curl. You've got some erroneous preconceptions—"

"When they start using four-syllable words, I always know they're stalling," Curl said blandly.

Lucifer swallowed. "This isn't a good idea," he said. "Suppose somebody walked in?"

"They won't."

"Now, Curl, you're embarrassing our guest again," Dimpleby said mildly.

"No, it's all right, Professor," Lucifer said worriedly. "She's quite right. After all, I'm supposed to be a sort of, ahem, mythic figure. Why should she believe in me without proof?"

"Especially when you blush so easily," Curl said.

"Well . . ." Lucifer looked around the room. His eye fell on the aquarium tank which occupied several square feet of wall space under a bookcase. He nodded almost imperceptibly. Something flickered at the bottom of the tank. Curl jumped up and went over. Lucifer followed.

"The gravel," she gasped. "It looks different!"

"Diamond, ruby, emerald, and macaroni," Lucifer said. "Sorry about the macaroni. I'm out of practice."

"Do something else!" Curl smiled in eager expectation.

Lucifer frowned in concentration. He snapped his fingers and with a soft *blop!* a small, dark purple, bulbous-bellied, wrinkle-skinned creature appeared in the center of the rug. He was some forty inches in height, totally naked, extravagantly male, with immense feet.

"Hey, for crying out loud, you could give a guy a little warning! I'm just getting ready to climb in the tub, yet!" the small being's bulging red eye fell on Lucifer. He grinned, showing a large crescent of teeth. "Oh, it's you, Nick! Howza boy? Long time no see. Anything I can do for ya?"

"Oops, sorry, Freddy." Lucifer snapped his fingers and the imp disappeared with a sharp *plop!*

"So that's a demon," Curl said. "How come his name is Freddy?"

"My apologies, Curl. He's usually most tastefully clad. Freddy is short for something longer."

"Know any more?"

"Er. . ." He pointed at Curl and made a quick flick of the wrist. In her place stood a tall, wide, huge-eyed coal-black woman in swirls of coarse, unevenly dyed cloth under which bare feet showed. Cheap-looking jewelry hung thick on her wrists, draped her vast bosom, winked on her tapered fingers and in her ears.

Lucifer flicked his fingers again, and a slim, olive-skinned girl with blue-black hair and a hooked nose replaced the buxom Sheban queen. She wore a skirt apparently made from an old gauze curtain and an ornate off-the-bosom vest of colored beads. A golden snake encircled her forehead.

Lucifer motioned again. The Egyptian empress dissolved into a nebulous cloud of pastel-colored gas in which clotted star-dust winked and writhed, to the accompaniment of massed voices humming nostalgic chords amid an odor of magnolia blossoms. Another gesture, and Curl stood again before them, looking slightly dazed.

"Hey, what was that last one?" she cried.

"Sorry, that was Scarlet O'Hara. I forgot she was a figment of the imagination. Those are always a little insubstantial."

"Remarkable," Dimpleby said. "I'll have to concede that you can either perform miracles or accomplish the same result by some other means."

"Gee, I guess you're genuine, all right," Curlene exclaimed. "But somehow I expected a much *older* man."

"I'm not actually a man, strictly speaking, Ma'am —Curl. And agewise, well, since I'm immortal, why should I look middle-aged rather than just mature?"

"Tell me," Curlene said seriously. "I've always wondered: what do you want people's souls for?"

"Frankly, Ma'am—Curl, that is—I haven't the remotest interest in anyone's soul."

"Really?"

"Really and truly; cross my heart. That's just another of those rumors *they* started."

"Are you sure you're really the Devil and not someone else with the same name?"

Lucifer spread his hands appealingly. "You saw Freddy. And those *are* noodles in the fish tank."

"But—no horns, no hooves, no tail—"

Lucifer sighed. "That idea comes from confusing me with Pan. Since he was a jolly sort of sex-god, naturally he was equated with sin."

"I've always wondered," Curlene said, "just what you did to get evicted from Heaven."

"Please," Lucifer said. "It . . . all dates back to an incident when I was still an angel." He held up a forestalling hand as Curl opened her mouth. "No, I *didn't* have wings. Humans added those when they saw us levitating, on the theory that anything that flies must have wings. If we were to appear today, they'd probably give us jets."

"Assuming you are, er, what you claim to be," Dimpleby said, "what's this about your needing help?"

"I do," Lucifer said. "Desperately. Frankly, I'm up against something I simply can't handle alone."

"I can't imagine what *I* could do, if you, with your, ah, special talents are helpless," Dimpleby said perplexedly.

"This is something totally unprecedented. It's a threat on a scale I can't begin to describe."

"Well, try," Curl urged.

"Stated in its simplest terms," Lucifer said, "the, ah, plane of existence I usually occupy—"

"Hell, you mean," Curl supplied.

"Well, that's another of those loaded terms. It really isn't a bad place at all, you know—"

"But what about it?" Dimpleby prompted. "What about Hell?"

"It's about to be invaded," Lucifer said solemnly. "By alien demons from another world."

2

It was an hour later. Lucifer, Curlene, and Professor Dimpleby were comfortably ensconced behind large pewter mugs of musty ale at a corner table in the Sam Johnson Room at the Faculty Club.

"Well, now," Dimpleby said affably, raising his tankard in salute, "alien demons, eh? An interesting concept, Mr. Lucifer. Tell us more."

"I've never believed in devils," Curlene said, "or monsters from another planet either. Now all of a sudden I'm supposed to believe in both at once. If it weren't for that Freddy . . ."

"Granted the basic premise, it's logical enough," Dimpleby said. "If earthly imps exist, why not space sprites?"

"Professor, this is more than a bunch of syllogisms," Lucifer said earnestly. "These fellows mean business. They have some extremely potent powers. Fortunately, I have powers they don't know about, too; that's the only way I've held them in check so far—"

"You mean—they're already *here?*" Curlene looked searchingly about the room.

"No—I mean, yes, they're here, but not precisely *here.*" Lucifer clarified. "Look, I'd better fill in a little background for you. You see, Hell is actually a superior plane of existence—"

Curlene choked on her ale in a ladylike way.

"I mean—not *superior,* but, ah, at another level, you understand. Different physical laws, and so on—"

"Dirac levels," Dimpleby said, signaling for refills.

"Right!" Lucifer nodded eagerly. "There's an entire continuum of them, stretching away on both sides; there's an energy state higher on the scale than Hell —Heaven, it's called, for some reason—and one lower than your plane; that's the one Freddy comes from, by the way—"

"Oh tell me about Heaven," Curlene urged.

Lucifer sighed, "Sometimes I miss the old place, in spite of . . . but never mind that."

"Tell me, Mr. Lucifer," Dimpleby said thoughtfully, "How is it you're able to travel at will among these levels?" As he spoke he pulled an envelope from his pocket and uncapped a ballpoint. "It appears to be that there's an insurmountable difficulty here, in terms of atomic and molecular spectral energy distribution; the specific heat involved . . ." he jotted busily, murmuring to himself.

"You're absolutely right, Professor," Lucifer said, sampling the fresh tankard just placed before him. "Heat used to be a real problem. I'd always arrive in a cloud of smoke and sulphur fumes. I finally solved it by working out a trick of emitting a packet of magnetic energy to carry off the excess."

"Hmmm. How did you go about dissipating this magnetism?"

"I fired it off in a tight beam; got rid of it."

"Beamed magnetism?" Dimpleby scribbled furiously. "Hmmm. Possibly . . ."

"Hey, fellas," Curlene protested. "Let's not talk

shop, OK?" She turned a fascinated gaze on Lucifer. "You were just telling me about Heaven."

"You wouldn't like it, Curl," he said, almost curtly. "Now, Professor, all through history—at least as far as I remember it, and that covers a considerable period—the different energy states were completely separate and self-sufficient. Then, a few thousand years back, one of our boys—Yahway, his name is—got to poking around and discovered a way to move around from one level to another. The first place he discovered was Hell. Well, he's something of a bluenose, frankly, and he didn't much like what he found there: all kinds of dead warriors from Greece and Norway and such places sitting around juicing it and singing, and fighting in a friendly sort of way."

"You mean—Valhalla really exists?" Curlene gasped. "And the Elysian Fields?"

Lucifer made a disclaiming wave of the hand. "There've always been humans with more than their share of vital energy. Instead of dying, they just switch levels. I have a private theory that there's a certain percentage of, er, individuals in any level who really belong in the next one up—or down. Anyway, Yahway didn't like what he saw. He was always a great one for discipline, getting up early, regular calisthenics—you know. He tried telling these fellows the error of their ways, but they just laughed him off the podium. So he dropped down one more level, which put him here; a much simpler proposition, nothing but a few tribesmen herding goats. Naturally they were impressed by a few simple miracles." Lucifer paused to quaff deeply. He sighed.

"Yes. Well, he's been meddling around down here

ever since, and frankly—but I'm wandering." He hiccupped sternly. "I admit, I never could drink very much without losing my perspective. Where was I?"

"The invasion," Dimpleby reminded him.

"Oh, yes. Well, they hit us without any warning. There we were, just sitting around the mead hall taking it easy, or strolling in the gardens striking our lutes or whatever we felt like, when all of a sudden—" Lucifer shook his head bemusedly. "Professor, did you ever have one of those days when nothing seemed to go right?"

Dimpleby pursed his lips. "Hmmm. You mean like having the first flat tire in a year during the worst rainstorm of the year while on your way to the most important meeting of the year?"

"Or," Curlene said, "like when you're just having a quick martini to brace yourself for the afternoon and you spill it on your new dress and when you try to wash it out, the water's turned off, and when you try to phone to report *that,* the phone's out, and just then Mrs. Trundle from next door drops in to talk, only you're late for the Faculty Wives?"

"That's it," Lucifer confirmed. "Well, picture that sort of thing on a vast scale."

"That's rather depressing," Dimpleby said. "But what has it to do with the, er, invasion?"

"Everything!" Lucifer said, with a wave of his hands. Across the room, a well-fleshed matron yelped.

"My olive! It turned into a frog!"

"Remarkable," her table companion said. "Genus *Rana pipiens,* I believe!"

"Sorry," Lucifer murmured, blushing, putting his hands under the table.

"You were saying, Mr. Lucifer?"

"It's them, Professor. They've been sort of leaking over, you see? Their influence, I mean." Lucifer started to wave his hands again, but caught himself and put them in his blazer pockets.

"Leaking over?"

"From Hell into this plane. You've been getting just a faint taste of it. You should see what's been going on in Hell, Proffefor—I mean Prossessor—I mean—"

"What *has* been going on?"

"Everything has been going to Hell," Lucifer said gloomily. "What I mean to say is," he said, making an effort to straighten up and focus properly, "that everything that *can* go wrong, *does* go wrong."

"That would appear to be contrary to the statistics of causality," Dimpleby said carefully.

"That's it, Professor! They're upsetting the laws of chance! Now, in the old days, when a pair of our lads stepped outside for a little hearty sword-fighting between drinks, one would be a little drunker than the other, and he'd soon be out of it for the day, while the other chap reeled back inside to continue the party. Now, they each accidentally knee each other in the groin and they both lie around groaning until sundown, which upsets everybody. The same for the lute players and lovers: the strings break just at the most climactic passage, or they accidentally pick a patch of poison ivy for their tryst, or possibly just a touch of diarrhea at the wrong moment, but you can imagine what it's doing to morale."

"Tsk," Dimpleby said. "Unfortunate—but it sounds more disconcerting than disastrous, candidly."

"You think so, Professor? What about when all the

ambrosia on hand goes bad simultaneously, and the entire population is afflicted with stomach cramps and luminous spots before the eyes? What about a mix-up at the ferry, that leaves us stuck with three boat-loads of graduated Methodist ministers to entertain overnight? What about an ectospheric storm that knocks out all psionics for a week, and has everyone fetching and carrying by hand, and communicating by signlanguage?"

"Well—that might be somewhat more serious . . ."

"Oh—oh!" Curlene was pointing with her nose. Her husband turned to see a waiter in weskit and kneepants back through a swinging door balancing a tray laden with brimming port glasses, at the same moment that a tweedsy pedagogue rose directly behind him and, with a gallant gesture, drew out his fair companion's chair. There was a double *oof!* as they came together. The chair skidded. The lady sat on the floor. The tray distributed its burden in a bright cascade across the furs of a willowy brunette who yowled, whirled, causing her fox-tail to slap the face of a small, elaborately mustached man who was on the point of lighting a cigar. As the match flared brightly, with a sharp odor of blazing wool, the tweedsy man bent swiftly to offer a chivalrous hand, and bumped by the rebounding waiter, delivered a smart rap with his nose to the corner of the table.

"My mustache!" the small man yelled.

"Dr. Thorndyke, you're bleeding on my navy blue crepe!" the lady on the floor yelped. The waiter, still grabbing for the tray, bobbled it and sent it scaling through an olde English window, through which an indignant managerial head thrust in time to receive a glass of water intended for the burning mustache.

Lucifer, who had been staring dazedly at the rapid interplay, made a swift flick of the fingers. A second glass of water struck the small man squarely in the conflagration; the tweedsy man clapped a napkin over his nose and helped up the Navy blue crepe. The waiter recovered his tray and busied himself with the broken glass. The brunette whipped out a hanky and dabbed at her bodice, muttering. The tension subsided from the air.

"You see?" Lucifer said. "That was a small sample of their work."

"Nonsense, Mr. Lucifer," Dimpleby said, smiling amiably. "Nothing more than an accident—a curiously complex interplay of misadventures, true, but still—an accident, nothing more."

"Of course—but that sort of accident can only occur when there's an imbalance in the Randomness Field!"

"What's that?"

"It's what makes the laws of chance work. You know that if you flip a quarter a hundred times it will come up heads fifty times and tails fifty times, or very close to it. In a thousand tries, the ratio is even closer. Now, the coin knows nothing of its past performance—any more than metal filings in a magnetic field know which way the other filings are facing. But the field *forces* them to align parallel—and the Randomness Field forces the coin to follow the statistical distribution."

Dimpleby pulled at his chin. "In other words, entropy."

"If you prefer, Professor. But you've seen what happens when it's tampered with!"

"Why?" Dimpleby stabbed a finger at Lucifer and grinned as one who has scored a point. "Show me a motive for these hypothetical foreign fiends going to all that trouble just to meddle in human affairs!"

"They don't care a rap for human affairs," Lucifer groaned. "It's just a side-effect. They consume energy from certain portions of the trans-Einsteinian spectrum, emit energy in other bands. The result is to disturb the R-field—just as sunspots disrupt the earth's magnetic field!"

"Fooey," Dimpleby said, sampling his ale. "Accidents have been happening since the dawn of time. And according to your own account, these interplanetary imps of yours have just arrived."

"Time scales differ between Hell and here," Lucifer said in tones of desperation. "The infiltration started two weeks ago, subjective Hell-time. That's equal to a little under two hundred years, local."

"What about all the coincidences before then?" Dimpleby came back swiftly.

"Certainly, there have always been a certain number of non-random occurrences. But in the last two centuries they've jumped to an unheard-of level! Think of all the fantastic scientific coincidences, during that period, for example—such as the triple rediscovery of Mendel's work after thirty-five years of obscurity, or the simultaneous evolutionary theories of Darwin and Wallace, or the identical astronomical discoveries of—"

"Very well, I'll concede there've been some remarkable parallelisms." Dimpleby dismissed the argument with a wave of the hand. "But that hardly proves—"

"Professor—maybe that isn't what you'd call hard scientific proof, but logic—instinct—should tell you that Something's Been Happening! Certainly, there were isolated incidents in Ancient History—but did you ever hear of the equivalent of a twenty-car pile-up in Classical times? The very conception of slap-stick comedy based on ludicrous accident was alien to the world until it began happening in real life!"

"I say again—fooey, Mr. Lucifer." Dimpleby drew on his ale, burped gently and leaned forward challengingly. "I'm from New Hampshire," he said, wagging a finger. "You've gotta show me."

"Fortunately for humanity, that's quite impossible," Lucifer said. *"They* haven't penetrated to this level yet; all you've gotten, as I said, is the spill-over effect—" he paused. "Unless you'd like to go to Hell and see for yourself—"

"No thanks. A faculty tea is close enough for me."

"In that case . . ." Lucifer broke off. His face paled. "Oh, no," he whispered.

"Lucifer—what is it?" Curlene whispered in alarm.

"They—they must have followed me! It never occurred to me; but—" Lucifer groaned, "Professor and Mrs. Dimpleby, I've done a terrible thing! I've led them here!"

"Where?" Curlene stared around the room eagerly.

Lucifer's eyes were fixed on the corner by the fire. He made a swift gesture with the fingers of his left hand. Curlene gasped.

"Why—it looks just like a big stalk of broccoli—

except for the eyes, of course—and the little one is a dead ringer for a rhubarb pie!"

"Hmmm," Dimpleby blinked. "Quite astonishing, really." He cast a sidelong glance at Lucifer. "Look here, old man, are you sure this isn't some sort of hypnotic effect?"

"If it is, it has the same effect as reality, Professor," the Devil whispered hoarsely. "And something has to be done about it, no matter what you call it."

"Yes, I suppose so—but why, if I may inquire, all this interest on your part in us petty mortals?" Dimpleby smiled knowledgeably. "Ah, I'll bet this is where the pitch for our souls comes in; you'll insure an end to bad luck and negative coincidences, in return for a couple of signatures written in blood . . ."

"Professor, please," Lucifer said, blushing. "You have the wrong idea completely.

"I just don't understand," Curlene sighed, gazing at Lucifer, "why such a nice fellow was kicked out of Heaven . . ."

"But why come to *me?*" Dimpleby said, eyeing Lucifer through the sudsy glass bottom of his ale mug. "I don't know any spells for exorcising demons."

"Professor, I'm out of my depth," Lucifer said earnestly. "The old reliable eye of newt and wart of toad recipes don't faze these alien imps for a moment. Now, I admit, I haven't kept in touch with new developments in science as I should have. But *you* have, Professor: you're one of the world's foremost authorities on wave mechanics and Planck's law, and all that sort of thing. If anybody can deal with these chaps, *you* can!"

"Why, Johnny, how exciting!" Curlene said. "I didn't know matrix mechanics had anything to do with broccoli!" She took a pleased gulp of ale, smiling from Lucifer to her husband.

"I didn't either, my dear," Dimpleby said in a puzzled tone. "Look here, Lucifer, are you sure you don't have me confused with our Professor Pronko, over in Liberal Arts? Now, his papers on abnormal psychology—"

"Professor, there's been no mistake! Who else but an expert in quantum theory could deal with a situation like this?"

"Well, I suppose there is a certain superficial semantic parallelism—"

"Wonderful, Professor: I knew you'd do it!" Lucifer grabbed Dimpleby's hand and wrung it warmly. "How do we begin?"

"Here, you're talking nonsense!" Dimpleby extracted his hand, used it to lift his ale tankard once again. "Of course," he said after taking a hearty pull, "If you're right about the nature of these varying energy levels—and these, er, entities *do* manage the jump from one quantum state to the next—then I suppose they'd be subject to the same sort of physical laws as any other energetic particles . . ." He thumped the mug down heavily on the tabletop and resumed jotting. "The Compton effect," he muttered. "Raman's work . . . The Stern-Gerlack experiment. Hmmm."

"You've got something?" Lucifer and Curlene said simultaneously.

"Just a theoretical notion," he said off-handedly,

and waved airily to a passing waiter. "Three more, Chudley."

"Johnny," Curlene wailed. "Don't stop now!"

"Professor—time is of the essence!" Lucifer groaned.

"Say, the broccoli is stirring around," Curlene said in a low tone. "Is he planning another practical joke?"

Lucifer cast apprehensive eyes toward the fireplace. "He doesn't actually do it intentionally, you know. He can't help it; it's like, well, a blind man switching on the lights in a darkroom. He wouldn't understand what all the excitement was about."

"Excuse me," Dimpleby said. "Ale goes through me pretty rapidly." He rose, slightly jogging the elbow of the waiter pouring icewater into a glass at the next table. The chill stream dived precisely into the cleavage of a plump woman in a hat like a chef's salad for twelve. She screamed and fell backward into the path of the servitor approaching with a tray of foaming ale tankards. All three malt beverages leaped head-first onto the table, their contents sluicing across it into Lucifer's lap, while the overspill distributed itself between Dimpleby's hip pockets.

He stared down at the table awash in ale, turned a hard gaze on the fireplace.

"Like that, eh?" he said in a brittle voice. He faced the Devil, who was dabbing helplessly at his formerly white flannels.

"All right, Lucifer," he said. "You're on! A few laughs at the expense of academic dignity are fine—but I'm damned if I'm going to stand by and see good beer wasted! Now, let's get down to cases. Tell me all you know about these out-of-town incubi. . . ."

3

It was almost dawn. In his third floor laboratory in Prudfrock Hall, Professor Dimpleby straightened from the marble-topped bench over which he had been bent for the better part of the night.

"Well," he said, rubbing his eyes, "I don't know. It might work." He glanced about the big room. "Now, if you'll just shoo one of your, ah, extra-terrestrial essences in here, we'll see."

"No problem there, Professor," Lucifer said anxiously. "I've had all I could do to hold them at bay all night, with some of the most potent incantations since Solomon sealed the Afrit up in a bottle."

"Then, too, I don't suppose they'd find the atmosphere of a scientific laboratory very congenial," Dimpleby said with a somewhat lofty smile, "inasmuch as considerable effort has been devoted to excluding chance from the premises."

"You think so?" Lucifer said glumly. "For your own peace of mind, I suggest you don't conduct any statistical analyses just now."

"Well, with the clear light of morning and the dissipation of the alcohol, the rationality of what we're doing seems increasingly questionable—but nonetheless, we may as well carry the experiment through. Even negative evidence has a certain value."

"Ready?" Lucifer said.

"Ready," Dimpleby said, suppressing a yawn. Lucifer made a face and executed an intricate dance step. There was a sharp sense of tension released—like the popping of an invisible soap-bubble—and *something* appeared drifting lazily in the air near the precision scales. One side of the instrument dropped with a sharp *clunk!*

"All the air concentrated on one side of the balance," Lucifer said tensely.

"Maxwell's demon—in the flesh?" Dimpleby gasped.

"It looks like a giant pizza," Curlene said, "Only transparent."

The apparition gave a flirt of its rim and sailed across to hover before a wall chart illustrating the periodic table. The paper burst into flame.

"All the energetic air molecules rushed to one spot," Lucifer explained. "It could happen any time—but it seldom does."

"Good lord! What if it should cause all the air to rush to one end of the room?" Dimpleby whispered.

"I daresay it would rupture your lungs, Professor. So I wouldn't waste any more time, if I were you."

"Imagine what must be going on outside," Curlene said. "With these magical pizzas and broccoli wandering loose all over the place!"

"Is *that* what all those sirens were about?" Dimpleby said. He stationed himself beside the breadboard apparatus he had constructed and swallowed hard.

"Very well, Lucifer—see if you can herd it over this way."

The devil frowned in concentration. The pizza drifted slowly, rotating as if looking for the source of some irritation. It gave an impatient twitch and headed toward Curlene. Lucifer made a gesture and it veered off, came sailing in across the table.

"Now!" Dimpleby said, and threw a switch. As if struck by a falling brick, the alien entity slammed to the center of the three-foot disk encircled by massive magnetic coils.

It hopped and threshed, to no avail.

"The field is holding it!" Dimpley said tensely. "So far . . ."

Suddenly the rippling, disk-shaped creature folded in on itself, stood on end, sprouted wings and a tail. Scales glittered along its sides. A puff of smoke issued from tiny crocodilian jaws, followed by a tongue of flame.

"A dragon!" Curlene cried.

"Hold him, professor!" Lucifer urged.

The dragon coiled its tail around itself and melted into a lumpy black sphere covered with long bristles. It had two bright red eyes and a pair of spindly legs on which it jittered wildly.

"A goblin?" Dimpleby said incredulously.

The goblin rebounded from the invisible wall restraining it, coalesced into a foot-high, leathery-skinned humanoid with big ears, a wide mouth, and long arms which it wrapped around its knees as it squatted disconsolately on the grid, rolling bloodshot eyes sorrowfully up at its audience.

"Congratulations, Professor!" Lucifer exclaimed. "We got one!"

4

"His name," Lucifer said, "is Quilchik. It's really quite a heart-rending tale he tells, poor chap."

"Oh, the poor little guy," Curlene said. "What does

he eat, Mr. Lucifer? Do you suppose he'd like a little lettuce or something?"

"His diet is quite immaterial, Curl; he subsists entirely on energies. And that seems to be at the root of the problem. It appears there's a famine back home. What with a rising birth rate and no death rate, population pressure long ago drove his people out into space. They've been wandering around out there for epochs, with just the occasional hydrogen molecule to generate a quantum or two of entropy to absorb; hardly enough to keep them going."

"Hmm. I suppose entropy *could* be considered a property of matter," Dimpleby said thoughtfully, reaching for paper and pencil. "One can hardly visualize a distinction between order and disorder as existing in matterless space."

"Quite right. The curious distribution of heavy elements in planetary crusts and the unlikely advent of life seem to be the results of their upsetting of the Randomness Field, to say nothing of evolution, biological mutations, the extinction of the dinosaurs just in time for Man to thrive, and women's styles."

"Women's styles?" Curlene frowned.

"Of course," Dimpleby nodded. "What could be more unlikely than this year's Paris modes?"

Lucifer shook his head, a worried expression on his regular features. "I had in mind trapping them at the entry point and sending them back where they came from; but under the circumstances that seems quite inhumane."

"Still—we can't let them come swarming in to upset everything from the rhythm method to the Irish Sweepstakes."

"Golly," Curlene said, "couldn't we put them on a reservation, sort of, and have them weave blankets maybe?"

"Hold it," Lucifer said. "There's another one nearby . . . I can feel the tension in the Rfield . . ."

"Eek!" Curlene said, taking a step backward and hooking a heel in the extension cord powering the magnetic fields. With a sharp *pop!* the plug was jerked from the wall. Quilchik jumped to his large, flat feet, took a swift look around, and leaped, changing in mid-air to the fluttering form of a small bat.

Lucifer threw off his coat, ripped off his tie and shirt. Before the startled gaze of the Dimplebys, he rippled and flowed into the form of a pterodactyl which leaped clear of the collapsing white flannels and into the air, long beak agape, in hot pursuit of the bat. Curlene screeched and squeezed her eyes shut. Dimpleby said, "Remarkable!," grabbed his pad and scribbled rapidly. The bat flickered in mid-air and was a winged snake. Lucifer turned instantly into a winged mongoose. The snake dropped to the floor and shrank to mouse form scuttling for a hole. Lucifer became a big gray cat, reached the hole first. The mouse burgeoned into a bristly rat; the cat swelled and was a terrier. With a yap, it leaped after the rat, which turned back into Quilchik, sprang up on a table, raced across it, dived for what looked like an empty picture frame—

A shower of tiny Quilchiks shot from the other side of the heavy glass sheet. Lucifer barely skidded aside in time to avoid it, went dashing around the room, barking furiously at the tiny creatures crouched behind every chair and table leg, squeezing in behind filing cabinets, cowering under ashtrays.

"Lucifer, stop!" Curlene squealed. "Oh, aren't they *darling!*" She went to her knees, scooped up an inch-high mannikin. It squatted on her palm, trembling, its head between its knees.

"By Jimini," Dimpleby said. "It went through a diffraction grating, and came out centuplets!"

5

"The situation is deteriorating," Lucifer groaned, scooping up another miniature imp, and dumping it back inside the reactivated trap. "It was bad enough dealing with one star-sprite. Now we have a hundred. And if any one of them escapes . . ."

"Don't look now," Dimpleby said behind his hand to the Devil, now back in human form and properly clad, "but I have an unch-hay the magnetic ield-fay won't old-hay em-they."

"Eye-way ott-nay?" Lucifer inquired.

"Ecause-bay . . ." Dimpleby broke off. "Well, it has to do with distribution of polarity. You see the way the field works—"

"Don't bother explaining," Lucifer said. "I wouldn't understand anyway. The real question is—what do we do now?"

"Our choice seems limited. We either gather up all these little fellows and dump them back where they came from, and then hunt down the others and do likewise, which is impossible, or we forget the whole thing, which is unthinkable."

"In any event," Lucifer said, "we have to act fast before the situation gets entirely out of hand."

"We could turn the problem over to the so-called authorities," Dimpleby said, "but that seems unwise, somehow."

Lucifer shuddered. "I can see the headlines now: DEVIL LOOSE ON COLLEGE CAMPUS!"

"Oh, they've already worked that one to death," Curlene said. "It would probably be more like: PROF AND MATE IN THREE WAY SEX ROMP."

"Sex romp?"

"Well, Mr. Lucifer *did* reappear in the nude." Curlene smiled. "And a very nice physique, too, Mr. Lucifer."

Lucifer blushed. "Well, Professor, what do we do?" he asked hastily.

"I'll flip a coin," Curlene suggested. "Heads, we report the whole thing, tails, we keep it to ourselves and do the best we can."

"All right. Best two out of three."

Curlene rummaged in her purse and produced one of the counterfeit quarters in current production from the Denver mint. She tossed it up, caught it, slapped it against her forearm, lifted her hand.

"Tails," she said in a pleased tone.

"Maybe we'd better report it anyway," Dimpleby said, nibbling a fingernail and eyeing the tiny creatures sitting disconsolately inside the circle of magnets.

"Two out of three," Curlene said. She flipped the coin up.

"Tails again," she announced.

"Well, I suppose that settles it. . . ."

Curlene tossed the coin up idly. "I guess it's definite," she said. "Tails three times in a row."

Dimpleby looked at her absently. "Eh?"

"Four times in a row," Curlene said. Lucifer looked at her as if about to speak. Curlene flipped the coin high.

"Five," she said. Dimpleby and Lucifer drew closer.

"Six . . ."

"Seven . . ."

"Eight . . ."

"Oh-oh," Dimpleby said. He grabbed for the desk drawer, pulled out a dog-eared deck of cards, hastily shuffled, and dealt two hands. Cautiously, he peeked at his cards. He groaned.

"Four aces," he said.

"Four kings here," Curlene said.

"Here we go again," he said. "Now no one will be safe!"

"But Johnny," Curlene said. "There's one difference . . ."

"What?"

"The odds are all mixed up, true—but now they're in our favor!"

6

"It's quite simple, really," Dimpleby said, waving a sheet of calculations. "When Quilchik went through the grating, he was broken up into a set of harmonics. Those harmonics, being of another order of size, resonate at another frequency. Ergo, he consumes a different type of energetic pseudo-particle. Instead of draining off the positive, ah, R-charges, he now subsists on negative entropy."

"And instead of practical jokes, we have miraculous cures, spontaneous remissions, and fantastic runs with the cards!" Curlene cried happily.

"Not only that," Dimpleby added, "but I think we can solve their food-supply problem. They've exhausted the supply of plus entropy back on their own level—but the original endowment of minus R remains untapped. There should be enough for another few billion years."

Lucifer explained this to the Quilchiks via the same form of instantaneous telepathy he had employed for the earlier interrogation.

"He's delighted," the Devil reported, as the tiny creatures leaped up, joined hands, and began capering and jigging in a manner expressive of joy. There's just one thing . . ." A lone manikin stood at the edge of the table, looking shyly at Curlene.

"Quilchik Seventy-eight has a request," Lucifer said.

"Well, what does snookums-ookums want?" Curlene cooed, bending over to purse her lips at the tiny figure.

"He wants to stay," Lucifer said embarrassedly.

"Oh, Johnny, can I have him?"

"Well—if you'll put some pants on him—"

"And he'd like to live in a bottle. Preferably a bourbon bottle, one of the miniatures. Preferably still full of bourbon," Lucifer added. "But he'll come out to play whenever you like."

"I wonder," Dimpleby said thoughtfully, "what effect having him around would have on our regular

Saturday night card game with those sharpies from the engineering faculty?"

"You've already seen a sample," Lucifer said. "But I can ask him to fast at such times."

"Oh, no, no" Dimpleby protested. "Hate to see the little fellow go hungry."

"Mr. Lucifer," Curlene asked. "I hope I'm not being nosy—but how did you get the scar on your side that I saw when you had your shirt off?"

"Oh, ah, that?" Lucifer blushed purple. "Well, it, ah—"

"Probably a liver operation, judging from the location, eh, Lucifer?" Dimpleby said.

"You might call it that," Lucifer said.

"But you shouldn't embarrass people by asking personal questions, Curl," Dimpleby said sternly.

"Yes, dear," Curl said. "Lucifer—I've been wanting to ask you: What did a nice fellow like you do to get kicked out of Heaven?"

"Well, I, uh," Lucifer swallowed.

"It was for doing something nice, wasn't it?"

"Well—frankly, I thought it wasn't fair," Lucifer blurted. "I felt sorry for the poor humans, squatting in those damp caves . . ."

"So you brought them fire," Curlene said. "That's why you're called Lucifer."

"You're mixed up, Curl," Dimpleby said. "That was Prometheus. For his pains, he was chained to a rock, and every day a vulture tore out his liver, and every night it grew back. . . ."

"But it left a scar," Curlene said, looking meltingly at Lucifer.

The Devil blushed a deep magenta. "I . . . I'd better be rushing off now," he said.

"Not before we share a stirrup cup," Dimpleby said, holding up the Old Crow bottle from the desk drawer. Inside, Quilchik, floating on his back with his hands folded on his paunch, waved merrily, and blew a string of bubbles.

"Luckily, I have a reserve stock," Dimpleby muttered, heading for the filing cabinet.

"Er, Lucifer, how can we ever thank you?" Curlene sighed, cradling the flask.

"Just by, uh, having all the fun you can," Lucifer said. "And I'll, er, be looking forward to seeing you in Hell, some day."

"I'll drink to that," Dimpleby said. He poured. Smiling, they clicked glasses and drank.

DOORSTEP

Steadying his elbow on the kitchen table serving as desk, Brigadier General Straut leveled his binoculars and stared out through the second-floor window of the farmhouse at the bulky object lying canted at the edge of the wood lot. He watched the figures moving over and around the gray mass, then flipped the lever on the field telephone at his elbow.

"How are your boys doing, Major?"

"General, since that box this morning—"

"I know all about the box, Bill. So does Washington by now. What have you got that's new?"

"Sir, I haven't got anything to report yet. I have four crews on it, and she still looks impervious as hell."

"Still getting the sounds from inside?"

"Intermittently, General."

"I'm giving you one more hour, Major. I want that thing cracked."

The general dropped the phone back on its cradle and peeled the cellophane from a cigar absently. He had moved fast, he reflected, after the State Police notified him at nine forty-one last night. He had his men on the spot, the area evacuated of civilians, and a preliminary report on its way to Washington by midnight. At two thirty-six, they had discovered the four-inch cube lying on the ground fifteen feet from the huge object—missile, capsule, bomb—whatever it was. But now—several hours later—nothing new.

The field phone jangled. Straut grabbed it up.

"General, we've discovered a thin spot up on the top side. All we can tell so far is that the wall thickness falls off there . . ."

"All right. Keep after it, Bill."

This was more like it. If Brigadier General Straut could have this thing wrapped up by the time Washington awoke to the fact that it was something big—well, he'd been waiting a long time for that second star. This was his chance, and he would damn well make the most of it.

He looked across the field at the thing. It was half in and half out of the woods, flat-sided, round-ended, featureless. Maybe he should go over and give it a closer look personally. He might spot something the others were missing. It might blow them all to kingdom come any second; but what the hell, he had earned his star on sheer guts in Normandy. He still had 'em.

He keyed the phone. "I'm coming down, Bill," he told the Major. On impulse, he strapped a pistol belt on. Not much use against a house-sized bomb, but the heft of it felt good.

The thing looked bigger than ever as the jeep approached it, bumping across the muck of the freshly plowed field. From here he could see a faint line running around, just below the juncture of side and top. Major Greer hadn't mentioned that. The line was quite obvious; in fact, it was more of a crack.

With a sound like a baseball smacking the catcher's glove, the crack opened, the upper half tilted, men sliding—then impossibly it stood open, vibrating, like the roof of a house suddenly lifted. The driver gunned the jeep. There were cries, and a ragged shrilling that set Straut's teeth on edge. The men were running back now, two of them dragging a third.

Major Greer emerged from behind the object, looked about, ran toward General Straut shouting. ". . . a man dead. It snapped; we weren't expecting it . . ."

Straut jumped out beside the men, who had stopped now and were looking back. The underside of the gaping lid was an iridescent black. The shrill noise sounded thinly across the field. Greer arrived, panting.

"What happened?" Straut snapped.

"I was . . . checking over that thin spot, General. The first thing I knew it was . . . coming up under me. I fell; Tate was at the other side. He held on and it snapped him loose, against a tree. His skull—"

"What the devil's that racket?"

"That's the sound we were getting from inside before, General. There's something in there alive—"

"All right, pull yourself together, Major. We're not unprepared. Bring your half-tracks into position. The tanks will be here soon."

Straut glanced at the men standing about. He would show them what leadership meant.

"You men keep back," he said. He puffed his cigar calmly as he walked toward the looming object. The noise stopped suddenly; that was a relief. There was a faint and curious odor in the air, something like chlorrine . . . or seaweed . . . or iodine.

There were no marks in the ground surrounding the thing. It had apparently dropped straight in to its present position. It was heavy, too—the soft soil was displaced in a mound a foot high all along the side.

Behind him, Straut heard a yell. He whirled. The men were pointing; the jeep started up, churned toward him, wheels spinning. He looked up. Over the edge of the gray wall, six feet above his head, a great reddish limb, like the claw of a crab, moved, groping.

Straut yanked the .45 from its holster, jacked the action and fired. Soft matter spattered, and the claw jerked back. The screeching started up again angrily, then was drowned in the engine roar as the jeep slid to a stop.

Straut stooped, grabbed up a leaf to which a quivering lump adhered, jumped into the vehicle as it leaped forward; then a shock and they were going into a spin and . . .

"Lucky it was soft ground," somebody said. And somebody else asked, "What about the driver?"

Silence. Straut opened his eyes. "What . . . about . . ."

A stranger was looking down at him, an ordinary-looking fellow of about thirty-five.

"Easy, now, General Straut. You've had a bad spill. Everything is all right. I'm Professor Lieberman, from the University."

"The driver," Straut said with an effort.

"He was killed when the jeep went over."

"Went . . . over?"

"The creature lashed out with a member resembling a scorpion's stinger. It struck the jeep and flipped it. You were thrown clear. The driver jumped and the jeep rolled on him."

Straut pushed himself up.

"Where's Greer?"

"I'm right here, sir." Major Greer stepped up, stood attentively.

"Those tanks here yet?"

"No, sir. I had a call from General Margrave; there's some sort of holdup. Something about not destroying scientific material. I did get the mortars over from the base."

Straut got to his feet. The stranger took his arm. "You ought to lie down, General—"

"Who the hell is going to make me? Greer, get those mortars in place, spaced between your tracks."

The telephone rang. Straut seized it. "General Straut."

"General Margrave here, Straut. I'm glad you're back on your feet. There'll be some scientists from the State University coming over. Cooperate with them. You're going to have to hold things together at least until I can get another man in there to—"

"Another man? General Margrave, I'm not incapacitated. The situation is under complete control—"

"It is, is it? I understand you've got still another casualty. What's happened to your defensive capabilities?"

"That was an accident, sir. The jeep—"

"We'll review that matter at a later date. What I'm calling about is more important right now. The code men have made some headway on that box of yours. It's putting out a sort of transmission."

"What kind, sir?"

"Half the message—it's only twenty seconds long, repeated—is in English. It's a fragment of a recording from a daytime radio program; one of the network men here identified it. The rest is gibberish. They're still working over it."

"What—"

"Bryant tells me he thinks there may be some sort of correspondence between the two parts of the message. I wouldn't know, myself. In my opinion, it's a threat of some sort."

"I agree, General. An ultimatum."

"Right. Keep your men back at a safe distance from now on. I want no more casualities."

Straut cursed his luck as he hung up the phone. Margrave was ready to relieve him, after he had exercised every precaution. He had to do something fast, before this opportunity for promotion slipped out of his hands.

He looked at Major Greer. "I'm neutralizing this thing once and for all. There'll be no more men killed."

Lieberman stood up. "General! I must protest any attack against this—"

Straut whirled. "I'm handling this, Professor. I don't know who let you in here or why—but I'll make the decisions. I'm stopping this man-killer before it comes out of its nest, maybe gets into that village beyond the woods. There are four thousand civilians there. It's my job to protect them." He jerked his head at Greer, strode out of the room.

Lieberman followed, pleading. "The creature has shown no signs of aggressiveness, General Straut—"

"With two men dead?"

"You should have kept them back—"

"Oh, it was my fault, was it?" Straut stared at Lieberman with cold fury. This civilian pushed his way in here, then had the infernal gall to accuse him, Brigadier General Straut, of causing the death of his own men. If he had the fellow in uniform for five minutes . . .

"You're not well, General. That fall——"

"Keep out of my way, Professor," Straut said. He turned and went on down the stairs. The present foul-up could ruin his career; and now this egghead interference . . .

With Greer at his side, Straut moved out to the edge of the field.

"All right, Major. Open up with your .50 calibers."

Greer called a command and a staccato rattle started up. The smell of cordite and the blue haze of gunsmoke—this was more like it. He was in command here.

Lieberman came up to Straut. "General, I appeal to you in the name of science. Hold off a little longer; at least until we learn what the message is about."

"Get back from the firing line, Professor." Straut turned his back on the civilian, raised the glasses to observe the effect of the recoilless rifle. There was a tremendous smack of displaced air, and a thunderous boom as the explosive shell struck. Straut saw the gray shape jump, the raised lid waver. Dust rose from about it. There was no other effect.

"Keep firing, Greer," Straut snapped, almost with a feeling of triumph. The thing was impervious to artillery; now who was going to say it was no threat?"

"How about the mortars, sir?" Greer said. "We can drop a few rounds right inside it."

"All right, try that before the lid drops."

And what we'll try next, I don't know, he thought.

The mortar fired with a muffled thud. Straut watched tensely. Five seconds later, the object erupted in a gout of pale pink debris. The lid rocked, pinkish fluid running down its opalescent surface. A second burst, and a third. A great fragment of the menacing claw hung from the branch of a tree a hundred feet from the ship.

Straut grabbed up the phone. "Cease fire!"

Lieberman stared in horror at the carnage.

The telephone rang. Straut picked it up.

"General Straut," he said. His voice was firm. He had put an end to the threat.

"Straut, we've broken the message," General Margrave said excitedly. "It's the damnedest thing I ever . . ."

Straut wanted to interrupt, announce his victory, but Margrave was droning on.

". . . strange sort of reasoning, but there was a certain analogy. In any event, I'm assured the translation is accurate. Here's how it reads in English . . ."

Straut listened. Then he carefully placed the receiver back on the hook.

Lieberman stared at him.

"What did it say?"

Straut cleared his throat. He turned and looked at Lieberman for a long moment before answering.

"It said, 'Please take good care of my little girl.'"

A RELIC OF WAR

1

The old war machine sat in the village square, its impotent guns pointing aimlessly along the dusty street. Shoulder-high weeds grew rankly about it, poking up through the gaps in the two-yard-wide treads; vines crawled over the high, rust-and guano-streaked flanks. A row of tarnished enamel battle honors gleamed dully across the prow, reflecting the late sun.

A group of men lounged near the machine; they were dressed in heavy work-clothes and boots; their hands were large and calloused, their faces weatherburned. They passed a jug from hand to hand, drinking deep. It was the end of a long workday and they were relaxed, good-humored.

"Hey, we're forgetting old Bobby," one said. He strolled over and sloshed a little of the raw whiskey over the soot-blackened muzzle of the blast cannon slanting sharply down from the forward turret. The other men laughed.

"How's it going, Bobby?" the man called.

Deep inside the machine, there was a soft chirring sound.

"Very well, thank you," a faint, whispery voice scraped from a grill below the turret.

"You keeping an eye on things, Bobby?" another man called.

"All clear," the answer came: a bird-chirp from a dinosaur.

"Bobby, you ever get tired just setting here?"

"Hell, Bobby don't get tired," the man with the jug said. "He's got a job to do, old Bobby has."

"Hey, Bobby, what kind o' boy are you?" a plump, lazy-eyed man called.

"I am a good boy," Bobby replied obediently.

"Sure Bobby's a good boy." The man with the jug reached up to pat the age-darkened curve of chromalloy above him. "Bobby's looking out for us."

Heads turned at a sound from across the square: the distant whine of a turbocar, approaching along the forest road.

"Huh! Ain't the day for the mail," a man said. They stood in silence, watched as a small, dusty cushion-car emerged from deep shadow into the yellow light of the street. It came slowly along to the plaza, swung left, pulled to a stop beside the boardwalk before a corrugated metal storefront lettered *Blauvelt Provision Company.* The canopy popped open and a man stepped down. He was of medium height, dressed in a plain city-type black coverall. He studied the storefront, the street, then turned to look across at the men. He stepped down into the street and came across toward them.

"Which of you men is Blauvelt?" he asked as he came up. His voice was unhurried, cool. His eyes flickered over the men.

A big, youngish man with a square face and sun-bleached hair lifted his chin.

"Right here," he said. "Who're you, Mister?"

"Crewe is the name. Disposal Officer, War Materiel

Commission." The newcomer looked up at the great machine looming over them. "Bolo *Stupendous*, Mark XXV," he said. He glanced at the men's faces, fixed on Blauvelt. "We had a report that there was a live Bolo out here. I wonder if you realize what you're playing with?"

"Hell, that's just Bobby," a man said.

"He's town mascot," someone else said.

"This machine could blow your town off the map," Crewe said. "And a good-sized piece of jungle along with it."

Blauvelt grinned; the squint lines around his eyes gave him a quizzical look.

"Don't go getting upset, Mr. Crewe," he said. "Bobby's harmless—"

"A Bolo's never harmless, Mr. Blauvelt. They're fighting machines, nothing else."

Blauvelt sauntered over and kicked at a corroded tread-plate. "Eighty-five years out in this jungle is kind of tough on machinery, Crewe. The sap and stuff from the trees eats chromalloy like it was sugar candy. The rains are acid, eat up equipment damn near as fast as we can ship it in here. Bobby can still talk a little, but that's about all."

"Certainly it's deteriorated; that's what makes it dangerous. Anything could trigger its battle reflex circuitry. Now, if you'll clear everyone out of the area, I'll take care of it."

"You move kind of fast for a man that just hit town," Blauvelt said, frowning. "Just what you got in mind doing?"

"I'm going to fire a pulse at it that will neutralize

what's left of its computing center. Don't worry; there's no danger—"

"Hey," a man in the rear rank blurted. "That mean he can't talk anymore?"

"That's right," Crewe said. "Also, he can't open fire on you."

"Not so fast, Crewe," Blauvelt said. "You're not messing with Bobby. We like him like he is." The other men were moving forward, forming up in a threatening circle around Crewe.

"Don't talk like a fool," Crewe said. "What do you think a salvo from a Continental Seige Unit would do to your town?"

Blauvelt chuckled and took a long cigar from his vest pocket. He sniffed it, called out: "All right, Bobby—fire one!"

There was a muted clatter, a sharp *click!* from deep inside the vast bulk of the machine. A tongue of pale flame licked from the cannon's soot-rimmed bore. The big man leaned quickly forward, puffed the cigar alight. The audience whooped with laughter.

"Bobby does what he's told, that's all," Blauvelt said. "And not much of that." He showed white teeth in a humorless smile.

Crewe flipped over the lapel of his jacket; a small, highly polished badge glinted there. "You know better than to interfere with a Concordiat officer," he said.

"Not so fast, Crewe." A dark-haired, narrow-faced fellow spoke up. "You're out of line. I heard about you Disposal men. Your job is locating old ammo dumps, abandoned equipment, stuff like that. Bobby's not abandoned. He's town property. Has been for near thirty years."

"Nonsense. This is battle equipment, the property of the Space Arm—"

Blauvelt was smiling lopsidedly. "Uh-uh. We've got salvage rights. No title, but we can make one up in a hurry. Official. I'm mayor here, and District Governor."

"This thing is a menace to every man, woman, and child in the settlement," Crewe snapped. "My job is to prevent tragedy—"

"Forget Bobby," Blauvelt cut in. He waved a hand at the jungle wall beyond the tilled fields. "There's a hundred million square miles of virgin territory out there," he said. "You can do what you like out there. I'll even sell you provisions. But just leave our mascot be, understand?"

Crewe looked at him, looked around at the other men.

"You're a fool," he said. "You're all fools." He turned and walked away, stiff-backed.

2

In the room he had rented in the town's lone boarding house, Crewe opened his baggage and took out a small, gray plastic-cased instrument. The three children of the landlord who were watching from the latchless door edged closer.

"Gee, is that a real star radio?" the eldest, a skinny, long-necked lad of twelve asked.

"No," Crewe said shortly. The boy blushed and hung his head.

"It's a command transmitter," Crewe said, relenting. "It's designed for talking to fighting machines, giving them orders. They'll only respond to the special shaped-wave signal this puts out." He flicked a switch, and an indicator light glowed on the side of the case.

"You mean like Bobby?" the boy asked.

"Like Bobby used to be." Crewe switched off the transmitter and put it aside.

"Bobby's swell," another child said. "He tells us stories about when he was in the war."

"He's got medals," the first boy said. "Were you in the war, Mister?"

"I'm not quite that old," Crewe said.

"Bobby's old, he's older'n Granddad."

"You boys had better run along," Crewe said. "I have to . . ." He broke off, cocked his head, listening. There were shouts outside; someone was calling his name.

Crewe pushed through the boys and went quickly along the hall, stepped through the door onto the boardwalk. He felt rather than heard a slow, heavy thudding, a chorus of shrill squeaks, a metallic groaning—a red-faced man was running toward him from the square.

"It's Bobby!" he shouted. He's moving! What'd you do to him, damn you, Crewe!"

Crewe brushed past the man, ran toward the plaza. The Bolo appeared at the end of the street, moving ponderously forward, trailing uprooted weeds and vines.

"He's headed straight for Spivac's warehouse!" someone yelled.

"Bobby! Stop there!" Blauvelt came into view, running in the machine's wake. The big machine rumbled onward, executed a half-left as Crewe reached the plaza, clearing the corner of a building by inches. It crushed a section of boardwalk to splinters, advanced across a storage yard. A stack of rough-cut lumber toppled, spilled across the dusty ground. The Bolo trampled a board fence, headed out across a tilled field. Blauvelt whirled on Crewe.

"This is your doing, damn you! We never had trouble before—"

"Never mind that! Have you got a field-car?"

"We—" Blauvelt checked himself. "What if we have?"

"I can stop it—but I have to be close. It will be into the jungle in another minute. My car can't navigate there."

"Let him go," a man said, breathing hard from his run. "He can't do no harm out there."

"Who'd of thought it?" another man said. "Setting there all them years—who'd of thought he could travel like that?"

"Your so-called mascot might have more surprises in store for you," Crewe snapped. "Get me a car, fast! This is an official requisition, Blauvelt!"

There was a silence, broken only by the distant crashing of timber as the Bolo moved into the edge of the forest. Hundred foot trees leaned and went down before its advance.

"Let him go," Blauvelt said. "Like Stinzi says, he can't hurt anything."

"What if he turns back?"

"Hell," a man muttered. "Old Bobby wouldn't hurt us. . . ."

"The car," Crewe snarled. "You're wasting valuable time."

Blauvelt frowned. "All right—but you don't make a move unless it looks like he's going to come back and hit the town, clear?"

"Let's go."

Blauvelt led the way at a trot toward the town garage.

3

The Bolo's trail was a twenty-five-foot-wide swath cut through the virgin jungle; the tread-prints were pressed eighteen inches into the black loam, where it showed among the jumble of fallen branches.

"It's moving at about twenty miles per hour, faster than we can go," Crewe said. "If it holds its present track, the curve will bring it back to your town in about five hours."

"He'll sheer off," Blauvelt muttered.

"Maybe. But we won't risk it. Pick up a heading of two hundred and seventy degrees, Blauvelt. We'll try an intercept by cutting across the circle."

Blauvelt complied wordlessly. The car moved ahead in the deep green gloom under the huge shaggy-barked trees. Oversized insects buzzed and thumped against the canopy. Small and medium lizards hopped, darted, flapped. Fern leaves as big as awnings scraped along the car as it clambered over loops and coils of tough root, leaving streaks of plant juice. Once they grated against an exposed ridge of crumbling brown rock; flakes as big as saucers scaled off, exposing dull metal.

"Dorsal fin of a scout-boat," Crewe said. "That's

what's left of what was supposed to be a corrosion resistant alloy."

They passed more evidence of a long-ago battle: the massive shattered breech mechanism of a platform-mounted Hellbore, the gutted chassis of what might have been a bomb car, portions of a downed aircraft, fragments of shattered armor. Many of the relics were of Terran design, but often it was the curiously curved, spidery lines of a rusted Axorc microgun or implosion projector that poked through the greenery.

"It must have been a heavy action," Crewe said. "One of the ones toward the end that didn't get much notice at the time. There's stuff here I've never seen before, experimental types, I imagine, rushed in for a last-ditch stand."

Blauvelt grunted.

"Contact in another minute or so," Crewe said. As Blauvelt opened his mouth to reply, there was a blinding flash, a violent impact, and the jungle erupted in their faces.

4

The seat webbing was cutting into Crewe's ribs. His ears were filled with a high, steady ringing; there was a taste of tarnished brass in his mouth. His head throbbed in time with the heavy thudding of his heart.

The car was on its side, the interior a jumble of loose objects, torn wiring, broken plastic. Blauvelt was half under him, groaning. He slid off him, saw that he was groggy but conscious.

"Changed your mind yet about your harmless pet?"

he asked, wiping a trickle of blood from his right eye. "Let's get clear before he fires those empty guns again. Can you walk?"

Blauvelt mumbled, crawled out through the broken canopy. Crewe groped through debris for the command transmitter—

"Mother of God," Blauvelt croaked. Crewe twisted, saw the high, narrow, iodine-dark shape of the alien machine perched on jointed crawler-legs fifty feet away, framed by blast-scorched foliage. Its multiple-barreled microgun battery was aimed dead at the overturned car.

"Don't move a muscle," Crewe whispered. Sweat trickled down Crewe's face. An insect, like a stub-winged four-inch dragonfly, came and buzzed about them, moved on. Hot metal pinged, contracting. Instantly, the alien hunter-killer moved forward another six feet, depressed its gun muzzles.

"Run for it!" Blauvelt cried. He came to his feet in a scrabbling lunge; the enemy machine swung to track him—

A giant tree leaned, snapped, was tossed aside. The great green-streaked prow of the Bolo forged into view, interposing itself between the smaller machine and the men. It turned to face the enemy; fire flashed, reflecting against the surrounding trees; the ground jumped once, twice, to hard, racking shocks. Sound boomed dully in Crewe's blast-numbed ears. Bright sparks fountained above the Bolo as it advanced. Crewe felt the shock as the two fighting machines came together; he saw the Bolo hesitate, then forge ahead, rearing up, dozing the lighter machine aside, grinding over it, passing on, to leave a crumpled mass of wreckage in its wake.

"My God, did you see that, Crewe?" Blauvelt shouted in Crewe's ear. "Did you see what Bobby did? He walked right into its guns and smashed it flatter'n crock-brewed beer!"

The Bolo halted, turned ponderously, sat facing the men. Bright streaks of molten metal ran down its armored flanks, fell spattering and smoking into crushed greenery.

"He saved our necks," Blauvelt said. He staggered to his feet, picked his way past the Bolo to stare at the smoking ruins of the smashed adversary.

"That thing was headed straight for town," he said. "My God, can you picture what it would have done?"

"Unit nine-five-four of the line, reporting contact with hostile force." The mechanical voice of the Bolo spoke suddenly. "Enemy unit destroyed. I have sustained extensive damage, but am still operational at nine point six percent base capability, awaiting further orders."

"Hey," Blauvelt said. "That doesn't sound like . . ."

"Now maybe you understand that this is a Bolo combat unit, not the village idiot," Crewe snapped. He picked his way across the churned-up ground, stood before the great machine.

"Mission accomplished, Unit nine-five-four," he said. "Enemy forces neutralized. Close out Battle Reflex and revert to low alert status." He turned to Blauvelt.

"Let's go back to town," he said, "and tell them what their mascot just did."

Blauvelt stared up at the grim and ancient machine; his square, tanned face looked yellowish and drawn. "Yeah," he said. "Let's do that."

5

The ten-piece town band was drawn up in a double rank before the newly-mown village square. The entire population of the settlement—some three hundred and forty-two men, women, and children—were present, dressed in their best. Pennants fluttered from strung wires. The sun glistened from the armored sides of the newly-cleaned and polished Bolo. A vast bouquet of wild flowers poked from the no longer sooty muzzle of the Hellbore.

Crewe stepped forward.

"As a representative of the Concordiat government I've been asked to make this presentation," he said. "You people have seen fit to design a medal and award it to Unit nine-five-four in appreciation for services rendered in defense of the community above and beyond the call of duty." He paused, looked across the faces of his audience.

"Many more elaborate honors have been awarded for a great deal less," he said. He turned to the machine; two men came forward, one with a stepladder, the other with a portable welding rig. Crewe climbed up, fixed the newly-struck decoration in place beside the row of century-old battle honors. The technician quickly spotted it in position. The crowd cheered, then dispersed, chattering, to the picnic tables set up in the village street.

6

It was late twilight. The last of the sandwiches and stuffed eggs had been eaten, the last speeches declaimed, the last keg broached. Crewe sat with a few of the men in the town's lone public house.

"To Bobby." A man raised his glass.

"Correction," Crewe said. "To Unit nine-five-four of the line." The men laughed and drank.

"Well, time to go, I guess," a man said. The others chimed in, rose, clattering chairs. As the last of them left, Blauvelt came in. He sat down across from Crewe.

"You, ah, staying the night?" he asked.

"I thought I'd drive back," Crewe said. "My business here is finished."

"Is it?" Blauvelt said tensely.

Crewe looked at him, waiting.

"You know what you've got to do, Crewe."

"Do I?" Crewe took a sip from his glass.

"Damn it, have I got to spell it out? As long as that damned machine was just as oversized half-wit, it was all right. Kind of a monument to the war, and all. But now I've seen what it can do—my God, Crewe—we can't have a live killer in the middle of our town, us never knowing when it might take a notion to start shooting again!"

"Finished?" Crewe asked.

"It's not that we're not grateful—"

"Get out," Crewe said.

"Now, look here, Crewe—"

"Get out. And keep everyone away from Bobby, understand?"

"Does that mean—?"

"I'll take care of it."

Blauvelt got to his feet. "Yeah," he said. "Sure."

After he was gone, Crewe rose and dropped a bill on the table; he picked the command transmitter from the floor, went out into the street. Faint cries came from the far end of the town, where the crowd had gathered for fireworks. A yellow rocket arced up, burst in a spray of golden light, falling, fading. . . .

Crewe walked toward the plaza. The Bolo loomed up, a vast, black shadow against the star-thick sky. Crewe stood before it, looking up at the already draggled pennants, the wilted nosegay drooping from the gun muzzle.

"Unit nine-five-four, you know why I'm here?" he said softly.

"I compute that my usefulness as an engine of war is ended," the soft, rasping voice said.

"That's right," Crewe said, "I checked the area in a thousand mile radius with sensitive instruments. There's no enemy machine left alive. The one you killed was the last."

"It was true to its duty," the machine said.

"It was my fault," Crewe said. "It was designed to detect our command carrier and home on it. When I switched on my transmitter, it went into action. Naturally, you sensed that, and went to meet it."

The machine sat silent.

"You could still save yourself," Crewe said. "If you trampled me under and made for the jungle it might be centuries before . . ."

"Before another man comes to do what must be done? Better that I die now, at the hands of a friend."

"Good-bye, Bobby."

"Correction: Unit nine-five-four of the line."

Crewe pressed the key. A sense of darkness fell across the machine.

At the edge of the square, Crewe looked back. He raised a hand in a ghostly salute; then he walked away along the dusty street, white in the light of the rising moon.